'Having enjoyed both *The Healing* [...] be offered the chance to read an [...] fascinating to learn more about E[...] briefly in *The Healing* but had a hu[...] Philip de Braose. Here we learn [...] were forcibly separated, and watch her respond to suddenly being put in charge of a household she had not chosen and having to care for children from her husband's previous marriage. She grows in confidence, and learns how to forgive and find joy in the everyday, particularly as she comes to accept God's loving hand in her life. While the story is set many centuries ago, I found Efa's growing spirituality and gentle responses to those around her challenging, and was rivetted to the story – desperate to find out what would happen to her. I won't spoil the ending, but rather would encourage people to read the book for themselves! It is a delight.'
Claire Musters, writer, speaker, editor and host of the Woman Alive Book Club

'Joy Margetts has an incredible gift for storytelling and *The Bride* is arguably her best book yet. It is beautifully written, with wonderful descriptions of the medieval Welsh landscape that forms the backdrop to the tale. I found myself gripped as I journeyed with each of the characters into a deep and profound understanding and experience of love – love for themselves, love for others and God's love for them. I recommend *The Bride* if you want to be encouraged, inspired and filled with faith.'
Joanna Watson, speaker and author of Light through the Cracks: How God Breaks In When Life Turns Tough

'A delightful and exquisite read. Joy tenderly transports us back to medieval Wales and with a gentle gallop we find ourselves in the abbey with the Cistercian monks in their white robes. You can almost hear their chanting and the stillness of the air as Joy takes you deeper into the story and deeper into God's heart. Here is Efa. She is mistreated and her dreams shattered and yet her faith and her love shine out as she chooses to forgive. In her pain and in her search for God's heart we are drawn to reflect on our own journey.

'Joy somehow manages to weave her beautifully written poignant tale into our hearts, where it stays and lingers long after the last line is read. It is a tale of forgiveness, of loving ourselves and of loving others in the same way despite the hurtful ways in which they treat us. Will she once again find love? You will have to read it to find out.'

Revd Jo Regan, Baptist minister and co-founder of Book Blest

'In *The Bride*, Joy Margetts has once again created an immersive and evocative story of love, power and faith set in thirteenth-century Wales. A parallel tale to her first two books, *The Healing* and *The Pilgrim*, we journey with Efa, ripped from the man she loves to be married for men's own political ends. Efa's story is one of not only of lost love but also of new purpose and the impact of encountering a God who loves her. *The Bride* is a page turner, but it's also a place to rest for a while and soak in beautifully written words that will remind you of your own true value. I warmly recommend it.'

Liz Carter, author of Valuable *and* Catching Contentment

'Joy Margetts' *The Bride* pulls the reader into medieval Wales and into the life of a remarkable woman. We come to know Efa – her thoughts, her feelings, her world; and to experience all levels of society – the aristocracy, the peasantry and the Church. We sympathise with her as she makes hard choices, and cheer for her as she faces difficult situations with calm dignity. Through it all she grows and, eventually, triumphs.'

Donna Fletcher Crow, author of historical fiction, including Glastonbury, The Novel of Christian England

'In *The Bride*, Joy Margetts has tackled one of the deepest desires in the human heart – the need to be loved. In her uniquely gentle style, Joy takes us on the journey of Efa, who endures betrayal, rejection and a life without choices. Is she still able to find and extend love, when she has been deprived of it herself?

'*The Bride* doesn't shy away from asking the difficult questions, but it also offers hope and reveals deep eternal truths which are as powerful and real today as they were for Efa.

'This story will resonate with anyone who ever had their heart broken, and all who ask the question, "Am I loveable?"'

'As in her previous books, Joy Margetts has drawn on her own deeply personal journey and woven godly lessons throughout this captivating story. I wholeheartedly endorse this book.'
Joy Vee, Christian children's author of The Treasure Man

The Bride

Joy Margetts

instant
ap stle

First published in Great Britain in 2023

Instant Apostle
104A The Drive
Rickmansworth
Herts
WD3 4DU

if notified, will formally seek permission at the earliest opportunity.

The views and opinions expressed in this work are those of the author and do not necessarily reflect the views and opinions of the publisher.

This is a work of fiction. Names, characters, businesses, places, events and incidents are either the products of the author's imagination or used in a fictitious manner. Any resemblance to actual persons, living or dead, or actual events is purely coincidental.

British Library Cataloguing-in-Publication Data

A catalogue record for this book is available from the British Library.

This book and all other Instant Apostle books are available from Instant Apostle:

Website: www.instantapostle.com

Email: info@instantapostle.com

ISBN 978-1-912726-75-2

Printed in Great Britain.

*For Judah and Olivia, and all my children's children.
My inheritance in the Lord, and a blessing to my heart.*

Contents

Glossary of Welsh Words

Abergwyngregyn (*Aber-gwin-greg-in*) – Llewellyn's princely court on the North Wales coast

Annest (*An-nest*) – Cynan's first wife, means 'pure'

Blodyn (*Blod-in*) – 'flower'

Cantref (*Kan-trev*) – division of land in Medieval Wales for administration purposes

Cawl (*kowl*) – traditional Welsh savoury stew

Cymer (*ku-meh*) – Cistercian Abbey in South Gwynedd

Cynan (*kunn-ann*) – Efa's husband, means 'chief'

Dafydd (*Dav-ith*) – Cynan's second son. Welsh form of David

Derwen (*Der-wen*) – 'oak tree'

Efa (*Eh-va*) – Welsh form of Eve, meaning 'life'

Eluned (*E-lee-ned, or Lee-ned*) – Tregaron's cook and housekeeper

Ferch (*Verch*) – 'daughter of', as *ap* means 'son of'

Gerallt (*Geh-rallt*) – Cynan's youngest son. Welsh form of Gerald

Gerallt or Gerald Cambriensis – Gerald of Wales, renowned twelfth-century churchman, scholar and writer

Gruffydd (*Grif-idh*) – Cynan's eldest son, means 'prince'

Haf (*Ha-v*) – Cynan's youngest daughter, means 'summer'

Ifan (*Ee- van*) – Tregaron's steward, means 'gift of God'

Llewellyn Fawr (*Hluh-well-inn Vow-rr*) – thirteenth-century great (*fawr*) prince of Wales. Llewellyn means 'lion-like'

Llys (*Hlees*) – a Welsh princes' court/seat of power

Maelgwyn (*Mihl-gwihn*) – lord of Deheubarth, an ancient region of South Wales. Maelgwyn means 'prince of hounds'

Manon (*Ma-non*) – Cynan's eldest daughter. A Welsh form of Mary, meaning 'bitter'

Marared (*Ma-re-rehd*) – Llewellyn's daughter and wife to John de Braose. Welsh form of Margaret, meaning 'child of light'

Non (*Non*) – children's nurse and friend to Efa, means 'nun'

Siwan (*Siew-an*) – Efa's maid. Welsh form of Joan, meaning 'God is gracious'

Tregaron (*Truh-ga-ron*) – Cynan's home, now a town in Ceredigion

Ystrad Fflur (*Is-trad F-lur*) – the Welsh name for Strata Florida, a Cistercian Abbey in Ceredigion. *Ystrad Fflur* means 'valley of flowers'

Part One

1
Bride

Efa slumped hard against the wall behind her, the rough stones tearing through the thin silk of her borrowed gown as she sank heavily to the floor. She felt it rip, felt the painful scrape of stone against flesh, but she did not care. She shut her eyes and clamped her hands to her ears, the thump of her heartbeat sounding loud in her head. If she could have hoped that this was all some sick dream, the painful tightening in her chest brought her back to reality. She knew she could not unhear what she had just heard or unsee what she just had seen. Even now she could still hear the echo of the laughter that had rung around the great hall. A cruel, abrasive laughter that turned her heart to stone.

She had sat on show at the top table, uncomfortable, and not just because of the dress not made for her. Alongside her sat a man she did not know, but who she would soon know well enough. She had sat and watched, her hands gripping each other so hard that her fingernails had left marks in her palms. Watched as Philip had stepped boldly up to face his brother, John, and her uncle, Llewellyn, the Welsh prince. He had promised her he would do it, fight for them, for their love and their future together. Pride had almost burst her chest as she had watched him stand resolute, his hand on his heart, his words spoken with conviction. But he had chosen the wrong moment, that had become obvious. Perhaps pride and anger had muddled his thinking, and if he felt as she did now, then that pride and anger would soon give way to betrayal and despair.

The moment of confrontation had not been wise. Philip should have known that John would never dare to counter Llewellyn, or to lose face in front of a room of Welsh nobles. She knew John, knew he loved his brother, but also knew that he was not brave or foolish enough to anger his powerful father-in-law. She knew Llewellyn too, all too well. He was not without feeling, but he would not be crossed when his mind was set. Politics and power won over sentimentality every time.

So she had watched as John de Braose had stepped down from the dais to meet Philip, staggering slightly from the effects of the celebratory ale, and grabbed him in what looked like a good-natured hug. Only his fingers had been white where they gripped Philip's shoulder, his eyes blazing a warning as he spoke.

'What do you know about love, boy? You are not man enough. You have no idea of the world and how it works.' He glanced around the room at stunned faces, and made some other coarse remark which had the desired effect. Men banged the table and clapped each other's shoulders and downed their drinks, and laughed as the 'boy' stood shaking with rage before them.

She had fled then, her face blazing and her heart breaking. How could she have kept her seat at that table, her uncle on one side and her betrothed on the other? The banquet had been set to honour her and Cynan, their upcoming marriage, but she would not be missed. It wasn't about her, she knew that. The match was nothing more than a political move on her uncle's part, a sop to keep the Deuheubarth princes as his allies. She was just a fortuitous asset, a nameless pawn, and he had played her. That was what had angered Philip most. Not just that his love for her and his own intention to wed her had been thwarted. But that her feelings had not been considered by her own uncle as he dictated her future. Efa in contrast saw things for how they were, outside the dream the pair had created for themselves and believed in with a passionate naïveté. After all, she was a woman, and fatherless; what more could she expect for her life than to be married off at another's will?

For a short while, Efa had dared to believe she could have had a different future, one of her own choosing. How foolish and reckless to let herself get attached to a young man who made her laugh and shared her dreams? It had happened naturally, an affection grown out of friendship. John and his wife, her cousin Marared, Philip and herself – the four of them had been happy together at Swansea. They had no reason to believe that Llewellyn would have opposed the match either. That was until the great prince himself had arrived at Swansea, with his retinue of lesser princes, and the fantasy had been swept away.

So now she was to marry Cynan, a man old enough to be her father. She had caught him watching her, not lasciviously, rather more like he was examining a fine tapestry, or maybe a new horse. He had spoken kindly to her, his voice soft and his accent thick. But he was old. The skin of his face was roughened red, thick dark bristles spotted his sagging chin, and grey hairs grew long from his nose and ears. The only things that had hinted that he had once been a handsome man were his eyes. Surrounded by still dark lashes, the colour of his eyes was the most unusual grey-green she had ever seen. She had found herself staring, mesmerised, and perhaps that was all the interest he had been waiting for. He had asked Llewellyn for her hand then and there, and in that moment her life had changed forever.

She felt someone approach her where she crouched, leaning against the cool stone in a dark corner. Hidden, she had hoped. She heard a swish of skirts and smelled the scent of roses. Marared.

'Efa.' Soft hands gently pulled her own away from her ears, and kept tender yet firm hold of them. 'Efa. Come now. You do not need to return to John's table. They will not miss you now they are all well into their cups.'

'I cannot leave. Philip will come for me.'

'No, my love. He would not dare,' she whispered firmly.

'But I need to see him. Speak to him.'

'Philip was angry, Efa, very angry. It was good that he left when he did. Perhaps in the morning you may see him. Chaperoned, of course. You are soon to be another man's wife.'

Efa raised pleading eyes to her cousin's kind face. She read understanding there, but something else too. Something she wasn't saying.

'Come.' Marared pulled on her hands to help her to her feet, and placed a soothing arm around her shoulders. Her fingers must have found the rip in the silk as she did so and she let out a gasp.

'What is it?'

'A tear. I can't see how bad it is, but we must get this dress off you and see if it can be mended.' She seemed flustered. It wasn't like Marared to be worried about a damaged gown. There were very many more at her disposal.

They started to walk towards the spiral stone stairway that led to Marared's private solar above. As they entered the room, the noise from the hall was beginning to subside. There were noises outside too. The sounds of shouts and horses being readied. And then the sound of hooves clattering over the stones and across the drawbridge. Efa stopped dead in her tracks as she realised what it was that Marared had hidden from her. She felt her knees begin to give way, and felt Marared's arm tighten around her shoulder.

She swallowed hard. 'He has gone?' she whispered.

Marared took her time answering. 'Yes. Philip has left Swansea.'

'You knew?'

Marared did not answer her, not until they had awkwardly negotiated the winding stairs and entered the welcoming warmth of the room with its rich tapestry-lined walls. Marared helped her sit on the bed and took her trembling hands into her own.

'He was so angry, Efa. I was only grateful that he did not have his sword on his belt when he approached John tonight. He might have done something he would have regretted, something that would have cost him his life. You have to see that he is better away from here. Better to cool off somewhere where he can do no harm.'

'He did not come to find me first.' It was not a question. Efa closed her eyes. One more promise not kept, one more betrayal. 'So be it,' she whispered, releasing her hands from Marared's and standing up to remove the dress as torn as her heart was. The tear in the silk could be mended, although she supposed that a scar in the fabric would always be visible. The wound in her heart would not be so easily mended, and to prevent it tearing further she swore to herself that she would never give her heart freely again.

When she woke, she felt chilled. The thick hangings of the bed had been disturbed and the space beside her was empty. If John had managed to stagger drunkenly up the stairs in the dark hours, he would have found his wife's door locked to him. Marared had stayed, lying down beside her, stroking her hair as she would have a child, and eventually exhaustion had taken hold and Efa had slept fitfully. As she roused herself now she felt far from refreshed, the dullness of her heart and the dread of what the new day held weighing heavy on her. She sat and swung her legs over the side of the bed.

'You are awake!' Marared was seated at a small table positioned in front of the window embrasure. The shutters had been unfastened but not swung fully open, allowing a single stream of morning sunlight to illuminate the small private solar. It brought little warmth with it. 'I have had Bethan bring us some victuals to break our fast. I'm in no mood to eat with my husband this morning, and I guessed you would rather stay away from the men also.'

'If this has caused a rift between you and John, I am sorry for it.' Efa walked over to the table and eyed the food; a fresh crusted loaf, some soft goat's cheese and a dish of honey. It looked good but she had no appetite for it.

Marared stood and placed a hand reassuringly on her arm. 'I will not have you worrying about John and I. I will give him a few days of the silent treatment and he will know how displeased I am with him. But you have to see that he really had no choice in it all. He could not have gone against my father, Llewellyn, most especially in front of the Welsh lords.'

'That may be so.' Efa reached out and tore off a piece of bread but it did not reach her mouth. Instead it was crushed mindlessly in her fingers.

'Come, sit and try to eat. You have a long day ahead of you.' Marared pulled a chair over to their makeshift breakfast table and guided Efa into it. She sat herself opposite and poured milk into a beaker, handing it to Efa. She was still talking, while Efa sat staring into the creamy liquid.

'Bethan has done a good job on the green silk. I am pleased as it looked so good on you. You will wear your hair down for the ceremony, of course, but then I have a gold-threaded barrette that I want you to have to clip back your hair, and my best gossamer veil. Oh, and my miniver-lined cloak. You can have that too, to wear for the journey.'

'It is too much, Marared. I can wear my own clothes.'

She longed for the familiarity of soft wool skirts. Not as fine as silk, but good quality enough for the ward of a Welsh prince. The silk had constrained her. It had already been let out and lengthened; she was not a slight woman, or elegant like her cousin. But her height and build had long since ceased to bother her because Philip hadn't cared. He was not tall and handsome like his brother. They had felt happy in their ordinariness together. Love had made them beautiful to each other.

Marared was watching her intently and Efa could see her sadness reflected in her cousin's eyes. Efa cursed herself for letting her mind go back to Philip.

'Let me do this for you. I cannot stop this marriage, Efa, and I cannot come with you.' Marared paused, her eyes filling. Her voice wavered. 'Let me at least send some of my things with you.'

Efa took Marared's hand in hers and squeezed it, allowing the corners of her mouth to lift in the semblance of a smile. She was going to find their separation hard, too. She would take Marared's proffered gifts as welcome reminders of their love for one another.

They could not linger long over their shared sadness. There was much to be done. Efa had belongings to gather and pack. Farewells to make. Then she needed to bathe and be dressed in her finery so that she could stand with Cynan before the priest for their wedding Mass, here in Swansea's chapel. The chapel had been a familiar place where she had prayed many times. But today she would not pray. She would mouth the words but her heart would not engage. As great as the betrayal she felt from Llewellyn and John, and now also from Philip, it was nothing compared to the pain of knowing God had neither heard nor answered her prayers.

When she finally stood ready to enter the chapel, Efa felt less like herself than she had ever felt, in her borrowed green silk with its wide brocaded sleeves, topped with the heavy miniver-lined mantle. Her hair had been brushed until the waves shone like sun-ripened corn, and a simple gold circlet crowned her head, securing Marared's gossamer veil in place. She guessed she must look like a bride; she had even seen the odd look of admiration as she had passed through the hall still full of Llewellyn's retinue. She should have been happy. Weren't brides supposed to glow with happiness on their wedding day?

The day was bitterly cold, but it wasn't the chill air that caused Efa to shiver, standing there at the threshold. The urge to rip off all the finery and run was overwhelming. But then the bulk of Llewellyn was suddenly stood beside her, and her hand taken and pulled to rest in his elbow.

'Courage, Blodyn.' He whispered her pet name and patted her cold hand with his rough one. She glanced up. Was it regret she read in his eyes, a soft sadness? Why then had he forced this marriage? For a moment she wondered if he was being forced to play her against his will also? No, she reminded herself. He alone wrote the rules of this particular game. He was the one intent on consolidating his power over the whole of Wales. Her back stiffened and she tried to pull her arm from his, but Llewellyn's hand tightened. And the look he now gave her had lost its softness. He looked as if he would drag her down the aisle if she resisted further. That would not happen. She would not give him, or any of them, the satisfaction of thinking they had broken her spirit. Even if her once soft heart now lay in tiny icy shards.

Cynan had greeted her with his odd, crooked smile, as she had come to stand beside him in front of the priest. He had taken her hands in his and said the words that bound them. She had answered in turn and knelt with him for the priest's blessing. She had taken the sacraments of the Mass and bowed her head in a sign of obeisance. But through it all she had felt nothing. Just an aching numbness that had nothing to do with the cold stone floor she stood on, or the wind whistling under the church door.

Her new husband was uttering words of love that meant nothing to him or to her. Llewellyn had been the only father figure she had ever known, and she had loved and trusted him. But he had bartered her without a second thought and would no longer hold any place in her heart. She knew Marared cared for her, but she had her husband, and remained loyal to him. John had done nothing to show that he had any concern for Efa's feelings. Even Philip had gone, abandoning her to her fate, and that betrayal stung deepest. So here she stood at an altar that was supposed to represent divine love, and she knew the truth. She was not loved, not loved enough by any of those she had loved. It was best that she felt nothing. That would sustain her going forward.

After the ceremony, she sat at that same high table she had sat at the night before, but now the stranger sitting beside her was her wedded husband. She sat while ale was supped and steaming dishes were paraded around the room. She heard the laughter and the ribald jokes. She pasted a smile on her face and spoke one-word answers when spoken to. She ducked her head demurely and forced herself to put food into her dry mouth. Soon enough the company rose to take their leave. Only then she felt the panic, remembering that she was leaving too.

As they made their farewells she held perhaps a little too tightly to Marered's soft hands as she saw the wince of pain cross her cousin's fair face. And then she had cause to curse that borrowed dress again as she struggled to mount and sit side-saddle on the horse that had been provided for her. She wasn't a natural horsewoman at the best of times and this just felt ludicrous. She perched in an ungainly fashion, struggling to keep her seat. If she could have worn her customary linen and wool, she would have sat much more comfortably astride. She would do so on the morrow, uncaring as to what impression that would give. At least her hair was now tied up out of the wind, Marered's beautiful gold barrette securing it, tucked beneath her married woman's wimple. She pulled up the hood of Marared's fur-lined mantle, grateful for its warmth, and still more grateful that it hid her face. She shed no tears, but her face felt cold and tight and her head pounded as she turned her horse to ride away from Swansea.

Cynan's home at Tregaron was some two days' journey north. They had been joined by Llewellyn and his retinue, which would likely slow them further, for at least part of their journey. They left with the clatter of hooves and rattle of wagon wheels echoing loud. Efa determined she would not look back. A petite, dark-eyed little girl also accompanied them. She came as a companion for Efa. Not a chaperone of her own status but a poor girl from the family of one of John's tenants. She did not seem to be leaving Swansea willingly either; her pale face was streaked with tears. With a frail frame and chestnut hair that might have been pretty if it had been touched with a comb, she looked little more than ten or eleven years old. She rode on the seat of one of the wagons, holding on white-knuckled, with a look of perpetual terror on her face.

Efa tried not to think of the girl's grief or to feel compassion for her. But it was impossible not to. And as soon as the party reined into the yard of the inn that was going to be their stop for that first night, Efa made a point of going to her. The girl was whimpering and shaking, whether with fear or from the cold, as flakes of light snow began to fall from the darkening sky.

'Here, come with me,' Efa took hold of the girl, helping her down from her seat and covering her with the edge of her mantle. They followed the men into the inn and into the wide, low room that had been made available for their use. The landlord was fussing around the prince, so Efa quietly pulled the child to a small pallet bed in the far corner of the room and made her sit on it. She knelt in front of her, not caring that her silk now rested in damp-stained rushes. It was not her dress anyway.

'What is your name?' she asked gently.

'Siwan.' It was barely a whisper, her eyes wide as they searched Efa's face.

'Siwan, I am Efa. I will look after you and you will look after me. We will stay together. We will keep each other safe. Do you understand?'

The small head nodded but the eyes never left Efa's face. Efa leaned in closer and smiled so that Siwan could see it. She had both the girl's frozen hands in hers. The inn was not very much warmer than being outside, but at least they were out of the cutting wind. As she glanced around at the men noisily eating and preparing themselves to sleep, she caught sight of her new husband. Suddenly she was thankful that this poor child had been forced to journey with them. She had no need of a maid and as soon as she could, she would send this girl back to her family. But for tonight she was grateful for her presence. She did not know if she was supposed to demand a private room for herself, or whether her husband was even yet enquiring after one for them both. She did know that she did not want to sleep alone, and she did not want to be available to her new husband either. Not tonight. Tonight she would stay with Siwan, unnoticed, hopefully.

She laid Siwan down and, unbuckling her own soft mantle, took it from her shoulders to lay it over the girl's shivering body. Efa carefully removed her wimple and veil, took Marared's barrette from her hair and tucked it with her boots under the pallet, before settling herself down beside Siwan on the narrow bed and pulling the edge of the mantle over to cover them both.

Draw me into your heart.

We will run away together ...

Song of Solomon 1:4, TPT

2

Tregaron

The skies were heavy with dark clouds as they approached the gates of what Efa could see was a substantial complex of buildings. Apart from those few flurries on the first night, the snow had held off for the remainder of their journey, although the wind had continued to bite. Now, however, the threat of snow felt inevitable and Efa was glad to see solid stone walls ahead of them.

Theirs was a much smaller party, now that they finally approached Tregaron. Llewellyn and his sizeable retinue had parted company with them, leaving Cynan and Efa with just eight armed men, a sole wagon with its driver, and Siwan. That morning Efa had hidden behind her cloak, held aloft by her little companion, and awkwardly removed her silk overdress, exchanging it for a much more sensible travelling dress of thick, red-dyed wool. It meant she had ridden astride, Siwan sitting in front of her on the poor, tired horse. The girl had attached herself to her like a limpet on Swansea's rocky seashore. Efa was thankful for the fine miniver that covered both her and the girl. With a wry smile she realised that appearing in the fur mantle would perhaps help her introduction as Cynan's new bride; it would cover her plain dress at least. She felt the bile rise to the back of her throat at the thought of who or what might greet her as they rode their mounts through Tregaron's heavy wooden gates.

Cynan dismounted and was there beside her horse ready to help her do likewise. He had been attentive enough during their journey, leaving her in the company of her diminutive shadow, seeing that they were served and well guarded, and not demanding of her in any way. Efa shook Siwan from her doze and handed the sleepy child down to Cynan. She was surprised to see a softness in his face as he helped the girl find her feet and pointed her in the direction of the house. He offered Efa the same kind look as he turned back to help her dismount, his strong hands supporting her waist as she slid down to place shaky feet on the ground. *Strange*, she thought to herself, *the look he gave was the same look a father might give his child.* It was definitely not the look of a lover, or a lascivious-minded husband.

She shook away the thought of what sort of husband he might yet be, as Cynan took her hand and led her towards the house. She could not see much of the exterior of it in the dimming evening light apart from the wide-open lamplit door, into which Siwan had disappeared. As she stepped across the threshold of that same door, she found herself in a wide hall, its stone walls lit by well-spaced torches. A large fire was roaring to one side and she could see a long table lined up parallel to the back wall. The rushes on the floor smelled clean, and there was a very welcoming aroma of cooked meat hanging in the air. Glancing up, she could make out the fine wooden-beamed ceiling. The building did not look old. And it spoke of wealth and comfort. It reminded her somewhat of Llewellyn's *Llys* at Abergwyngregyn. The thought should have comforted her, but her memories of that life were now marred by her uncle's betrayal.

A large, tall man and a small, round woman approached. Both were smiling in welcome.

'Ifan, Eluned, this is the Lady Efa, my wife.'

If the pair were surprised by Cynan's words they did not show it. Eluned dipped in an awkward attempt at a curtsey. She wore a simple cap that did nothing to control the wild, dark, curly hair beneath. The stained apron tied loosely around her waist indicated that she had come from the kitchen.

Ifan stepped up and took Cynan's hand in a firm grasp, before turning his attention to Efa.

'You are most welcome, my lady.' The tall man bent his long body in welcome, his blue eyes twinkling as he lifted a head well thatched with thick, grey hair. He turned his attention to Siwan, who had found her way to stand close at Efa's side. He bowed even more dramatically to greet her, 'And you, too, my little lady.' He smiled, but when he got none in response he put one knee on the floor so that his face was level with Siwan's. He made no attempt to touch the girl who was staring at him with wary eyes.

'I am glad you have come, because Eluned has been very busy cooking and we have far too much food to feed just us. I don't suppose you are hungry?' He was addressing Siwan but as Efa's stomach rumbled audibly, he glanced up at her and winked, sending her face pink in the torchlight.

Ifan persevered with Siwan. 'I dare say you are weary to your bones as well. Well, I suggest we get you fed and to a comfortable bed. The other children are long abed, but you will meet them in the morning.' He glanced up at Efa again and across to Cynan. The master of the house nodded his assent and moved away towards the table that was now being furnished with an assortment of edibles from the kitchen.

Ifan stood awkwardly to his feet. He was plainly dressed in a working man's tunic. He spoke to her directly this time, and she was surprised how his smile made the corners of her own mouth twitch to respond in kind. Who was this man who radiated with such kindness?

'I have the pleasure of being steward of this house, and long-time friend of Cynan. He is brave enough to entrust the keeping of Tregaron to me, and that includes the welcome of new family members to our door. I am very pleased to welcome you and hope that you will soon feel at home here with us. When the master is away, we run a small and relaxed household. I am sure you will find us easy enough to live with.'

He was grinning now as he looked her up and down. Efa's face flushed warm again as she looked down and realised her dress was mud-splattered and her boots filthy. Her hair was escaping from her wimple and the fur of her once fine mantle was bedraggled and matted. What a sight she must have looked! What must the steward think of his master's fine new wife? She opened her mouth to apologise for her dishevelled state but Ifan was already turning away to lead a suddenly wide-awake Siwan towards the laden table.

Efa followed, tucking the wayward strands of her hair back into her wimple and releasing the catch of her heavy mantle so that she could remove it from her shoulders and lay it over the bench beside her as she sat. The top part of her dress was clean and dry at least. She straightened her back. Whatever their first impression of her, she was now lady of this manor; if only she could make what felt like a pretence stick.

The smell of the feast before her was mouth-watering and she nearly forgot herself completely, reaching to avail herself of a good portion of the lamb *cawl* that had been placed in front of her. It was only as she heard Cynan mention Llewellyn and realised he was talking about how their betrothal had come about that she remembered why she was there. And the betrayal and loss that she had suffered to get there. The piece of meat she had just swallowed stuck in her throat and she had to take a deep swallow of ale to dislodge it, just as the steward looked in her direction, his eyes knowing. She felt her face warm again. She really wasn't doing a great job of introducing herself favourably to Cynan's household.

Efa made a point of looking away, letting her gaze take in the rest of the room. A doorway behind the table must lead to a kitchen of some sort, as Eluned's food had appeared through it. A third, smaller door was fitted into the west wall, and three high windows were spaced at regular intervals along the back wall, shuttered against the night air. Unusually for a ground floor room there was also a larger arched window next to the door they had entered by. It was wide and low with well-made shutters and set deep enough into the wall to accommodate a sizeable window seat. The floor beneath her feet was well covered with fresh rushes, and the room was pleasingly warm thanks to a well-stoked fire blazing within a circular stone hearth.

As the warmth filtered into her chilled body, Efa felt her back sagging. She ached from the hours in the saddle. She wondered and worried where she would be resting her head. And would it be beside her new husband, who was sat opposite her, his full attention taken by the well-roasted capon he was devouring? She felt a warm presence behind her and realised she had sagged yet further into the soft plumpness that was Eluned.

'Come, let us get you to bed, my lady,' she whispered softly into Efa's ear. 'Your young companion has already been carried to her bed, and I am about ready for mine. Let us leave the men to their talk. I will bring you something warm to drink to help you rest when I have you settled.'

All the time she had been talking, Eluned had been helping Efa to stand and quietly move away from the table. She had an arm around Efa's back and was propelling as much as leading her towards the west end of the hall. Eluned released a torch from its sconce and held it aloft so that Efa could make out a set of stairs, made of wood, not stone. They led to a galleried landing, also made of wood, and as they slowly reached the landing, Efa could see two small doors leading from it. The workmanship was finer than any she had seen, even at Swansea. Eluned led her to the first door and opened it. Efa stepped through, ducking slightly to save her head from hitting the low, curved door frame.

She almost gasped in surprise at what awaited her. It was a large square room, finely wood panelled on all sides, except for the exterior wall, which was built of white-washed stone and contained a large recessed window. Within the window embrasure a cushioned bench seat had been made to fit the space exactly. The centre of the room was dominated by a fine canopied bed, with rich brocaded hangings. There were other pieces of fine furniture, including a side table and carved chair and several wooden chests. There was a tapestry hanging on one wall, the design impossible to make out in the low light, and sheepskin rugs dotted about the wooden floor. This was the room of a noble lady, and instinctively Efa stepped back as if she were trespassing. Perhaps this was Cynan's room? She swallowed back the sudden panic.

'Now then, there is nothing to be afeared of.' The firm solid arm of Eluned had come around her back again as she was led over towards the bed. 'You will be safe here, from those without.' She nodded towards the heavy shutters that covered the window. 'And from those within, I daresay.' She gave Efa a small smile. Efa could not quite fathom her meaning, but let herself be led until she felt the edge of the bed against the back of her legs. She sat down gratefully and felt the softness of the mattress sink beneath her weight. 'Now you stay right there.' There was a soft authority in the voice. 'And I will send Non to you with some warm milk. She will help you to bed.'

Efa watched her leave and close the door behind her. *And then my husband will join me, no doubt*, Efa thought to herself. It was an inevitability she ought to be preparing herself for. Her tired, muddled thinking wasn't helping. She desperately wanted to lie down and lose herself in the softness of the bed beneath her, but she needed to get these damp clothes and boots off first. As she bent to release the fastenings of her boots, she felt the whole room spin. At the same time she heard the door hinges creak and she started in fear. Cynan? Come already? She wasn't ready for him.

'My lady! Forgive me for startling you. Here, let me help you.'

It wasn't Cynan's voice, nor Eluned's. Efa kept her head down, willing the room to stop spinning and her breathing to calm. She was aware of the light-footed scurrying of feet, something being placed on a table and the door being shut softly. Then a concerned face appeared beneath her own. It was a round and pleasant face, and youthful. The hair was dark and cropped unfashionably short; the young woman wore no veil. And there was something vaguely familiar about her eyes.

Her voice was soft and calming. 'I can't imagine what you must be feeling, and what fears must be flitting through your head. I am sorry not to have been there to greet you with the others, but I was with the children. They will be happy to meet you in the morning, I am sure of it.'

Efa lifted her head slowly, and the girl stood up from where she had been kneeling. She was not tall, but by her form and her confident manner, definitely not a child. She was looking directly into Efa's eyes and had taken hold of one of her hands. It felt like she was somehow reading her. All Efa knew was that her closeness felt reassuring. And her words as she continued even more so.

'This is now your chamber, not Cynan's. It has never been his, and probably never will be. He will never step over the threshold uninvited. I think you understand my meaning?'

The grasp on Efa's hand had tightened. Efa nodded her understanding. So Cynan would not come to her bed tonight? Would not come uninvited? She would think more on what that meant later. But for now, the relief was immense and overwhelming. She felt tears prick and closed her eyes. No. No tears. She took a deep breath and breathed out a whispered, 'Thank you.'

The young woman was already back on her knees and loosening Efa's boots. She then helped her to stand to untie her dress fastenings. Efa let the weight of the wool fall to the floor, feeling suddenly chilled in the linen shift she stood in. Her new friend gently pushed her shoulders firmly so that she sat again on the side of the bed, and expertly removed her headdress and wimple, releasing her curls from Marared's barrette.

'Here,' Efa snatched it. 'Let me have that.' It came out harsher than she intended, with a desperation to hold on to one thing that reminded her of her past life. She held the barrette close to her chest as she laid down on the soft pillow and drew her legs up. She felt the weight of covers pulled up over her shoulders and allowed herself to relax into the bed. Her eyes were so heavy and her head so tired. Her body ached and her heart ached still more. She felt a soft hand rest gently on her shoulder and in her half-awake state thought she heard whispered words of blessing. She forced her eyes open again, but the room was now dark. Was she alone?

'I did not ask your name?' she whispered into the darkness.

Silence and then, a soft whisper in response. 'Non. My name is Non. And I hope to be a friend to you, if you let me. God grant you peace and rest.'

Efa let the tiredness take her.

She woke to find the pillow beneath her damp. Her body was warm and the covers over them dry: no dampness had infiltrated in the night. So it seemed that the tears she had denied in the light had flowed unbidden in the dark. She could not remember crying, but she could recall snippets of a dream, where she was in the sunlit gardens at Swansea, and Philip was laughing. Only she was tied up in a net, suspended from a tree, and Philip wasn't laughing with her, but at her.

She shook the memory away and sat up, parting the bed curtains. The room was still dark but she could see a fine line of sunlight through the crack where the window shutters met. She pulled the covers up, sitting with her knees raised and her back leaning against the bedhead. She was grateful that the night was over, but the dawning day meant new things to face. And she suddenly felt very, very alone. Even Siwan's quiet company would have been a comfort. The bed she lay in, with its fine fabrics and soft down filling, was wide enough for more than her. It was surely designed for lovers to share. She brushed the space beside her and just for a moment imagined Philip lying there, smiling up at her. She closed her eyes and willed the painful thought away. That was never going to happen now. Never. He had left her to her fate, and she would try to forget that they had even loved each other. Try to forget what could have been.

No, the space beside her was for her husband. She shivered involuntarily. She would have to accept it. Thousands of other women had been in the same position. A pawn, an object of desire, an acquisition to be used, abused even, at a man's whim. She was grateful enough that it hadn't happened yet. That she had slept at least the first night in her new home untouched.

She remembered then the softly spoken Non. The kindness that had soothed her and reassured her the night before. She was thankful for that. What was it that she had heard her say? That she would be a friend to her? Efa wasn't sure if she could be a friend in return. Friendship demanded care, love even. Her heart felt incapable of any feeling at all. Surely it was better not to care and so not to feel it when the inevitable betrayal came? Her life experience had proved her vulnerability. All the people she had loved or trusted had abandoned her or let her down somehow. Perhaps she was cursed, never to be truly loved for herself. She would take care to not expose herself to hurt again. No, she didn't need a friend, but she did need someone to serve her breakfast. Her stomach ached from hunger.

She heard the door open and soft feet cross the floor.

'I am awake, Non, if that is you.' Her voice sounded supercilious even to herself.

'My lady.' Non's smiling face appeared around the bed curtain. She was carrying a trencher holding a steaming beaker and a hunk of bread.

'Put them on the table. I will rise to eat.' She sat up and swung her legs around. Non reappeared, still smiling, with a soft woollen blanket that she draped around Efa's shoulders.

'I'm afraid there is no fire in this room. There is a charcoal brazier but it has not been added to this morning as no one wanted to disturb you. It was thought you might stay abed but if you would rather rise, I can bring you hot water to refresh your hands and face and then help you dress. The fire is well lit down in the hall and you will find it warmer there. The rest of the household is long awake. The children are eager to meet you.' Non crossed over to the window and unfastened the shutter enough to let a wider beam of light in. The air that came with it was wintry despite the blue sky beyond. Efa shivered again and regretted her rash insistence on rising to eat.

Efa pulled the wool tighter about her and made her way over to the small table where her breakfast was laid out. The beaker contained warm milk sweetened with honey. The bread was also warm, and was served with a small round of white cheese. She had sat and sampled both before she had truly registered Non's words. The children. Cynan's children. Did they expect her to be their mother? How was she equipped for that? She was barely out of childhood herself! True, she had dreamed of being a mother once, to children born out of the love Philip and she shared. But now, broken as she was, how could she be what these children needed?

'Their mother? She died?' Her voice had lost its hard edge. She could not pretend that she did not need more from Non than to serve her breakfast and help her dress. She needed information from her too.

'Yes. Five years hence. But I will tell you more once you have met the family. For now, I think you should eat and then dress.' It was said smartly, and like that, Non was gone from the room and Efa was left alone to contemplate her breakfast and her attitude. Efa felt ever so slightly as if she had been chastised. Had Non seen through her already? When she returned with a pitcher and bowl, Efa made a decision to put things right.

'I am sorry for the way I spoke to you earlier. Will you forgive me?'

Non smiled in response. 'Do not concern yourself, my lady. This is strange and new for you, and for us here too. We all have to get used to each other.'

'Efa. My name is Efa... Please call me by my name. And Non,' she reached out her hand to lightly grip Non's arm, sighing deeply, 'I too hope that we can be friends.'

Jerusalem maidens, in this twilight darkness

I know I am so unworthy – so in need. …

Yet you are so lovely!

I feel as dark and dry as the desert tents

of the wandering nomads. …

Yet you are so lovely –

like the fine linen tapestry hanging in the Holy

Place.

Song of Solomon 1:5, TPT

3
Secrets

Non had been busy.

'Your travelling chests have been brought up. I took the liberty of sorting through to find you something clean to wear. Your clothes from yesterday are still in the process of drying out,' Non chuckled. 'And as for that screwed-up piece of fine green silk, I have left that with Eluned to see whether it is at all salvageable! I thought this would do for today.'

She held in her arms one of Efa's favourites. Made of the softest wool and dyed a rich, warm blue, it was a tunic dress that hung loosely and comfortably with wide sleeves. And yet it was elegant enough when decorated with her best belt – a cord twisted with gold and threaded with ruby red beads. This dress would have been Efa's choice to wear at fine gatherings in the past. It was more to her style that the fragile silk. And yet, she mused to herself, as Non helped her to dress and secure her hair under her wimple and veil, by the luxury of the room she stood in, it would seem that she could well be the wife of a wealthy man now. Perhaps she would be expected to wear silk and furs more often.

'Are you sure this is fine enough?' She fingered the skirt of the gown.

'What, to meet the children?' Non laughed then. 'We don't judge people by what they wear here. And in my opinion, you look lovely. Quite the lady.'

Non stood back, satisfied with her work, and then, picking up the used pitcher and bowl, she turned to lead the way out of the bedroom door. As Efa followed her out onto the landing, the warmth of the hall below hit her. She could see Eluned fussing around the fire and Ifan sat at the table in Cynan's chair. But there was no sign of her husband. She could also see three small figures dotted around the hall engaged with various activities.

As she descended, five pairs of eyes were suddenly trained on her, and Efa wanted to turn and fly back up to her room. But she steeled herself, determined to meet her anxiety head on. They were only children, after all; what had she to fear?

And then, as she reached the base of the stairs, Non had gathered them, all three, to stand before her. The elder two stood stiffly, their hands by their sides, eyes studying Efa intently. Their appraisal of her was unnerving and Efa's hands felt suddenly clammy as she gripped them tightly together in front of her stomach.

'It is nice to meet you all. I am Efa. Perhaps you could tell me your names?' Her voice was not as steady as she had hoped either. She pasted a smile on her face.

There was one boy and it was him she turned to first. He looked to be about seven or eight, maybe older, but it was hard to tell as he was slightly built and not tall. His hair was dark, and his features fine in a strikingly pale face. He wore a serious look but at least he spoke.

'I am Gerallt.' The voice was thin and quiet. His pale face turned pink as he stepped forward and made a small bow, before hastily stepping back to stand with his sisters.

The taller of the girls stepped forward but made no attempt to bow or bob. She was older, taller, and dark-haired and fine-featured like her brother. The look on her face as she examined Efa was decidedly disdainful.

'I am Manon. I will soon be old enough to marry. This is our sister, Haf. She is five years old.' She pulled the little one close to her in a protective gesture. 'We were not expecting my father to bring home a wife. We are not sure why you are here.'

Her statement threw Efa for a moment. But before she could think of a reply that satisfied both Manon and indeed herself,

41

the littlest girl extricated herself from her sister's hold and ran into Efa's legs. She buried a head of golden curls into her skirts and, after squeezing her legs for a moment, she turned a little face up as Efa bent down. The face was round and soft and full of smiles. She looked very different from her siblings, except for her eyes. All three children had their father's dark-framed grey-green eyes.

'Are you going to be our new mother?'

'Haf!' Manon growled and stepped forward to pull her sister away. But Efa had moved faster. She had sunk to her knees and grasped the little girl's hands in her own. She smiled, and this time it came easily.

'Little one, I would love to have been your mother, but you had a mother who loved you very much. I could not replace her. So what I would like to be is your friend. A friend who can perhaps look after you at times? Play with you, show you new things, and even comfort you when you are sad? Would that be acceptable?' She glanced up at Manon and Gerallt, knowing they had heard her words and hoping they had taken them in the sincerity with which they had been spoken, wondering if they would also accept her on those terms. She turned her attention back to Haf.

The little girl had turned her head to one side and was examining Efa's face closely. 'Yes,' she said eventually. 'Yes, that would be 'sceptible. As long as you like animals. Because I like animals, and if you did not like animals, then I do not think I could be your friend.'

Efa nodded solemnly, trying to keep the smile from returning to her face. 'I understand. And I do like animals very much, although you might have to teach me what you know about the animals you have here at Tregaron. Could you do that?'

'Oh yes!' Haf said excitedly. 'We are going to see some puppies in the stables right now. Ifan promised to take us if we were polite and kind in our welcome. Were we?'

Efa glanced over at the other children, still stood apart from her. Gerallt looked unsure and Manon was positively glowering.

42

Efa could well understand their feelings towards her, the suspicion and distrust. She may not have felt welcomed with open arms by them all, but she decided on diplomacy.

'Yes. You all welcomed me well,' she said with a nod.

'So will you come and see the puppies with us?' Haf was now jumping from foot to foot with excitement.

'Now, children. Let us leave the Lady Efa to settle into her new home.' Ifan had appeared beside her. 'Well done,' he murmured, before adding in a louder voice, 'My lady, we have carried your belongings into your chamber. Perhaps Non will help you sort and find places to store them.'

She turned to him and dipped her head, smiling gratefully. 'Thank you, Ifan.'

Non had gone, and returned with outdoor clothing for the children. As she began to help them dress with mantles and gloves, Efa realised another small person had appeared. Siwan! Efa felt a wave of shame. She hadn't thought once about the girl and how she had fared since their arrival at Tregaron. She didn't even know where she had slept. But looking at her now, she could see that Siwan looked rested and clean. Her long chestnut hair was brushed to a shine and her cheeks were rosy. Someone had found clothes for her too. The ones she wore looked of a far finer quality than those she had travelled in, and fitted her form well. Presenting like that she seemed older than Efa had first thought, maybe even the same age as Manon. She was smiling shyly.

'You are happy for Siwan to come and see the puppies with us?' Ifan asked. 'She has been very helpful to Eluned in the kitchen this morning.'

'Of course, yes. Yes, go, Siwan. Thank you, Ifan.'

She was thankful that at least someone had given the girl some care and attention while she had been wallowing in her exhaustion and self-pity.

Non encouraged all four children to follow Ifan's tall form out of the door, and then returned to Efa with a smile.

'I suspect you were as unprepared to look after Siwan as you were to become a mother... or a *friend*... to three strange children. If they seemed less than welcoming, don't take it to heart.' Non was leading the way back to the stairs. 'And in case you were wondering, Siwan slept with Eluned in the warmth of the kitchen. And she seemed quite at home in helping her to prepare and serve breakfast this morning. Before being subjected to a bath, by the look of things!'

'She was sent to serve me. I really should have taken more care over her well-being. But in all honesty, I don't really think I will need her here.'

'Because you have me?' They had reached the landing.

'Well, yes. But I am not used to having anyone help me wash and dress. Except my cousin Marared, of course. We helped each other.'

Non laughed. 'Well, I'm not your cousin, but I'd like to help you. We can unpack these together.' They were now inside the chamber, faced with a selection of wooden chests and travelling bags. The charcoal brazier had also been restocked and the room definitely felt warmer for it. It meant they could leave the window partially unshuttered, and Efa was glad for the sunlight that brought life and colour into the room.

They worked companionably together to sort, fold and arrange her clothes and to store her possessions. Surprisingly, it did help make it feel more like home to have her familiar things around her. She stopped to watch Non place carefully folded garments into a large wooden chest. She felt a wave of gratitude for the young woman's attentiveness.

'There is something I want to thank you for, Non. Well, besides caring for my person and possessions, of course. I want to thank you for greeting me with such kindness. I have not shown you the appreciation you deserved in return. There seems to be much kindness in this house. You, Ifan, Eluned.'

Non glanced up and Efa saw her gently touch a small wooden cross that hung from her neck.

'That is good to know, that you have found kindness here. It is as it should be.'

Efa thought to the children's introduction to her.

'Manon wasn't so sure how to welcome me. I suppose she will not feel kindly to me usurping her mother's place?'

Non stood and closed the lid on the chest, and then perched herself on top of it.

'I did not want to talk to you about the children and their mother before you had the chance to meet them. They are real people and not just products of the things that have happened to them. And now that you have met the children for yourself, and spoken kindly to them, I am happy to answer any questions you may have.'

Efa sat down on the side of her bed and folded her hands. Non let out a breath and continued.

'Manon is slow to trust anyone. She carries a lot of sadness, understandably perhaps, and has been forced, in her own mind at least, to grow up too quickly. That quip about being of an age to marry,' Non chuckled. 'That was just to challenge you, so that you do not dare to treat her as a child. And yet, I feel that to be a child is what she really needs to be, for a while at least.'

'And Gerallt, he seemed shy, and... frail. Is that the right word?'

'He is quiet and thinks deeply. And yes, he has been sickly for much of his young life. He certainly isn't half as robust as his two elder brothers. And very different from them in his interests too. He has no desire to fight, or run, or ride. So much so that his father has despaired of him at times. He does not know how to relate to the boy.'

Non had said something that Efa had picked up on. There were more children! As if three weren't enough for her to get used to. She tried not to show her discomfiture, but her voice was suddenly shaky. 'I didn't know there were two more boys. Will I get to meet them also?'

Non glanced up from where she had been fiddling with her apron hem and grinned. 'I daresay you will meet them eventually, Efa. But you will not need to worry about being a mother to them in any way. Gruffydd is almost a man, in years anyway, and Dafydd is but two years younger. Both are learning to be fighting men like their father. Gruffydd is attached to the household of Lord Maelgwyn *ap* Rhys, Prince of Deuheubarth. Dafydd left last year to join Llewellyn's retinue in the north.'

'One has gone to Llewellyn and the other stays with Maelgwyn. That sounds like Cynan is playing at diplomacy. One of his sons in each camp. Obviously I am familiar with Llewellyn, but I know little of Maelgwyn.'

'Maelgwyn inherited Deuheubarth from his father, the Lord Rhys. Cynan faithfully served the Lord Rhys for years. Unfortunately, Maelgwyn is not nearly so great or so loved as his father was. He has a vicious side and does not respond well when crossed. He has even treated family members with vile cruelty. I fear for Gruffydd in his company. I have already noticed him changing from the likeable boy he once was.' She sighed heavily then and stood to wander over towards the window, her arms held crossed tight in front of her. 'And Llewellyn holds the reins of power here now. He only allows Maelgwyn to keep the lordship of a single *cantref* south of here, and has trusted Cynan with the oversight of the *cantref* that Tregaron sits in. Placing one of his sons with each of the two men holding most power here proves Cynan's allegiance to both, I suppose. I only wish for Gruffydd's sake that it hadn't been necessary. And Dafydd – well, he now lives far from home and we will see little of him.'

Efa did not dare to imagine what Cynan's older sons would think to find their father's new wife was a girl near to their own age. She shuddered at the thought, but that was another day's battle. She would only see them when they visited and was secretly glad of it.

'Their mother died when Haf was born, then?'

Non turned and plonked herself on the window seat, motioning for Efa to join her.

'There is much that you probably need to know, Efa. Some of it might shock you, but I have been given permission to answer all your questions honestly.' Non placed a hand over Efa's. 'But these are things only known within this family. And I trust you to keep the things I tell you safe as secrets to stay within these walls.'

'I understand. You have my word.' Efa was both curious and nervous now. She had not seen Non so serious in the short time she had known her. Surprisingly, she realised that she already liked this young woman who sat beside her. Liked her very much. And now she was to be trusted with secrets, and that must mean that Non had judged her worthy.

'Annest was a beautiful woman. She was slight and had the same fine features you saw in Manon and Gerallt but with hair not dissimilar to yours, fair and curling to her waist. Haf is the only one of her children to have inherited her colouring. Cynan's father had built this hall and prospered the estate and Cynan was set to inherit it all. His father was determined to add wealth to Tregaron in the choice of bride for his son. Annest did not disappoint. She came from a prominent family and with a significant bridal dowry, enough to make improvements to both building and lands. It was all arranged and she was probably much the same age as you when she entered this house. But it was not a love match, nor ever would be, because Cynan had already given his heart elsewhere. There was already another woman, one he could never marry, and there was already a child on the way.'

Non paused and lifted her head. Efa met her gaze and then suddenly there was a moment of clarity, why Non's appearance had been familiar to her. She too had inherited her father's grey-green eyes.

'You?' She whispered, trying to suppress the surprise in her voice.

Non nodded and released her hand, looking away and dipping her head.

'Efa, you must understand that Cynan... my father... is not a bad man.'

No, Efa thought, *just a man who abandoned the woman he loved and married one he didn't. Oh, and then years later forced another young woman he didn't love to marry him, when she could have married the one she loved.* Not bad? Not particularly good either, the way she judged it. But could she judge him? Non had said that he hadn't had any choice in whom he married the first time. Perhaps he had been forced to give up on love, as she had. At least his bastard-born daughter had been given a home.

'I can see that this has shocked you, as I thought it might.' Non raised her head to look at Efa again. 'But there is more. And you do need to know it. It might explain why things are as they are now. It might help you to see how you can fit into our lives here, and maybe even help you to forgive Cynan for bringing you to Tregaron.'

Efa closed her eyes and bowed her head, clutching the edge of the seat that extended either side of her. Did she want to know more? She already had much to process. Revelations about her new husband that she had not expected to hear, and about the new friend who sat quietly beside her. It was a strange arrangement, to be sure. What exactly was Non's status in this house?

'We can talk more later, if you would feel more comfortable.'

Non's offer was kind, but Efa knew leaving her with unanswered questions would not be good for the quietness of her mind when she finally found herself alone. For her own sake, and that of her relationship with the family of this house, she needed to know all; needed to know exactly what sort of household she had been wedded into. She lifted her face to Non again.

'Your mother, the woman Cynan loved, does she still live?'

Non gave a funny little half-laugh. 'Oh yes, she well and truly lives.' And then her face grew more serious. 'My mother, Iola, and Cynan knew each other from childhood. Ifan is Iola's brother, and my uncle. The three of them grew up together here. The friendship between Iola and Cynan grew into love, and they hid it well, although I think Ifan always knew of it. It was when the relationship was finally discovered that Cynan's father stepped in and arranged the marriage with Annest. Neither Cynan or his father knew at the time that my mother was already carrying me in her womb. Cynan could not, would not, stand up to his father and refuse to wed his wealthy bride. Iola was secreted away to another place, and Cynan welcomed Annest into this house. It was only when he learned that Iola had given birth to a child and was desperately ill that he went looking for her, abandoning his new wife here. He stayed with us until he knew my mother would survive. And then, desperate not to be separated from her again, he moved us back nearer to Tregaron and continued to care for us, while also trying to keep his new wife happy and his father in the dark.

'By the time his father died and Cynan inherited, Annest knew enough to understand that she was not her husband's first love. She was used to fine things, so Cynan tried to make things better for her by providing her with the best of everything. He built the tower that houses these rooms, and they were furnished to Annest's design. She did her duty in providing him with children, and there grew a genuine respect and fondness between them. She was a brave and good woman to endure what she did with such good grace. I suppose there are very many like her who have had to make the most of marriages forced upon them.' She reached across to squeeze Efa's hand.

'But his wife was unloved!' Efa's words had a bitter edge to them.

'No, she was not! Not by her children, nor by the others in this house, and even Cynan loved her in his own way. He certainly mourned genuinely when she died, not long after Haf was born. The whole community did, her absence was so keenly felt. But there were the children to consider too. I had not lived here until that point, although I had never been unwelcome. I offered to come and stay and help to care for the little ones, as they were then. I have been here since.'

'Cynan did not move your mother in?' Again Efa couldn't disguise the critical tone of her words.

'My mother did not want that. And it would not have been right for the children. Iola and my father have their own longstanding arrangement. She has never wanted to be the mistress of this house, and he prefers to spend his nights in her humble home than here with its memories of Annest. I think you must understand now, Efa? He has not married you to bed you. He has no desire for any other woman than my mother, or for any more children. He has married you for his children's sake.'

Efa took in what Non was saying. Relief vied with disbelief. And another emotion – disappointment? Not disappointment that there would be no true marriage between herself and Cynan. She did not desire him in any way. Did not even really know the man. Rather, she now knew that she might never know the true intimacy of the marriage bed with any man. She was a wife, but might as well have stayed a spinster, become a nun even. And that was not a future she had ever seen for herself. She had always dreamed of giving herself fully to a man that she loved.

As her thoughts spun unwanted back to Philip, waves of pain at the loss of what would never be threatened to overwhelm her. She willed herself to fight those feelings down. It would not help her to give into them. Better still that she hardened her heart and accepted her lot, as Annest had before her. She looked around the room with its fine finishes, and imagined its former occupant perhaps spending many hours there, alone maybe. It was a beautiful room, but had it become a prison, a place of regret and loss, she wondered?

She was jarred out of her sad imaginings by the sound of running feet and excited voices. Two grinning faces appeared at her door, one ringed with golden curls, the other with windblown chestnut hair. Both faces were flushed with the cold, and with excitement.

'Lady, lady, come and see! You must come. Oh, please come,' Haf was wriggling excitedly. Siwan was stood slightly behind her, saying nothing but nodding enthusiastically.

'What now? What's all this excitement?' Non had already stood to waylay the girls, who were threatening to step muddy feet onto the fine rug that lay just inside the threshold of the room.

'Yes. Haf, Siwan. What is it we must come and see?' Efa rose from her seat and walked towards the girls, smiling despite herself.

'A puppy!' The girls squealed in unison.

'A puppy? In the house?' Non didn't seem thrilled with the idea.

'Oh yes, but we had to bring him inside. He is so little and was so cold, and Ifan said he would probably die, and that was the way of things if his mother couldn't feed him with his brothers. And I said that I would be his mother, and feed him, and make him warm again. He will not die then, will he?' Haf hardly took a breath.

Efa and Non exchanged a glance. Neither wanted to answer that particular question.

'Well, we must just come and see.' Efa spoke first. She hoped very much for the little girls' sake that this new little adventure was not going to end in grief.

Won't you tell me, lover of my soul,

where do you feed your flock?

Where do you lead your beloved ones

to rest in the heat of the day?

Why should I be like a veiled woman

as I wander among the flocks of your shepherds? …

Listen, my radiant one —

if you ever lose sight of me,

just follow in my footsteps where I lead my

lovers.

Come with your burdens and cares.

Come to the place near the sanctuary of my

shepherds.

Song of Solomon 1:7-8, TPT

4

Cynan

There was indeed a puppy. Laid in style in a basket that probably once held bread, on a sheepskin quite as fine as any in Efa's room. He was small, granted. A little ball of white fluff, with matching brown patches, one over each eye. A thin tail wagged pathetically as Efa and the girls approached. The newcomer had gathered quite an audience with Eluned, Ifan and Gerallt all stood around the basket that had been placed as close to the fire as was safe. Manon was the only one who held back, but even she was surreptitiously inching nearer to see more.

'He has a poorly leg. See?' Haf had knelt down and with surprising gentleness lifted the puppy's rear left paw so that Efa could see the leg was misshapen. 'Ifan said that is why he could not fight for his place with the others, to feed from the mother dog. But *we* can feed him now, and he doesn't have to move at all if he doesn't want to.'

Efa was concerned as to whether the poor mite would ever be able to move, or indeed walk or run as a dog should. Would it not be kinder perhaps to leave the puppy to its sad fate? She glanced over at Ifan, and their eyes met over the children's heads. His forehead creased and he shook his head slightly. She wondered why he had agreed to bringing the puppy inside, to giving the girls hope, however frail a hope that might be. She sensed a softness in the big man, bordering on indulgence maybe. It might not have been the wisest of decisions to give into the girls' pleas. It might yet all end in heartbreak.

Eluned was all business. 'Some warm milk with softened bread, I think. And shall we try him with some cooked capon? I have some roasted that we can shred up. If he has teeth already, of course.'

As if on cue the puppy opened his mouth with a large yawn, showing a very fine set of pinprick teeth. Eluned laughed. And Efa smiled despite herself. Haf was clapping her hands in excitement and the wagging tail sped up in response. Eluned whispered something to Siwan and the two disappeared, returning only moments later with the dish of milk and bread, and a trencher with the scraps of roast capon meat. Siwan knelt to offer the dish to the puppy who obliged by raising his head just enough to lap with a small pink tongue. Haf was soon beside the older girl, using her fingers to feed morsels of bread and meat to the dog. He didn't seem to be lacking in appetite.

The whole of the household was engrossed in this little scene; none of them heard the door of the hall open and close, until suddenly another figure was standing in the circle with them.

'Now, what have we here?'

Every one of them started in surprise at the authoritative tone. Haf and Siwan stood quickly to their feet, the older girl sliding to half-hide herself behind Eluned.

'Tad! You are home!'

Haf flung herself against Cynan's legs and he staggered slightly, laughing at her exuberant welcome. He patted her curls and placed his hand under her chin, lifting her face to place a small kiss on her forehead. 'Hello, my littlest one. And where is my boy, and my more-sensible daughter?'

Gerallt and Manon had moved closer to their father, but their welcome was decidedly less demonstrative, as if they were more unsure of how to approach him. Cynan held out his arms towards them, and slowly first Manon and then Gerallt stepped stiffly into his embrace. It was all very awkward and both children seemed relieved when he released them. Haf was still clinging to his legs but he extracted her gently.

'Thank you for your welcome, little one. But I still need an explanation as to why there is a small white dog lying like royalty by my fire and being hand-fed from my kitchen. And why no one seems to have anything more important to do than entertain it?' He glanced around and even Efa felt her face flush under his gaze. But his eyes were smiling.

Ifan laughed. 'Well, if you had seen your daughter's face as she pleaded with me to save the poor puppy dog's life, you too would have brought him inside to live like a king.'

'I give you that!' Cynan snorted. He bent down to tickle the small white muzzle, and the little pink tongue snaked out and licked his hand.

'Well, I suppose he can stay. But that doesn't mean that he gets so much attention that everyone forgets to do their more important tasks. Like preparing me some food! It is past noon and I am ready to eat. If you wouldn't mind?' He turned his pointed gaze to Eluned, who sniffed and tossed her head before turning and leaving the room, at half the speed she had moved when going to fetch the puppy his meal. Siwan trailed behind her.

Cynan turned his attention to his children. 'You can go to the kitchen and eat there today. Ifan, Non, will you see to them?' They were all being dismissed bar Efa. She sensed the change in the atmosphere as they all left, and shivered in anticipation of being left alone with her husband.

'My lady,' Cynan turned and seemed to be appraising her, taking in her blue woollen gown and simple white head covering, finishing his perusal with an approving nod. Efa let out the breath she didn't know she had been holding. From the moment Cynan had entered and made himself known, she realised she had been on guard. This was the first time she had ever been fully alone with her husband. She had never spoken more than a few polite words with him.

Non had told her that he was not looking for a lover, but she was Cynan's wife now and other things would be expected of her. She was surprised at how much she wanted to prove herself worthy. She didn't think she had married a harsh man, from what she had seen and heard, and from the very atmosphere of his household here at Tregaron. But she had married a wealthy, powerful man, who dealt with princes, and that required her to be a certain kind of wife. She would have to host nobles at his table, she would have to stand proud under their scrutiny; she didn't want to let herself down.

Cynan was standing holding his hand out to her. After a moment of hesitation, she lifted hers to meet his, and allowed him to lead her to the table. This time she did not sit opposite him on the backless bench as she had the night before; instead, he led her to a chair that had been placed beside his own. Both chairs were similar in design, dark wood with finely carved wooden backs, both shiny and worn with age. The only difference was that her chair was slightly narrower than his. *Annest's chair*, she realised with sudden apprehension. His wife's chair.

Efa felt the enormity of it as she lowered herself to take her seat. The feeling of being a usurper of sorts. She was too young, too inexperienced for this role that had been forced upon her. Yes, she had been raised in the court of a prince, but never as a person of note, always in the background. She had not dreamt of nobility as her cousin Marared, Llewellyn's daughter, had. She had been happy enough to be a companion, a servant even, to live a simpler life. Until Philip. But even marriage to him would not have elevated her much. He was a second son, with no inheritance of his own. They would have lived dependent on his elder brother, John, for any wealth or status. Now, here she was, lady of the manor of Tregaron, married to a man of influence, and young enough to be his daughter.

Cynan was talking to her, she realised. She had been sat lost in her thoughts, her hands gripped white in her lap. He was sitting in his chair, leaning towards her.

'I hope you have found it comfortable in my house, and that you have been well served.'

She nodded, mutely, not meeting his gaze.

She felt him shift his position and move yet closer to her. She could smell the scent of horses on his clothes. He did not touch her, but his hand lay on the arm of her chair. And when he spoke again it was quieter, softer.

'I am sorry, Efa, if you are not happy.'

She glanced up then, and in his face saw a look of genuine concern.

'My lord,' she swallowed hard, wanting to reassure him. But it was true, what he said. She was not happy. Not happy to be in his house, sitting at his table, despite the kindness she had been shown and the comfort afforded her here.

'Everyone has been very kind and attentive,' she said quietly. That was the truth.

'I am glad of it.' He leaned back and removed his arm from her chair, as Eluned appeared with Siwan trailing behind her. A selection of food was presented, and a shared trencher placed between them.

'Will you eat with me?' Cynan asked as he began to load his side of the trencher with meat and bread. She automatically reached to help herself, her stomach twitching more with nerves than hunger. She picked at her food as he tucked heartily into his.

If she had thought that he was satisfied with their short conversation, she was wrong. As soon as they were alone, he addressed her again. He at least politely finished his mouthful and took a deep swig of ale first.

'The girl who travelled with you, she seems to have attached herself to Eluned. Was she not sent to serve you?' It was not accusatory, just an enquiry.

'Her name is Siwan, my lord. I do not need her to serve me, and if she is happier in the kitchen, then I am happy for her to stay there. And to play with your children at times, if you agree? To help look after the puppy, at least.'

Cynan nodded with a deep chuckle. 'It seems my children, well, the youngest of them anyway, may very well be running this whole household. A puppy, indeed! Ifan is soft with them. We all are.' He looked markedly at Efa. 'My children have need of a steadying influence.'

Efa looked away. His children needed something – a more present father, maybe? She felt a twinge of something. Anger? Frustration? Panic? Was he about to shift responsibility for his children over to her? She swiftly changed the subject back to Siwan.

'I mean to talk with Siwan and give her the chance to return to her home in Swansea, if it can be arranged? She was distraught to have been dragged away from her home against her will.' Efa's voice had taken on an edge, and she felt suddenly close to tears. The knife she had been holding was gripped tightly in her fist.

Cynan stopped eating and took another deep swig of his ale. He stood, pushing back his chair from the table.

'If you have eaten all you require, would you join me for a walk? I would love to show you more of Tregaron. I suggest you put the knife down first,' he added quietly.

Efa released her hold on the utensil and it clattered to the table, the sound echoing around the hall. She reached for her own cup and swallowed the ale, and her tears with it. Cynan was standing by the door, throwing a thick wool mantle around his shoulders. Non appeared from nowhere with Efa's miniver laid over her arm. Efa rose from the table to meet her.

'It is dry and now more resembles the animal it was made from, rather than a drowned rat,' Non chattered cheerily as she held the mantle up to place it around Efa's shoulders. 'It is dry outside and the sun shines, but the air is still cold. You will be thankful for this.' She caught Efa's eye as she helped fasten it at Efa's neck. Her look was so kind that Efa had to swallow again, and shut her eyes momentarily against the prick of tears. She felt Non's hand clasp her arm and squeeze it reassuringly. 'Do not fear, Efa. All will be well,' she whispered.

Cynan had the door open and was waiting for her to pass through. Efa stepped out into the sun. The sky was pale blue with a few stringy white clouds hanging like whispers in the air. Her first sight of the outside of Tregaron startled her somewhat. It really was impressive. The gatehouse they had entered through the night before was a substantial stone-built tower, with arrow slits on the outside walls, but small high windows on the inside walls. Either side of the gatehouse a tall stone wall swept around in a wide arc to meet either end of the building they had just stepped out of. The area enclosed was sizeable. To one side was a wooden stable complex, those same stables where a certain puppy had lately been residing. Between the stable and the house was a kitchen garden, more brown soil than green growth. But Efa could see herbs and turnip tops, and a few forlorn-looking cabbage plants still growing. A wide, cobbled path divided this side of the enclosure from the other, and Cynan was leading her down it. He stopped and reached out for her, taking her elbow to turn her around so that she could see the full aspect of the building they had just left.

Her jaw dropped. The hall she had only seen from the inside the previous night stood before them. It was built with well-cut stone. Both the entrance door and the mullioned window beside it were decorated with fine stone arches. The hall alone would have been a worthy home for a wealthy man, except that at either end also rose two towers. They were not identical. At the east end the tower that accommodated Efa's room was square, and boasted several good-sized windows on the upper floor. In contrast, the tower at the west end was taller and circular, with familiar castellations, and arrow slits visible on the levels above the height of the enclosure wall. The west tower was reached by an external wooden stairway to a door some feet off the ground. It was obviously built for defence.

'My father added the west tower not long after the hall was finished. I added the gatehouse and stone wall when the east tower was completed.'

'When you married the first time?' Efa blurted the words out, while thinking, *with your wife's money.*

Cynan turned to her, his eyes seeming to drum into her. He held her gaze long enough for Efa to begin to shift uncomfortably. She felt like a child being assessed for her level of maturity and found severely wanting. He did not answer her question.

'We live in turbulent times and in a turbulent land, where your friends can quickly become your enemies, and your enemies, friends. Ambitious lords vie with each other for power, and there are losers and winners, and there are also those caught in the middle. It seemed sensible to make sure we could defend ourselves and that my family would remain safe. Tregaron is a more secure place than many of the homes of those far nobler than we. We have loyal men who would lay down their lives to guard this place and my family. They man the gatehouse and they man the tower. You will meet them and they will treat you with respect. Or hear from me.'

Cynan continued as he led her past the stables. 'You will find horses to choose from here and grooms to prepare them for you. But I would advise that you do not ride out alone at any time. Ask Ifan and he will accompany you, or he will find a trustworthy man to go in his stead. If you would rather not ride, the wagon can be made available for you. Or if you like to walk, of course.' They had reached the main gates, which stood open. Cynan walked through them and waited for her to follow. A narrow path wound along the outer side of the east wall towards an area marked by a line of reeds, and a large weeping willow. Efa could hear the sound of water splashing over rocks.

'Behind the house runs the River Brennig. It is a wide enough stretch of water to act as a defence, as much as any moat would. On a pleasant day the riverside also provides a good place to walk. As long as you do not stray out of sight of the walls, you should be safe. I do not allow the children to wander alone to the riverbank, however, as the water can run fast and full. In fact, they are forbidden from going outside these walls alone at any time. But I do not want them to live as prisoners so hope you will find time to venture out with them.'

He had turned back towards the gates, so Efa followed, taking it all in. It felt a bit like he was laying all this out for her and hoping for her approval. Not to impress her so much as to reassure her of Tregaron's comfort and safety.

They had walked back through the gates. To the left of the cobbled path Efa could see a collection of established fruit trees, six or seven of them, bare branched but with early buds appearing. The grass beneath them was well kept. As they walked nearer the house, they came to a tall hedge, dense and well trimmed. Efa could see it took the shape of a three-sided square, with the stone wall creating a fourth. Cynan led her down a path that followed the edge of the square until they came to a gap in the hedge. He stopped there and stood back to let her enter the enclosed garden herself. It was a beautiful space, even in its winter state, with evergreen shrubs and tall ornate grasses. Efa could see rose bushes and, in the soil beneath them, tiny white snowdrops and pale yellow crocuses littering the ground. The whole garden was thoughtfully laid out and obviously tended.

She stopped at a stone bench and Cynan encouraged her to sit. He sat as well but leaving a man's width between them. Efa breathed in deeply and closed her eyes, lifting her face to look for warmth from the watery sun that was still commanding the sky. She could hear birds grubbing around for worms, or maybe it was for sticks to build their nests. The garden felt like an oasis.

'This was Annest's special space. More so even than that fine room you now occupy. She would spend hours here; it made her happy. And she deserved to be happy, as God knows she did not get the love she deserved from me.'

Efa looked up at him. His face was surprisingly sad.

'The children you gave her must have brought her joy?'

He smiled a small smile. 'Yes, they did. But they also shortened her life.'

They sat in silence for a few moments, both lost in their thoughts, before he shifted and turned towards her.

'Efa, it is my wish for you to be happy here at Tregaron,' he paused and rubbed a hand absent-mindedly over his stubbly chin. 'When you spoke of Siwan before, I knew it was not just her you felt had been brought here, into this situation, against her will. I knew, when I witnessed that lovestruck boy make his foolish protest before Llewellyn, and saw your reaction, that you had been given to me against your will. I even thought to renege on my deal with Llewellyn for your sake. I understand what it

61

means to be forced to marry one that you do not love, and to love one that you must be separated from.'

He paused, and Efa felt herself flush. Did he know that Non had told her his own story?

'But Llewellyn would not have taken well to me pulling out of our agreement. Our marriage solidifies my relationship with the prince. And staying in his favour means I can enjoy being left alone to govern this *cantref*. He affords me that privilege, and my son is also now in his service.' He paused. 'I also needed a wife for my children's sake.'

Efa shook her head. 'You may have chosen me as a wife to stay on good terms with Llewellyn, but you did not choose well if you wanted me to be a mother. I am barely out of childhood myself. Perhaps you have made a mistake in bringing me here.'

'What's done is done, Efa. And cannot, will not, be undone. You are my wife now, and your lover has abandoned you.' He was clearly riled as he had stood to his feet and was pacing. He must have realised the harshness of his words as he stopped his pacing and came to stand before her. Efa sat motionless, feeling the chill of the cold stone bench go right through her.

When Cynan spoke again his tone was softer. He let out a long breath. 'They do not need a mother, Efa. You will never replace Annest, particularly for Manon and Gerallt. Haf never knew her mother, so may yet attach herself dearer to you, but not the older children. They have also been shown much love and care, mothered well by Eluned and Non these past years. What they need now is to be prepared for the world that they will have to live in, outside these walls.

'Manon is soon of marrying age but she has none of the attributes looked for in a wife of status. You can train her in those things, prepare her. Gerallt – well, I just do not understand the boy, he is so different in his interests, and I fear for him, that he will not be strong enough of character to survive life in the real world. Perhaps he might respond better to you than he has to me. I fear that all three have been coddled and I am not here often enough to supervise them properly.'

'You are their father. I am a stranger to them. You really think I can be more use to them than you? Perhaps you should be here more.' Efa added the last under her breath, out of sheer frustration. He must have heard her and for the first time she saw anger flicker across his face.

'I owe you no explanation for how I choose to live my life.'

He was right, and she felt chastened. As her husband he did not have to excuse his actions to her, to defer to her in any way. If he chose to spend his nights away from his family, and months away from home courting the powerful, that was his due. She had no rights here. In fact, he had offered her far more than many women in her situation would ever hope to get. He had just offered the whole of his home and the use of all she needed there, to be content. There was fine food on her table and luxurious furnishings in her chamber. All he wanted in return was for her to invest a little time and care into three motherless children.

Could she do this? Could she make this lovely place her home, and find contentment in caring for Cynan's family? She weighed up the imagined future with Philip she had dreamed of against the reality of what was being asked of her now. Her heart still longed for the former, but her head told her she had to accept the inevitable. She had little choice but to stay, and it was going to be up to her to make the best of it, to snatch what happiness she could from it. She might never know true love again, but perhaps like Annest before her, she could find a place of peace here.

She breathed deeply and took a moment to calm herself. He had resumed his seat and now sat silent beside her. She knew she deserved some response.

'My lord husband,' she chose formality. 'I will repay the generosity of your kindness in welcoming me into your home by becoming a friend to your children. Only time will tell if my influence on them will be what you have hoped for.'

He studied her face for a moment and then nodded. 'We all have much to discover about how we will influence one another here, so that is enough for me. There is but one more thing,

Efa.' His face had softened again. 'I heard you laugh at Swansea. It is my hope to one day hear you laugh that way again, here at Tregaron.'

My dearest one,

let me tell you how I see you –

you are so thrilling to me.

Song of Solomon 1:9, TPT

5

Siwan

He had escorted her back inside the house, and then her new husband was gone. Efa felt strangely bereft to be left alone. There was no sign of Non, and she didn't feel she could yet interrupt the children in their scattered pastimes. Who was she to them? She had been here for less than a day. She needed to find her feet as mistress of this house somehow, and then observe the workings of the household and indeed observe the children to see how best she could fulfil her promise to Cynan. She would try, she knew that much, however inadequate she felt for the task. At a loss as to what else she could do, she purposed to find Siwan, a comforting connection with her old life. She had things she wanted to say to the girl and she owed it to her to check on her well-being.

She found Siwan in the kitchen. A stone-built addition to the back of the main house, it was a good-sized room, stone-flagged with a large, well-worn table filling much of the central space. Along the back wall was a fireplace and hearth, with a smoke hole opening out of the roof above. There was also a simple oven to one side of the fire, and it was there she found the bent figure of Siwan.

'Siwan.'

The girl started and spun around to face Efa. Her face was flushed from the heat and there was a very obvious dab of white flour on her nose. She was wearing an apron too big for her tied several times around her slight waist. In her hands she held a clay dish.

'Now, now, my lady. Don't be disturbing the chief baker at her work!' Eluned bustled into view with a chuckle. 'Siwan, get that pie in the oven and then go and fetch some water for me, if you wouldn't mind.' She waited as the girl slid her dish into the oven and skittered away, before turning her attention back to Efa, her hands on her wide hips and one eyebrow raised.

'Welcome to my kitchen, Lady Efa. What can I get for you?'

Eluned wasn't brusque exactly. Nonetheless, Efa suddenly felt like she had stepped uninvited into the other woman's domain, and she felt her face flush.

'My apologies, Eluned, if I am disturbing you. I will leave you to your work. Please excuse me.' Efa held up her hands and then lifted her skirts to turn back the way she had come. She was surprised to find her eyes pricking. And then there was a soft hand on her arm.

'Now, now then, no need to hurry away.' Eluned had softened her tone. 'Come, come and sit here.' She gestured to the table and pulled out a stool for her to sit on. Efa did as she was told. 'It is just that I am not used to the lady of the house deigning to visit us here in the kitchen unannounced. You surprised me, 'tis all. I guess you were just finding your way around your new home. In need of some friendly company, perhaps?'

Efa felt the intensity of Eluned's gaze and heard the note of concern in her voice. She closed her eyes briefly against the threatening tears. It would do no good for her to cry. She had already decided that. But she really was very glad of some friendly company. She still felt lost in this strange new life of hers. She swallowed hard and struggled to find her voice.

'You are not used to unannounced visits and I am not used to being the lady of the house, either, Eluned.' She looked over to find the older woman nodding her understanding. 'I actually feel quite at home in hot kitchens and muddy gardens alike.' She laughed nervously, forcing a smile. 'Nevertheless, please accept my apologies. I feel that I really do need to learn the ways of things here and what my place is to be. To be honest with you, I don't know how to act or behave. All I do know is that at this very moment I feel more comfortable here at your table than sitting upstairs in my fine room alone. But I really don't want to keep you from your work. I only came looking for Siwan… and… what *is* that tantalising smell?'

Efa heard her stomach rumble and Eluned must have heard it too. She chortled.

'That my lady, is one of the pies that our little Siwan has just baked. I cannot tell you how fine a little cook she is. Her pie crust is the best I think I have ever tasted. She has already proved her worth in my kitchen.' She suddenly flushed pink herself and rubbed her hands nervously down the sides of her skirt. 'Of course, I do not want you to think that I have stolen your maid from you to bake for me. I understand that she came here to serve you, and if you need her, of course she must leave my kitchen. But,' she sighed heavily, 'I have to tell you that she has really been a Godsend, even in the short time she has been here. I have been delighted to look after her for you and she in turn has really taken to helping me. To be very honest, my old bones have been very grateful, especially in lifting and carrying. The boy who is supposed to help me is more than useless at times. Siwan, however, is a natural in the kitchen. She knows instinctively how best to help. And as I say, her baking skills are… well, see for yourself…'

Before Efa had a chance to respond to Eluned's little speech she was away, returning with a trencher holding a slab of pie. The crust was a rich golden brown, and the warm filling oozed with tender pieces of meat and deliciously savoury-smelling juices. Efa's mouth was suddenly watering and she found herself raising her hand to her mouth to check she wasn't actually drooling.

'Now, I have seen how little you have allowed past your lips since you have been with us, so I suggest you get some of that down you.' Eluned plonked the pie down on the table in front of Efa and then pulled up a second stool, sitting down heavily on it with another loud sigh. She wiped her glistening brow with a corner of her apron.

Efa forgot for a moment all the reasons why she hadn't had an appetite. Before she knew it, she had scooped up a handful of warm deliciousness into her mouth. She closed her eyes to savour it and lost herself in the moment. She followed the first mouthful with a second, and a third, before looking up to see Eluned watching her with a bemused expression on her face.

'Seems we might well have to sell these pies of Siwan's as a cure for heartache.'

Efa looked down at her sticky fingers, and the now almost empty trencher lying on the table before her, feeling suddenly mortified. But as she glanced up and saw Eluned's beaming face she couldn't help but smile in response. If pies could cure heartache, that would be simple indeed. Except, she mused, she would end up very portly indeed. She had forgotten the pain in her heart for a moment to satisfy the cravings of her stomach; it wasn't a permanent cure, though, she knew it, for now that her hunger was satisfied, the dull ache in her heart had returned. No, she wouldn't be looking to food to cure her, however good it was. She licked her fingers to savour the last of the pie, and looked about for something to wipe them on.

'Here.' Eluned handed her an almost clean-looking rag and poured her a beaker of milk. 'Drink this up too, then at least I know you have had one decent meal today.'

Efa was pleased for the milk, as the pie was now sitting heavily in her stomach. She was thankful for the woman's kindness too. But she had come here to speak with Siwan. She had been grateful enough for Siwan's company on the journey from Swansea, but realised, to her shame, that she knew little about the shy girl who did not speak much, and who just then had appeared noiselessly beside her.

'I will leave you two to speak.' Eluned levered herself up from the stool with a grunt, and gestured for the girl to take her place. Siwan chose to remain standing, her hands held tightly clasped in front of her, her eyes large in a face now pale, and not just from errant flour.

Efa felt a sudden wave of compassion and reached out to take the girl's arm gently, smiling reassuringly. 'Please sit, Siwan.

There is no need to be worried. I am not angry with you, or disappointed in any way. And I have just had a piece of the most wonderfully cooked pie I have ever eaten.'

At that the girl blushed and the shadow of a smile crossed her lips. She sat as directed, but her hands lay clasped tight in her lap and her head dropped. She shifted nervously in her seat.

'Siwan, I need to apologise to you. You were very good to keep me company on our journey here, and I think we consoled each other, did we not?'

The girl did not reply. She glanced up once, and then lowered her eyes again.

'Siwan?' Efa reached forward and lifted the girl's chin so that she was forced to look at her. 'You were rightly sad to be dragged away from your home, for my sake. And I am sorry for that. I know how it feels to be forced to leave the place and people you love against your will. I am also sorry that I did not think of your feelings enough to make sure you were cared for when we arrived here. I was too tied up in my own grief, and that was wrong of me. Will you forgive me?' Efa released her chin.

Siwan held her gaze. Her lips parted and she took a breath, but then seemed to reconsider and let the breath out. She nodded her head once.

Efa smiled, and continued, 'Nor did I ask you about your family, what you were leaving behind, not on the whole of our journey. I am also sorry for that. You may think me a fine lady and that I should not have to deign to speak to you, but I want you and I to be friends, Siwan. We came here together, and we will always share that. Two strangers together in a new home, trying to find our way.'

Siwan unclasped her hands but continued to fiddle with her fingers, squeezing fingertips between finger and thumb.

'I left my tad and my brothers.' She spoke so softly that Efa had to lean closer to hear her.

'And that made you sad?'

Siwan nodded again and a solitary tear ran down her cheek.

'I am sorry.' Efa placed her hands over Siwan's, stilling them with a gentle squeeze. The girl seemed to find her courage.

'My tad worked the land for Lord John, but Mam worked in the castle kitchens. I did much of the caring for my family. I could cook, when there was food. Often after my brothers had eaten there wasn't much left for me. Mam used to bring things home from the kitchens, food that would have been given to the pigs, and that kept us from starving. That stopped when she...' Siwan swallowed and released her hands from Efa's grasp, raising one to her cheek to dash away another tear. 'My tad wanted me to come with you. He thought I would learn to be a maid to a fine lady and that with you I would always have food in my belly and a roof over my head. I agreed to come because I knew it would please him. But I didn't really want to leave my family.' She paused, and sank into herself again, seemingly exhausted with the effort of speaking.

'Thank you for telling me your story, Siwan.' Efa placed her hand gently on a hunched shoulder. 'And you seem to have inherited your mother's cooking skills, at least according to Eluned. So, tell me, Siwan, do you want to be a maid? Or would you rather stay here with Eluned and learn to be an even finer cook than you already are?'

'I have a choice?' The look she gave Efa was a startled one.

In that instant Efa realised why the girl had been so anxious. She thought she was about to be forced again, against her will, to leave the kitchen and serve Efa instead. Efa also realised the gift that was in her hands to give her the freedom to choose for herself.

'Siwan, I want you to choose what makes you happiest. I can help you to learn to be my maid, but I do not need you to be. I would be just as happy to see you stay here with Eluned. Especially if you make more of those pies!'

Siwan's eyes had filled with moisture again but now a smile lit her face. 'I do like being with Eluned. She reminds me of Mam. And I can help her... I'm stronger than I look.' She had jumped to her feet as if to demonstrate.

'Then of course you can stay here.' Efa reached out to guide the girl back down onto the stool. 'But I have something else I want to say to you, Siwan. I want to make a solemn pledge to you – I promise you that if you want to go back to Swansea, I will find a way to make that possible. It might not be today, or for many days, but if you are unhappy here, you can go back. Do you understand?'

The girl was watching her, screwing her forehead in thought.

'I like Eluned, she has been kind if a bit bossy at times.' Siwan let out a little giggle. 'And I do like Haf, she is sweet. And if I left, I could not help her look after the puppy. Will I be able to play with Haf and the puppy if I stay?'

Efa laughed gently, with the realisation that this girl who might be considered on the brink of womanhood was actually still a child at heart. One who perhaps had never known the freedom of play, or indeed known comfort or a full belly before.

'I am sure you can play with Haf and the puppy. As long as you don't forget your duties to Eluned.' Efa tried to sound stern but it was hard to, watching the girl in front of her beaming.

'Then I think I will stay here, for now at least.'

'That is fine, as long as you remember that I have promised to help you return home if ever you feel you need to. And I swear I will keep that promise.' Efa squeezed the girl's hand once more and the girl fidgeted in her seat.

'Do you think I could go and find Haf and the puppy now?' she half-whispered to Efa, looking over her head to see if Eluned was there.

'Oh, I think that would be fine,' Efa leaned forward to whisper in response. 'I'm sure Eluned will find you if she needs you.'

And with that the girl was gone, leaving Efa to muse to herself. Siwan seemed to be getting over her homesickness rather rapidly. Seemingly a friend and a small dog, and of course a job to do, and some kindness from a mother figure was enough for a lost little girl to feel at home. What would it take for her, she wondered? Yes, there was kindness in this house. And maybe helping Cynan's children would give her a purpose.

But, she thought, it would take much more than that, or a delicious pie or a sweet puppy dog, to get her to forget her longing for what might have been. And there was no going back to Swansea for her. No freedom of choice. Unlike Siwan, she had to stay, and take on a role she hadn't looked for.

She rose from her stool reluctantly. She needed to find something to occupy herself. She felt suddenly wearied and seriously contemplated returning to the warmth and comfort of her fine bed. She could pull up the covers and close her eyes and imagine herself somewhere else. An image of Philip's smiling face flashed through her mind and the stab of pain almost caused her to double over. She grabbed the edge of the table to steady herself.

'My lady?' It was Non's soft voice, and her steadying hand on Efa's arm. 'Are you well?'

Efa took a deep breath and loosened her grip on the tabletop. Non was standing there and her presence alone was strangely soothing.

'I am well, forgive me, Non. Just a little overcome with the heat in here, perhaps.'

'Shall I help you to your chamber to rest a while?'

Suddenly the thought of lying alone in a strange room and dreaming dreams that could only hurt her further was no longer appealing. A new resolution was forming. She needed to keep herself busy. Busy enough that when she did have to return to her bed later that night she would sleep dreamlessly.

'Non, can you help me find something to occupy myself with? Or accompany me on a walk, or a ride, or something?' She couldn't hide the note of desperation in her voice.

'My lady…'

'Efa, call me Efa… please!' The desperation exploded. She was immediately ashamed of her sharp tone, but Non seemed unfazed.

'Efa… The skies have just opened so I don't think we can leave the house for a while. But I have this.' She held out the garment that was draped over her arm. It was Efa's red travelling dress. It was no longer mud-spattered, but it still looked a bit worse for wear. 'There are some small tears and the seams have come apart in places from your horse ride here. But this is a fine dress and I was going to repair it for you. Perhaps we could do it together? The fire is warm in the hall. The light from the windows today is not ideal for needlework but we can light wall torches. We could lay the dress out on the table to examine it properly at least.'

'Yes. Thank you, Non.' Efa sighed in relief. That was a perfect plan. Something to do, and someone to do it with.

The girl laughed. 'Who would have thought a mending job would be so welcome?' But the look that passed between them was one of mutual understanding.

Efa blessed Non silently as the girl sat by her and they worked together. They spoke little but it was both comfortable and comforting to have a task to focus on and a kind person to keep company with. And it gave Efa the opportunity to observe what else was going on in the house. The children occupied themselves separately from one another and in a strange near silence. Apart from Haf. The young girl was occupied with the puppy, who seemingly had found a new lease of life with all the attention he was receiving. He was even attempting to stand on wobbly legs, and half-jump as Haf teased him with a stick. His antics were making her laugh, and Siwan had joined her, giggling. But the other children were seemingly uninterested in the dog.

The shutters of the high windows had been opened but the clouded sky outside meant that little natural light was available in the dark room. Gerallt sat perched on a stool, a small desk in front of him, by the still shuttered large window to the front of the house. He had a quill in his hand but no ink or parchment and seemed to be tracing with the feather on the tabletop, the lack of light not seeming to bother him. He stopped periodically to walk over to the window and open the shutters enough so that he could see outside, standing there for a few moments before closing the shutters and resuming his seat. Efa longed to go closer to try to see what it was that he was doing. Whatever it was, it was taking all of his concentration. But it did seem a little odd.

Manon sat on a chair to the other side of the hall. She had a small upright loom set up in front of her with some half-finished piece of work on it, but she seemed distracted. Efa watched her for some moments and never actually saw her lift her fingers to the threads once. At one point one of the men-at-arms walked in from the door that accessed the west tower, stopping to bow a greeting to Efa, and then headed towards the kitchen. But Efa had noticed a change in Manon the moment the young man had appeared. The girl had stood up with a very audible sigh and straightened her dress so that it tightened noticeably over her form, before flicking her long dark hair over her shoulder. It was coquettish and disturbing in one so young. When the guardsman took no notice of her, she returned to her seat, a scowl on her face; a scowl that deepened when she noticed Efa watching her. It seemed it wasn't a show for that particular man either, as she sat upright and started smiling and singing under her breath when one of the stable lads came to the main door looking for Ifan. He did notice her, apparent by the blush that flooded his cheeks. He did not linger long.

Had Cynan noticed his daughter's worrying flirtatiousness, Efa wondered? And Gerallt's rather strange behaviour? Was that why she had been brought here? Yet again the enormity of what she had been asked to do loomed large. What if she couldn't be what Cynan's children needed? What if her presence in this house would make things worse? Her instinct was to run. But to where? This was her home now, and this her life.

My darling,

you are so lovely!

You are beauty itself to me.

Your passionate eyes are like gentle doves.

Song of Solomon 1:15, TPT

6
Non

Efa felt strongly that she should speak to Cynan about the children. The uneasy feeling that she carried having observed the older two would not leave her. She was at a loss as to how to even begin to get to know them. But Cynan did not reappear that evening, or indeed the next day, or the day following. The children spent hours doing very little as far as Efa could see. Gerallt barely left his little desk, and Manon spent a good deal of time wandering aimlessly, sighing loudly. When they did venture outside it was to wander around their mother's garden, and that not for long. There were no toys or games that held their interest, and there was definitely no learning going on.

At last, Efa knew she had to do something. She too had taken to wandering aimlessly. She also escaped to the garden when the weather allowed her to. And to the kitchen, where observing Siwan busying herself just evoked feelings of jealousy at the girl's purposeful industry. She was desperate for some occupation. Eluned had no need of Efa's help to plan meals or prepare them. The running of the house and estate was well taken care of by Cynan's steward, Ifan. Efa was listless and bored, and something had to change.

It was Non she finally confided in, on the evening of her fourth day in Tregaron, when once more Cynan had not appeared to share supper with his family. Non was helping her unlace her dress so that she could retire. She wasn't particularly looking forward to the comfortable bed that stood ready to receive her. Her body was not tired and her mind was far too preoccupied. And any hope she had harboured of nights of dreamless sleep had been quickly dashed. Her dreams had been vivid and disturbing, the sleep fragmented.

Efa felt herself on the edge of some kind of dark abyss. If she couldn't find some purpose for her being here, some consolation for her broken heart, what was the reason for living at all? Her husband was obviously absent by choice, preferring the company of another woman. She didn't know whether to feel pleased or offended by that. She sat heavily on the edge of the bed as Non gathered up her discarded outer clothes.

'Non, I must talk to someone about Manon and Gerallt. I am concerned for them, and I am lost as to how I can help them.' *I am just lost*, she added in her own thoughts.

Non came over and sat on the bed next to Efa, reaching out to cover Efa's hand with her own.

'Yes, we do need to talk about the children. Efa,' she waited until Efa turned her head to look at her, 'I know their behaviour may seem a little strange to you, but there are reasons for it. And they are not bad children, or even, in my opinion, peculiar. They have just had to deal with a lot in their young lives. Their mother dying…'

'And an absent father.' Efa ground out her frustration.

Non did not reply. Instead, she released Efa's hand and stood to continue folding Efa's day clothes, laying them carefully in the open chest. Efa wondered if her words had offended. She thought perhaps the conversation was over so she laid her head down and pulled her legs up and under the covers.

To her surprise Non began speaking again, quietly and thoughtfully.

'Manon loved her mother deeply. Idolised her, even. The feeling was mutual, and the two were rarely apart. They were so similar, not in looks maybe, but in temperament and in giftings. When Annest died, it was devastating to Manon. She was not close to her father, and there is distance between them still. And she struggles to be a kind sister to Haf… well, in her mind the poor babe caused her mother's death. And I believe she also perceives that her father carries more affection for her younger sister than he does for her.'

'I understand her feelings of loss, and how they must continue with her. But why the coquetry? Does she not realise how she presents herself?' Efa levered herself up against the pillows, grateful to be able to talk about her concerns at last.

'She is looking for attention, as I perceive it. Perhaps in her own mind she thinks that by attracting a young man she might get the male affection she feels is lacking from her father. You are right to show concern; I, too, worry about her. She does not know the consequences of her behaviour. She is safe here – none of the young men of the household would dare to dally with her, for fear of Cynan. But once she is old enough to leave this house, or when her brothers start to bring other young men back here, then... well, then I fear for her. Genuinely.'

Non was now standing back beside the bed so Efa encouraged her to sit. This time she was the one to reach out and take Non's hand in hers. Non's loving concern for Manon was evident; there were tears in the young woman's eyes. Of course, Efa remembered, this was her sister by blood she was talking about. A child whose upbringing she had played a large part in.

'And Gerallt?'

'Gerallt is a sweet and gentle soul.' Non smiled briefly. 'As I explained before, he has never been robust like his brothers, and never wanted to be like them. He is an anomaly to his father in that he does not want to enjoy the things most boys of his age do. He has a very quick mind, though, and is so observant. He can tell you all about the birds and the trees and the flowers, having never read a book or had a tutor.'

Efa had noticed that no tutor visited Tregaron. That was strange in itself.

'What is he doing when he traces patterns on his desk?' It seemed to occupy the boy for hours.

'On the occasion that he has been able to borrow ink and a scrap of parchment, he has used the quill to draw intricate representations of the things he observes from the window. It is the only time I have seen his pale face light up with joy. His pictures are really very good. When he does not have ink or parchment, he practises his drawing by tracing on the table, seeing in his imagination what he is drawing, I suppose.'

Efa felt deep sadness and frustration on his behalf. Surely ink and parchment could be found for him, at little cost? And if he was so bright, he really did need a tutor.

'The children, there is something else I have observed. I have noticed that there is no structure to their days?'

'No.' Non sighed heavily. 'No structure, and no discipline to enforce it. I can care for their physical needs and Eluned can feed them, but neither of us can make them do anything they do not want to do. We cannot lord it over them; we have no authority to do so.'

Efa looked at the young woman sitting beside her and understood her a bit better. Non obviously felt deeply for her siblings and was devoted to the household, but by means of her birth could hold no position over them.

'I am sorry you find yourself in such a difficult position.'

At her words, Non turned her head sharply.

'I am not discontent with my place – in this house, or in the children's lives. I want no more than I have here. I do not envy your fine clothes and comfortable bed. Believe me. I do not want to be a mistress, or a parent to my brothers and sisters. And I do not need my father to place me on an equal footing with his heirs, as some are wont to do in our land.'

She spoke vehemently, and then to Efa's distress dropped her head into her hands, her shoulders shaking and silent tears seeping through her fingers. Efa leaned in to her and put her arm around her shoulder.

'I'm so sorry to have upset you, Non. I did not mean to imply that you have not done well in caring for your family. Forgive me.'

She watched as the girl took deep breaths to calm herself. Non sat for a moment with the heels of her hands pressed against her eyes. Eventually she spoke, dragging her sleeve across her face to dry it.

'No, Efa, forgive me. It was nothing that you have said.' She rose and smoothed her skirts, and made to leave.

'Non, please, wait. You have been so kind to me. Is your sadness anything I can help with?'

Non stopped, her hand on the handle of the door. 'My hope is that you being here will help more than the children.' She spoke so softly, Efa almost missed it.

'Come, please, sit and talk with me. We are becoming friends, are we not?'

Non paused for a moment before turning and taking her place again, perched now a little more uncomfortably on the edge of Efa's bed.

'Efa, thank you for your kindness,' she whispered. 'I love my family, deeply and truly. It has not been hard to be here and help to raise them. They love me too, in their own way. But the reason I want no more than to be what I have been is that I have no desire to be a mother, or even a wife. I have been content to stay here, but now that you are here, once you are settled and the children... *if* the children... are happy to be led and loved by you, once I know I have done all that I can do, I will be leaving Tregaron.'

Leaving? The thought filled Efa with dread. Already she had realised her dependence on Non's sweet presence. 'Where will you go?'

Non turned her face and even in the candlelight, Efa could see that her eyes were shining, and not just with tears.

'Llanllugan.'

Efa racked her brains. She had heard the name before but couldn't remember where.

'Is that a place special to you?'

'I hope it will become so. It is a place special to God, and that is enough for me.'

The abbey! Of course, there was a nunnery at Llanllugan. Efa swallowed back the shock, registering what Non was saying.

'You are surprised, I can tell. I dare say my father will be surprised, and none too happy either. But it is a decision I made a long time ago.'

'You wish to enter the Church?' Efa hoped the incredulity she felt was not betrayed in her tone.

'With all my heart!'

Efa could not understand but desperately wanted to. What would make a young woman with her whole life ahead of her want to throw away her chances for love, home, family? And she was so kind and considerate, so loving; she had so much to give.

'Can I ask you why you want to give your life to the Church? I don't want to offend, but it is hard for me to imagine such a vocation as being fulfilling to one so young and full of life.'

Non laughed then. A sweet trill of a laugh.

'Believe me, when I consider all the alternatives, I am more determined than ever to go. What is there for me besides? I could stay here the few more years until Haf is grown and left and continue to serve this house willingly, but still my heart would long to be elsewhere. I could go home to my mother's house, but I would be unwelcome now that my father is more often there. Or I could marry. But if I were to marry, it would unlikely be to a man of my choosing. You understand that all too well. And I have never loved a man like you have.' Non reached out to squeeze her hand. 'Forgive me, Efa, but I have seen your tears and heard you cry out another man's name in your dreams. I have watched you since your arrival and seen the grief you carry. I did not have to have the whole story to know that your heart has been broken by your marriage to my father. And he a man who will not love you the way a woman deserves to be loved. I am deeply sorry for that.' She held Efa's gaze. 'You must see that I do not want that for myself.'

Efa nodded. That was something she well understood.

'This is not a difficult decision for me, Efa, because I have found love. A love that I know is more than I deserve, but which is freely given and without condition.' She was fiddling with the cross hung from her neck. 'And He who loves me will never leave me or let me down. I just want to be with Him for all of my days, serving my Saviour and living in His love alone.'

'But as a nun?' Efa asked quietly. She knew that such devotion to God existed in others. She did not comprehend it herself. She had not experienced the love of God in the way Non obviously had. Even so, surely she could love God and not have to sacrifice everything to serve Him?

'Let me explain it to you this way,' Non replied. 'For years I have watched my mother sacrifice everything for the love of a man. She sacrificed her good name, she endured scorn and shame, she gave up her chance of a home and family and a constant husband. I saw how when Cynan came she poured love and affection on him, doing anything she could to encourage him to stay. But then every time he left, she would shrivel and weep for days. Even now, when she has his company more than ever, she still has to endure the days, weeks and months that he is away. She will never be a true wife to him, never have the advantages you have of this home and its comforts, of status and honour. And she has been content with that – it was the life she chose. It still is.

'How different, then, is it that I choose to sacrifice everything, not for the inconstant love of a human being, but for the love of One who will ever be constant? What you see as sacrifice, to me is just embracing a life where I can be undistracted and undivided in my affections. I can give my all. Willingly. To the One who gave His all for me.'

'And it is truly what you want?' Efa could see the answer shining from Non's face.

'So much so that at times I feel my heart will break in the longing for it. I know He is here with me. I can pray here, and I can take myself away to be alone with my Lord. If ever you can't find me,' she laughed softly again, 'just know I am in my favourite place, and will return soon.'

'Where is that place?' Efa had seen no chapel here. A solitary *prie-dieu* stood in the far corner of her room, with its simple wooden knee and elbow rest. Perhaps Non made use of that for her private prayers.

Non laughed again. 'I need no particular place. It can be anywhere where I can be quiet and alone! Quiet enough for me to hear His voice and know His presence.'

Efa looked again at the woman sitting beside her, with a new kind of respect. She still didn't understand the devotion; that kind of relationship with an unseen God was a mystery to her. But Non carried something hard to describe. A peace, a gentleness, a serenity. Even when she was busy. She had heard no cross or harsh words come from her mouth, even when she could have been offended or upset. She gave so much of herself to the family, willingly, lovingly, and yet her heart was to be elsewhere. Efa resolved then and there to do all she could to help Non to achieve her heart's desire. But not yet. Selfishly she realised she could not bear for Non to leave yet.

'Now, I really must go.' Non rose to her feet again and smiled back at Efa. 'What I have told you is my secret longing, Efa. No one else knows of it. Be assured, I am in no hurry to leave you or the children. And I still have to choose my moment to ask my father's blessing. I feel the time will come sooner for me, now that you are here. It would not surprise me if even now he is looking for a match for me among the men of his acquaintance. Even though I am not his wife's daughter, I am Non *ferch* Cynan, and would still be considered a prize by many who want to keep in favour with him. You will keep my secret?'

'Yes, of course.'

Non nodded and was gone. Efa reached over to extinguish the candle and pull the bed curtains closed against the chill night air. But sleep did not come. She was strangely disturbed by her conversation with Non. She remembered the young woman's words and the look of joy on her face as she talked about her 'Saviour', and His love for her. How had she come to that place of such certainty? Not just about the life choice she wanted to make, but of how God felt about her? What did it feel like to know God that way, to have no doubts, to trust an unseen being with the whole of your life? With the whole of your heart as well? Efa knew she did not know Non's God. She had not even prayed once since the night Philip left her. The God she knew was a distant one, who must have been angry with her, or at the very least disinterested. He had not heard her cries for help. He had not stepped in to save her from the unhappy situation she now found herself in. Love her? Efa laughed to herself. No, He might love Non, whom everyone loved, but obviously He did not love her. Or if He ever had, like everyone else who had purported to love her, He had betrayed her and left her when she needed Him most. No, she was still unloved. Even her new husband felt nothing for her, that was obvious.

'Am I that unlovable?' she cried out loud, whispering to the darkness that surrounded her, as hot tears filled her eyes. 'Why, God? What have I done?' She sobbed then, stifling the sound in the softness of her lonely, luxurious bed. She cried until she was exhausted with it. She heard no voice, no reply to her complaint. Not that she had expected to. No, God would not speak to her. Non might be on good-enough terms with the Almighty to have intimate conversation with Him. She was envious of that, she realised. Envious that Non had that place for her heart to rest, that reassurance of God's love for her. But she, Efa, well; she would just have to do what she had already resolved to do. She would shut down her heart. Not even God would be able to penetrate it. That was the only way she was going to survive. Her heart had no more room for pain.

My beloved is to me
the most fragrant apple tree –
he stands above the sons of men.
Sitting under his grace-shadow,
I blossom in his shade,
enjoying the sweet taste of his pleasant, delicious
fruit,
resting with delight where his glory never fades.
Suddenly, he transported me into his house of wine –
he looked upon me with his unrelenting love divine.
Revive me with your raisin cakes.
Refresh me again with your apples.
Help me and hold me, for I am lovesick!
I am longing for more –
yet how could I take more?
His left hand cradles my head
while his right hand holds me close.
I am at rest in this love.
Song of Solomon 2:3-6, TPT

7

Changes

Efa rose early the next morning, before Non even came to wake her. She had slept only fitfully, and she was anxious to leave the bed that had lost any comfort as she had tossed and turned through the night hours. She needed to be occupied, distracted from her own thoughts and feelings, and she had resolved on what that occupation would be. Cynan had brought her here for his children's sake, and Non wanted to be released from her obligations here, so Efa would step up.

She had a plan. It had come to her in the dark hours, whirring around her brain, stealing sleep from her. She did not need the children to like the changes she wanted to make, or even to like her. She had said that she would be a friend to them, but it was obvious to her they needed more than a friend. Manon and Gerallt particularly were going to be in for a shock. She had already decided that she would not wait to ask Cynan's approval for the changes. As far as she was concerned, he had already abandoned responsibility for his children to her. But for certain things to be set in place, Efa would need help. She needed to speak to Ifan, and then to Eluned and Non. Yes, Non would have to help her too.

Efa realised then that one of the reasons she had been so swift to rise and dress herself was that she wanted to avoid Non's company, avoid the possibility that Non would want to continue their conversation of the night before. She did not think she could bear to see Non so alive and so 'in love' with God. Non carried the contentment and joy of a woman who knew she was loved. And that twisted the knife painfully in Efa's own heart. She would have to see her, of course, but later. No, she would seek out Ifan first.

As she descended the stairs, Efa could hear laughter coming from the open doorway that led to the kitchen, and female voices. Eluned and Non, probably. She hoped Ifan wasn't with them, but he wasn't in the main hall. In the early morning half-light, Efa could see that the fire had been tended to and was burning nicely. There were cups and empty trenchers on the table, so someone had broken their fast. There was no sign of the children; too early for them, perhaps. Efa stood in the middle of the rush-strewn floor and watched as the rising sun streamed through the high windows and danced light patterns on the wall and floors. There was a chill in the air still but Efa had been hoping for a dry, sunlit morning, and it looked like her wish had been granted. Not that she'd wished a wish, or prayed a prayer even... she shook her head to banish the unwelcome reminders of her contention with God. No, she needed to focus on her purpose, and a dry day would help with part of her plan at least.

She headed across the hall towards the door that gave access to the west tower. It was often left open during the day but this morning she found it shut. She had never been through the door, was not sure what exactly lay beyond. She did know that Ifan had a room somewhere, where he slept and did whatever estate business was his to do. She hesitated for a moment, wondering if she should just go instead to the kitchen and enquire after Ifan there. Just as she lifted her hand to the handle of the solid oak door it opened suddenly and the great bulk of Ifan filled its frame, looking as surprised as she felt.

'My lady Efa, well, you just about made me jump out of my skin!' He was smiling, but he was holding his hand over his heart dramatically.

'Ifan, my apologies!' Efa stepped back, flustered and almost tripping over her skirts. A firm hand reached out to steady her, and then just as quickly released her when she regained her balance.

'Now then, no harm done! Were you looking for something? I wouldn't suggest you venturing into that pit,' he gestured over his shoulder, 'alone, at this time of the morning. There are some very unsavoury smells and some very bedraggled half-dressed men through there. I have just given them orders to rise and make themselves useful.'

'Oh, no, I'm sorry.'

Ifan laughed as Efa felt her face warm with the thought of what she might have encountered if she had ventured through that door alone. She'd forgotten there were others who garrisoned within the tower – off-duty men-at-arms and other sundry retainers. In many great houses they would have bedded down in the main hall, but here at least they had separate quarters. It was an arrangement she was glad of. She was mortified by her thoughtlessness, but as she glanced up, she could see the steward's kind eyes. He was not laughing at her; he had just found the situation amusing.

'Will you sit, my lady?' Ifan gestured over to the table Efa had just walked past. 'Can I get you anything to break your fast? I have eaten, but Eluned and Siwan have been busy baking since before the crack of dawn and there are fresh honey-sweetened buns.'

'No. Ifan, thank you, but no. Please, I have no need of food.' The thought of sweet buns made her stomach turn. She was unexpectedly nervous about the conversation she needed to have, about the things she wanted to change, how the children's daily routine needed to be altered. And she didn't want to sit at the table eating and risk being interrupted or distracted by Eluned, Non, the children or anyone else. Ifan turned to face her, his eyes creased with concern.

Efa swallowed hard and straightened her back. She had gripped her skirts and was sure the sweat from her palms would be leaving them creased. She released her fingers and went to wipe her hands on her dress, before thinking better of it and bringing her hands together to clasp in front of her. It wasn't as if the tall steward intimidated her, but she had to take her place as mistress in this house, however young and unprepared for the role she felt. She needed courage to say what she needed to say. And he might or might not agree with her. She did not know what she would do if he didn't.

'I need to talk with you about the children.' She glanced over his shoulder as she spoke, up to the wooden landing to check that the door to the children's room was still shut. 'And not here. Somewhere where we can be undisturbed.'

He seemed to pause and think for a moment, before nodding his understanding.

'Come.' He laid his hand gently on her elbow and directed her back towards the door from which he had only a few moments ago emerged. 'If you would wait here a moment, I will make sure it is safe for you to enter.' He winked before disappearing through the door. She was not left standing alone for long. He returned, pushing the door open wide and leaving it that way. A short passageway led to another door the same size and shape as the one they had just passed through. But this one was firmly shut. A small unshuttered window illuminated the walkway with soft morning light, and opposite the window was another door. This one stood open, but was smaller, so that both Ifan and Efa had to duck their heads to enter. Again the door was left open and not closed behind them. Efa realised then that she had put the poor steward in an awkward position, insisting on speaking with him alone. She cursed her thoughtlessness and impropriety.

The room she stepped into was small and rectangular, with a small partially shuttered window in the far wall. Under the window was a side table, strewn with piles of parchment, an ink pot and quills. They were a reminder of one of the things she wanted to ask Ifan about. She wondered if Gerallt knew Ifan had the object of his desire so readily available here. Along the side wall was a pallet bed, its covers hastily pulled up. The other wall was lined with an assortment of wooden chests and coffers, each with its own locking device. There was no fancy wood panelling or finely hung tapestries here, but there was a well-made colourful wool rug on the floor. Ifan was stood watching her as she took in the room, a slightly bemused look on his face.

'It is none too tidy but it works for me.'

She felt her face flush again. He covered her embarrassment by offering her a stool to sit on, and perching his long frame on one of the larger chests.

'What is it that you need to speak to me about?'

'Gerallt.' That was an easy place to start. 'I notice you have ink and parchment here. Would you be able to spare some for Gerallt? I understand he loves to draw.'

Ifan raised a finger and tapped his chin. 'I do have ink, and I could find parchment for him, if he were happy with used pieces and scraps. We get our supplies from the monks at Ystrad Fflur, and we have to pay generously for them. I tend to try to use only what we need.'

So cost was an issue. That was surprising.

'Am I right that Cynan trusts you with the household accounts? But that perhaps he keeps a close eye on your spending? And perhaps he would not agree to spending extra to provide writing materials for a mere boy's amusement?'

Ifan looked back at her with surprise, and then grinned and dipped his head. 'You have the measure of things, to be sure! You are right, on all counts.'

'Well, as mistress of this house, I am authorising you to acquire the writing materials for the use of Gerallt, to aid with his learning. And if Cynan has a problem with it, I will answer to him.'

Ifan was looking at her now with what looked suspiciously like admiration. She sat straighter in her seat and cleared her throat to continue.

'What's more, things have to change here for the children's sake. I will be organising their daily routine from now on, and I will need your cooperation. It may mean you have to alter your own routines and habits.' She paused, worried she might have gone too far. But Ifan was sitting relaxed, his elbows resting on his knees, and his hands clasped loosely in front of him. He was listening intently, a small smile on his face.

She swallowed hard. 'I will be allocating the children tasks for the first two hours of their day. These will include helping with the chores involved in running this household. I will need you to take Gerallt with you and show him what you do, and encourage him to help you.'

He was still smiling, and now his eyes were definitely twinkling. He sat upright, stretching his long back, and nodded his consent. It gave her courage to go on.

'I will not have you and Eluned and Non doing everything for the children. They must be made to take responsibility for certain things. They have been cosseted too long. They need to learn these things in order to prepare them for the world outside these walls. I have seen and observed disturbing behaviour, and a lack of purpose in the children. I would like that to change.

'After they have finished their chores, I will insist that they apply themselves to learning. We will have to help in that for now. I have understanding of basic letters, and I assume you can read and write. We must help them learn accounting also. I intend to speak to Cynan about having a tutor visit, but until that can be arranged, we must do what we can do.'

All this time Ifan had said nothing, but at mention of a tutor he shifted and let out a long breath.

'I agree that a tutor would be good for Gerallt, but you will do well if you can persuade Cynan to allow one into the house. He does not see the need for his son to be educated in anything other than horsemanship and weaponry.' He laughed drily. 'And as for educating his daughters…'

'Well, I received an education of sorts, and it is not so unusual now for women of a certain rank to learn to read and write. Indeed, it is considered a good thing when it comes to marriageability. Cynan will have to accept that if he wants a good match for his daughters.'

'We will see. *You* may be able to persuade him.' Ifan sounded less than sure.

'There is one more thing I need you to agree on.'

'If I can.'

'I intend for the children to spend time outside every day, if the weather permits. We will walk, we will take rides and we will tend the garden together. Cynan was insistent that neither I nor the children leave the gates of Tregaron without company. So when we do have to venture outside of the gates, I would prefer if you were available to accompany us, over any of the younger men of the household... for Manon's sake.'

She shot him a look and saw that he had registered her meaning.

'Manon must be kept out of harm's way in every respect, until I have worked out how to teach her to behave more appropriately. I do not think I need to say more.'

'No. Indeed not.'

Efa was surprised to see a slight flush rise on Ifan's cheeks. She stood then. 'I hope you will take time to think on what I have asked. If you are in agreement, then I ask you to be ready at noon today to escort the children and I for a walk along the riverbank.'

She turned with a swish of her skirts and made to leave.

'My lady!' His tone caused her to stop and turn. He too was now on his feet and she watched as he bowed deeply from his waist. 'I am at your service.'

Efa emerged back into the hall to find bustling activity, as the children were now at the table and tucking into a pile of buns that had appeared, still warm, from the kitchen. If they noticed her they made no show of it. She needed to speak with Eluned; her plan was that she and Non would occupy Manon and Haf and involve them in the household chores while Ifan did the same with Gerallt. But first she needed to see for herself what Non actually did for the children. She had her suspicions, which were confirmed when she climbed the stairs and stepped through the doorway into the children's room.

Like her own, the chamber was light and well appointed, with walls adorned with wooden panelling and hung tapestries. It was narrower than hers, but also boasted a fine wide window with its own window seat. The room contained four pallet beds, lined up against the far wall. Two were pushed together at one end, and a third was placed close to it. The fourth was placed at the other end of the room, closest to the door, and a simple curtain was hung floor to ceiling to separate it from the others. The fourth bed was tidily made and the small wooden chest that stood beside it was closed. In contrast, the bed coverings of the others had been left dishevelled, and clothes spilled out of open chests and onto the floor.

Non appeared behind her and started with surprise as she saw Efa standing in the room. She was carrying a pile of clean linens, which almost toppled out of her grasp. Efa moved quickly, their eyes meeting as she bent to help Non keep hold of her load.

'My apologies if I startled you, Non. I wanted to see this room for myself.' She stood back to let the other woman pass. 'I have decided that the children need to learn how to be useful in this house, as well as to receive some instruction as to how to behave, and hopefully also to be educated.'

Non put down her load on the wide window seat. She quietly began to strip the two beds that were pushed together. Efa moved over to help her remove linen that was soiled, most likely by a small girl's dream-disturbed sleep. As they worked together to make and tidy the beds, she outlined her plan to Non, as she had to Ifan. Non said nothing until the beds were straightened and the clothing stowed neatly away in chests.

'Thank you for your help,' she said quietly as she bundled up the soiled linens.

'So you are happy that from tomorrow it will be the children helping you to tidy their beds and put their own clothing away? I know it will be hard for them at first, but I believe they need to learn to take some responsibility. And this is a good place for them to start.'

She expected a response, but Non was still standing, holding her burden, her head dipped. Efa had a moment of uncertainty. She suddenly found herself really wanting Non's approval for her plans.

'Do you think I am expecting too much of the children? Do you think it is beneath them?'

'No!' Non's face shot up, a wide smile on her face. 'No, I was just praying and thanking God for bringing you to this house. I think what you are planning to do is just what the children need. Have needed for a long time. It is going to be hard – for them and us – for all of us to get used to. And I am not sure what Cynan will make of his daughters doing the maid's tasks.'

'You are his daughter and you have been doing them, without complaint, for years.'

'This is true,' she laughed. 'I'm about ready for a change too!'

The kitchen was Efa's next stop and she again found herself being forced to sit and eat at Eluned's table. The soft, honey-sweetened buns were actually light and delicious, slathered with soft, creamy butter, and for a few moments Efa forgot why she had come to see Eluned. She allowed herself the moment to rest and nourish herself. She needed physical strength to match the determination she was forcing herself to find – needed to bolster herself before she faced the children. She was still so unsure of how they would respond to her. She could not come with the authority of a parent; she had not yet earned their respect for that. But at least if she could present her plans to them with the support of Ifan, Non and Eluned, that would help immeasurably.

Eluned listened to her ideas while busying herself working around her. She did not seem too shocked by the thought of working with the girls, and like Non, seemed pleasantly surprised and pleased that Efa was prepared to take such an active interest in the children's well-being. She pledged her support, laughing that it might mean some changes to the quality of the food that left the kitchen And stating, in no uncertain terms, that Jac, as the puppy had now been named, was not welcome in her kitchen at any time, however much Haf would plead his company.

At noon that day, Efa stood by the door, ready in her everyday wool mantle. Beside her stood three less-than-impressed-looking children, similarly dressed for the outdoors. Ifan had kept his word and stood holding the door open for them, a sheepish smile on his face, as Efa explained to Haf once more that Jac could not come with them and needed to grow in size and strength, and obedience, before he would be allowed to accompany them. But that, yes, of course, when he had fulfilled all three of those requirements he would be welcome to join them. Haf did not often pout, but her lower lip was definitely protruding as she reluctantly settled the puppy back into his basket by the fire. Jac, in contrast, seemed only too pleased to be left to snuggle and sleep in peace.

The day was thankfully still bright and dry, the sun high in the sky, although a cold breeze stung their cheeks as they walked together towards the gatehouse. Efa's stomach had twisted in apprehension as she had faced the children earlier, but she had given herself a good talking to. She did not want to show any signs of uncertainty of purpose to the children. They had to see she was serious. She had also tried to be kind in her explanation as to why things were having to change, and how they would change. But she was under no illusion that it was anything about her words or even her manner that had persuaded the children to comply with this particular outing. It was Ifan's enthusiasm and Eluned's promise of sweetmeats on their return that had got them to this point. Now it was up to Efa to make this walk enjoyable.

As they reached the gate, while they waited for the huge wooden latches to be lifted and the heavy doors to be opened for them, she asked for the children's attention.

'I have a challenge for you. I want you to help me find some treasure.'

Haf and Gerallt at least seemed to engage. Manon stood with her head down and, Efa noticed, was tracing patterns in the dirt with a soft silk-shod toe. Efa groaned inwardly. She would have to check that the girl even possessed more suitable footwear than those flimsy slippers she was wearing. Manon glanced up under her perusal and shot her a look so filled with challenge, she realised that the choice of footwear was most likely out of protest and that Manon was probably expecting to be allowed to opt out of the walk. But Efa was not going to give in to her.

It was dry enough underfoot, and if her feet hurt when they returned, at least she would learn to be more prepared the next time.

'What treasure?' Haf had forgotten her dismay at having to leave her doggy companion behind, and was jiggling up and down. Gerallt looked less excited but at least he managed a small smile.

'I want you to find three things. First, the most perfectly round stone you can find. Second, the straightest piece of wood. And third, one other item that you would consider treasure – that you think either beautiful or useful. Can you do that?'

There were enthusiastic nods, from the younger two at least. They made their way along the path, Ifan leading them, singing a jaunty little song, until they reached a spot on the riverbank where a small beach had formed among the reeds. Efa was surprised that actually all three children began to search around and pick up stones, checking them for roundness, feeling the weight of them in their hands. She took a deep breath of the fine cool air and released some of the tension she had been carrying, as the warmth of the sun touched her shoulders.

A copse of small trees further along the riverbank provided a great selection of sticks of all shapes and sizes, and soon Haf held in her hand a stick that was longer than she was tall. She was laughing as she tried to use it as a walking stick, until the end of it snapped away. Efa rushed to reassure her that it was still a fine, straight, strong stick, and tears were narrowly averted. Both Gerallt and Haf had rosy cheeks and shining eyes when they happily showed her their found treasures. Manon stood at a distance and watched as her siblings played and interacted with Efa. Her face was hard to read, but she was worrying her lower lip with her teeth, and her fingers fiddled constantly with her mantle clasp.

By the time they returned through Tregaron's gates they were all ready for Eluned's sweet treats, but before she allowed them to enter the hall, Efa guided the children to the stone seat in their mother's garden. It was the very same seat that she had shared with their father, when she had promised to do what she could for his children. She felt at least she had made a positive start, as the two younger ones sat happily either side of her. She felt even more reassured when she felt Haf lean into her to show her what she had collected. Manon perched on the far end of the seat on the other side of Haf. She held a stone in her hands. It was not round, Efa noticed, rather more heart-shaped, grey with a red line streaking across its surface.

Haf had collected a round white stone and showed it to Efa, with the remains of what had been a snowdrop, obviously plucked up by its roots. But she declared her straight stick as the most special of her treasures as it was going to be useful. She would give it to Jac to use as a walking stick, she explained. Efa laughed and gave her a small squeeze.

Gerallt had also collected a lovely round stone, and a good-looking twig, but to his delight had also found a fine, white bird feather. 'This is my treasure,' he said with a shy smile. 'It is both beautiful and useful, as a quill.'

'Of course,' Efa nodded knowingly. She was yet to surprise Gerallt with his own ink and parchment, and could not wait to see his response when she did so.

'And you, Manon? Did you find treasure?' Efa turned to smile at the girl.

Manon looked at the stone in her hand and then scowled and jumped to her feet, throwing the stone into the flowerbed in front of her.

'This is all so ridiculous. I am not a child and will not be treated as one.' She stamped her silk-shod foot, and it must have pained her, as tears came to her eyes and she fled towards the house.

Efa stood and ushered the children to follow their sister inside. She stooped to pick up the stone Manon had discarded. It was still warm from where it had been held and stroked. She knew, because the stone spoke to her too, that the tears and the anger that Manon had let loose were not just a childish tantrum, but rather the fallout of a still broken heart.

Listen! I hear my lover's voice.

I know it's him coming to me –

leaping with joy over mountains,

skipping in love over the hills that separate us,

to come to me.

Let me describe him:

he is graceful as a gazelle,

swift as a wild stag.

Now he comes closer,

even to the places where I hide.

He gazes into my soul,

peering through the portal

as he blossoms within my heart.

Song of Solomon 2:8-9, TPT

8

Ystrad Fflur

'You have drawn Jac so well, Gerallt!'

Efa was gratified to see the boy flush with pleasure. He really was very gifted, and she was so pleased that he now had ink and parchment in place of his finger and wooden desktop imaginings. Gerallt had shown such an affinity for the quill. He moved the ink with flowing confident strokes, keeping his illustrations small so as not to waste an inch of the precious parchment he had been gifted. Birds, animals and flowers all appeared in fine, clear detail. Ifan had also begun to teach him simple lettering. It was as if the boy was finally doing what he had been born to do, and he seemed happy in it. Yet Efa sensed he had the capacity for so much more and was determined to pursue tutoring for him.

More than a fortnight had passed since Efa had initiated the change of routine for the children. Mostly they had responded to it reasonably well. She smiled as she looked over to see Ifan teaching Haf to write her name. So as not to waste more parchment or ink, he had created an ingenious device – a shallow rectangular wooden box, filled with sand from the riverbed. Haf held a small stick and traced trails in the sand that bore some resemblance to the letters that spelled out her name. She could level the sand out and practise over and over again to perfect her script. Wooden counters also lay strewn across the table from where Efa had earlier made counting and adding numbers into a game for the child.

Even Manon was occupied. She had been less than enthusiastic in doing her share of the chores, and definitely not as much of a natural in the kitchen as Siwan, but she seemed to be good with a needle. She was working on a garment with Non guiding her. The fabric looked to be good quality, and in a lovely shade of purple. Efa walked over to take a closer look. Non and Manon had been talking animatedly but stopped and looked up as she approached. Manon shot Efa a resentful look.

'See what fine stitches Manon makes?' Non held the work up for Efa to inspect. She was right. The stitches were indeed finely made, small and even, and Efa commented so.

Manon lowered her head back to her work, saying nothing, but Efa was pleased to see a slight colour rise to the girl's cheeks at her praise.

'What will it be? The fabric is fine and a beautiful colour.'

'It will be a dress for Manon to wear. The fine wool came from a dress of her mother's. We chose it for the colour, as it will suit Manon well, I think.'

'I agree it will.' Efa fingered the soft material. 'And I have some gold thread if you would like to use it. Perhaps to embroider a motif around the neckline?'

Manon glanced up and took a breath as if she was going to reply. But then she pursed her lips and turned her attention again to her work.

'That would be very kind of you, Efa. Would it not, Manon?' Non nudged her companion.

'Yes,' Manon whispered, without looking up at Efa. 'Thank you.'

Some progress, Efa thought. *At least we are beginning to communicate.*

Cynan had not been seen for more than a fortnight either, so could not hide his look of surprise as he entered the hall, seeing his children all well occupied. Not even Haf ran to greet him, so focused was she on completing her crooked 'H'. Efa noticed Gerallt had responded to his father's entrance by guiltily dropping his quill and trying to hide his ink-stained fingers.

'Well, I see much industry here!' Cynan glanced over to where Efa was still standing beside Manon and Non. She realised she was holding her breath, waiting for his next words. He held her gaze for a moment or two, before giving her the slightest of nods. He removed his mantle and moved over to the table.

'Now, who is this sitting in my chair, and why is there sand on my dining table?' He chuckled at Haf's cheeky smile as she showed him her 'letters'. She jumped down to let him sit and then scurried away to wake a reluctant Jac from his doggy doze.

Eluned appeared, with ale and bread and cheese, and Ifan swept away a clear space for him to eat. Cynan gestured for Efa to join him at the table, and she picked up her skirts and willed her legs to carry her to her seat. She tried to read her husband's face, but could not judge whether he was pleased or concerned with what he had encountered on his return to his home.

'I think there have been some changes here, in my absence.' He took a bite of bread and chewed. He offered her his trencher but she could not take food until the knot in her throat eased. He glanced over and raised one eyebrow when she did not immediately answer him. Efa reached for a cup of ale and took a drink, and without daring to raise her head to meet his gaze, she began to tell him of all that she had initiated, and how the children were responding; of the chores and the learning and the outings; how Ifan and Eluned and Non had supported her plans, and how she had already seen improvement in the children's behaviour.

He listened intently as he ate, saying nothing. There was a slight creasing in his forehead as she mentioned the ink and parchment that had been procured for Gerallt's use, but he allowed her to finish her tale. When she had, he sat back and watched his children for a few minutes. Manon was laughing at something Non had said, but was still applying herself to her sewing. Haf was teaching Jac to 'count' using his three good legs. Gerallt had turned his back to his father and had bent his head again over his parchment, quill in hand. Cynan rose from the table and walked over to where his son sat. Gerallt stiffened at his approach and dropped his quill again. Efa found herself moving quickly to stand beside Gerallt's stool, placing her hand reassuringly on the boy's back, as he moved his arms to try to cover his work.

'Look here. See how gifted Gerallt is with the pen?' She pulled the sheet of parchment from under the boy's arm. Birds of all shapes and sizes dotted the page. The robin at his window, the buzzard he had observed from their ride yesterday, a goose and a cockerel, and many more. All recognisable from his depictions. The boy still hung his head, but Efa thrust the parchment under Cynan's nose, appealing to him with her eyes. He took the proffered page from her and seemed to study the images for a moment. Efa was surprised to see his eyes soften and a moment of sadness cross his face.

'These are really very good.' It was barely a whisper. And then he seemed to compose himself as he placed the parchment back down on the desk. He placed his hand on Gerallt's shoulder and the boy tensed.

'Gerallt, I am not angry.' The boy turned his face to meet his father, who gifted his son with a smile. Cynan then looked over the boy's head to meet Efa's gaze and nodded, before turning his attention back to his son. 'Your father longed to handle a quill and parchment like you do, Gerallt, but he was never given the opportunity. He was educated instead for war from as young as he could remember. I had forgotten...' He paused and took a deep breath. 'I have tried to rob you of the very dream I was robbed of.' He glanced back at Efa. 'I am sorry for that.' He squeezed his son's shoulder and then moved swiftly away. Efa bent to check on the boy. Tears dropped onto the parchment in front of him, but when he raised his face to hers, she saw that joy shone from his eyes.

'Dry your eyes,' she whispered close. 'Your tears are not needed. They will add nothing to your work, except perhaps the memory of this moment.' A child receiving a father's approval. Her heart swelled for the boy. She had forgotten how good it felt to be validated by the love of another.

Later, after supper, when the children had retired, Cynan sat with Efa by the fire. The wind was howling outside and a persistent rainstorm was making everything inside feel damp. Efa was glad of the chance to warm herself before she too escaped to her bed. She was surprised her husband had stayed. He seemed in no hurry to leave, and she found herself glad of his company. She still had things she wanted to ask for, for the children. She still wanted to be sure he approved of what she had started. If he had any doubts, she needed to know before he left again. She had found an odd satisfaction in seeing the children respond well to her ideas, and an increased sense of belonging. As if she was actually needed here in Tregaron. Was she happy? She mused to herself. That was hard to say. But she wasn't as unhappy to be there as she had been. She was beginning to find herself becoming quite attached to this family, her heart softening despite herself.

'I must leave Tregaron early in the morning, and I intend to take you with me.'

His words shocked her out of her reverie. Why was he taking her away so soon? Was he that against what she had done? Did he no longer want her at Tregaron influencing his children? Was he already regretting his decision to wed her and wanted to take her back to Swansea? A glimmer of hope rose within her momentarily, followed by a crushing reality. There was nothing for her back in Swansea. Would he take her back to Llewellyn, then? She was surprised to realise that she didn't want to go back there either. In fact, she would rather stay here at Tregaron. This placed that only a matter of days ago had felt like a prison was beginning to feel more like a home. A place where she had a role to play and people to care about.

'Where?' She couldn't hide the tremor in her voice.

He looked up from stirring the fire with a poker, and a look of puzzlement crossed his face.

'I will not force you to come, if you would rather not. I simply mean to visit the abbey at Ystrad Fflur, that is all. I go regularly to hear Mass for my late wife, and to pay my respects.

The abbey has some fine buildings, built to the glory of God, and I thought perhaps you might like to see it.'

Efa let out a long breath and ducked her head, berating herself for her misplaced pessimism. She looked up to smile gratefully at her husband.

'I would very much like to see the abbey. Thank you for your offer to take me.'

'Of course,' he smiled crookedly. 'We will need to leave at first light, so I must now find a bed.' He rose stiffly from his perch and came over to bow to her. She lifted her hand to him and he helped her to also rise.

'I too must retire.' She consoled herself that she would have much time to speak of the children with him on their journey tomorrow, to ascertain his thoughts and ask him for further indulgence. But as she turned to head for the stairs, a sudden thought crossed her mind. She spun to see him stood still, watching her, and the kind look on his face emboldened her.

'My lord husband, I have one request, which I cannot leave to the morrow.'

'What is it, my lady wife?' It felt strange to hear the formal greeting on his lips, but also reassuring.

'Can Gerallt accompany us tomorrow to Ystrad Fflur?' She continued without a pause, in case he should argue back. 'They have a fine library of manuscripts, I am led to understand, some even donated by Gerallt's namesake, the saintly Gerald Cambriensis? And they also have a scriptorium that produces the most magnificent documents. I'm sure Gerallt would love to see it, to be inspired by what the monks do?'

Cynan stood looking at her for a moment, weighing her words.

'He may come. But if you are asking if perhaps my son has a future with those scriptorium monks, I will not answer to that. So do not raise his hopes, if that is what he hopes for, Efa. But yes.' He paused and sighed. 'He may come.'

The early morning was damp and chilly after the storm that had blown itself out in the night hours. Mercifully, although the ground beneath their horses' hooves was soft in places, the rain did not return. Before the cock had even crowed, Efa had tiptoed into the children's room and roused Gerallt from his slumber, whispering to him to dress quickly and to pack up his precious writing materials. She glanced back at him now, sitting awkwardly on his horse but with such a look of excitement that she found herself unexpectedly swallowing back emotion. She hoped he would be inspired by what he saw at Ystrad Fflur, encouraged by those who used the same gift as he had for a higher purpose.

What she didn't expect was her own reaction as the impressive buildings of the abbey came into their view. She had seen her fair share of fine buildings, abbeys even, but nothing prepared her for this. It was the setting as much as the buildings, which although substantial and well constructed were simple in ornamentation. Ystrad Fflur stood in a broad green valley, already dotted with early spring wild flowers, on a slight rise, the wide sky expansive above it. The abbey church, with its high, narrow windows, stood regal and proud, the point of the roof of its simple tower seeming to punch into the very heavens. It was surrounded by an impressive range of stone and wooden buildings, no doubt including cloisters and the famous scriptorium. The abbey was somehow both imposing and welcoming, and Efa felt strangely drawn towards its embrace.

They were greeted by the friendly porter and relieved of their mounts. As they stepped through the abbey gates, a monk calling himself Brother Aled approached to welcome them. On hearing Cynan's purpose for bringing his son, he nodded enthusiastically and offered to take Gerallt to the scriptorium himself. The brother spoke quietly with Cynan for a few moments before smiling at them both, taking the boy gently by the arm and leading him away. Gerallt glanced back briefly, and it was to Efa the boy looked for reassurance, not his father. Efa responded with a smile, lifting her hand in a small wave. Cynan turned to her, his eyes narrowing slightly.

'The Mass for the Lady Annest will be said as part of the monks' Office at Sext. I have some business to attend to with the almoner here but will be back by noon. I am assured you are welcome to visit the church by yourself, but not to wander into any other of the abbey buildings unaccompanied. I will show you to the church door and return for you in time for the service.'

Cynan did not wait for a reply and was already leading her towards the church. He was used to giving orders, she supposed. How would he have responded if she had disagreed with his arrangements for her amusement? She wasn't sure a church building was where she wanted to spend any time. But then, she had agreed to come to the abbey, and deep down she knew it wasn't just for Gerallt's or Cynan's sake. And now as she stepped through the great wooden door, into the quiet space beyond, with its lofty arches and high glass-paned windows, she felt the need to take a deep breath, hoping perhaps the peace of the place would find its way deep into her soul.

Cynan looked at her for a moment, and then surprisingly reached out to clasp her fingers. 'You do not mind being left here?' He was concerned for her feelings after all.

'I do not mind,' she whispered in response, and he squeezed her fingers lightly before dropping her hand and taking his leave.

Efa pulled her thick mantle tight around her, suddenly feeling a little lost. It was not warm in the church, barely warmer than outside, and she was glad she had worn her miniver. The nave was huge and she wandered down the central space, looking up at the fine stone-carved roof arches, until her head began to spin. It was definitely a beautifully constructed building, the craftmanship of stonemason and glazier combining to create something wondrous. She was glad to experience it; glad to be here alone, too, for these few moments. She looked up towards the high altar, but did not approach it. She should perhaps have bobbed and genuflected and acknowledged God in this holy place, but she was still unsure of where she stood with the Almighty. And she had never been one to pretend devotion when it was not truly felt.

The great church had been built in cruciform shape and both transepts were lined with three small chapels. She continued her wanderings until she found herself in one of those chapels, drawn by a memorial bearing the image of a woman carved in stone. The name inscribed beneath that image made her gasp, so loudly that she spun around to check that she had not disturbed anyone. She stepped closer to run her fingers over the words *Maude de Braose, 1172-1210, wife of Grufydd ap Rhys, late Prince of Deuheubarth'*.

'*De Braose.'* Efa sunk to her knees, her hand still caressing the words. Philip's name. She leaned her head on the cold stone and let hot tears come. She had done well not to cry more over him. Done well to put her own heartache aside to care for Cynan's children. But now, alone, in that small serene space, hidden from the world, she could allow herself to grieve again, for a few moments at least.

As the wave finally subsided, she used the ends of her sleeves to dry her eyes. She stood awkwardly to her feet. The cold of the stone floor had caused her limbs to stiffen. She must have been there longer than she thought. She knew she should probably leave and go back into the main part of the church to wait for her husband, but something made her stay.

She looked again at the inscription. *Maude de Braose*, daughter of a noble Norman family, married into the family of a Lord of Wales. Had she had any say in it, Efa wondered? Or had she, too, been a pawn in the power game played by the men in her life? Had she been happy to live in a new land, learn a new language? Had she been content, loved, had the joy of bearing children of her own? She had lived and died, and here was her memorial. But what of that life, of those brief thirty-eight years? It was a fine memorial, carved into the abbey wall, befitting her status. But had it been laid with love, she wondered? Was true love ever possible for women of noble birth?

'She was a fine lady. I knew her. Kind, generous of spirit and brave.'

Efa spun around at the voice and found herself in the company of a slightly built monk, dressed in simple Cistercian white. His face was smiling, with warm hazel eyes beneath bushy white eyebrows and snow-white hair. His face was wrinkled with age, but there was a life and vitality about him. He did not stoop but stood tall, his hands clasped loosely in front of him, watching her.

'But was she happy and was she loved?' The words came unbidden, and immediately she regretted her rudeness. 'Forgive me, brother.' She dipped her head in apology. 'I will leave you to your prayers.'

'Don't leave on my account.' The monk stepped closer so that he too was in touching distance of the memorial. 'Your question is valid, my child. We all seek those things – to know happiness and to be loved.' He looked intently at her, perhaps seeing what she had tried to wipe away. 'Come, let us sit. My tired bones will thank me. If you don't mind my company, that is?'

He gestured towards the wall of the chapel, lined by three small, finely decorated stone alcoves, each containing a stone seat. She followed and perched herself in one, nervously straightening her skirts as she did so. She didn't know why this monk was so keen to sit with her, but felt it rude to deny his invitation. He sat with a sigh and leaned his head back against the smooth stone behind him, his eyes closed and his hands clasped in his lap. She waited for him to speak, and when he didn't, she thought perhaps she should.

'It is a beautiful space here.' It really was. Coloured tiles covered the floor in an intricate design, and the window above them let in sunlight that brought those colours to life.

'The chapel decoration was paid for in the lady's memory. I think perhaps she was loved. Certainly honoured in her death. But, forgive me, my lady, if we talk not of the one laid to rest here, but of your own reason for grieving. Did you know her? You would have been but a child when she died?'

He had opened his eyes and was now leaning forward, watching her.

'No.' She breathed deeply and let the breath out slowly. 'My tears were not for her.'

'Oh. Then for another you have lost, perhaps?'

'For a loss, surely. But you do not need to hear my woes, brother.'

'No. That is true. I do not need to, but I am here and I have ears. And it is good to sit here for a few moments, hopefully undiscovered.' He laughed then, a soft warm sound.

She wondered why he might want to hide, but actually found herself happy to have company. And he was a stranger. A man of God. Perhaps she could speak to him, and he would treat it as a priest would the confessional.

'The name on the tomb opened a wound that I thought was beginning to heal,' she began. And then before she knew it, she had told her quiet companion the whole tale. He sat listening, sometimes nodding his understanding, sometimes bowing his head and closing his eyes. Never did he interrupt or question her. When she was done, she felt exhausted but also strangely lighter. Only then did the monk speak.

'You have endured much heartache; for that I am sorry. But I believe that God will help you to find new purpose in life, and in time you will find healing for your heart and soul, in His care.'

Efa shook her head and the words came with vehemence. 'Forgive me, brother, but I have found God no help in any of this. I have been betrayed by the man who I considered a father, I have been let down by the family I trusted, and I have been abandoned by the man I loved. I now live in a family not my own, with a husband who does not love me and a future I did not envision. I cannot see God's hand in any of it. In fact, I feel He too has betrayed me.'

He didn't answer, just watched her, with a kind smile on his face. Efa began to feel uncomfortable under his gaze, and found herself speaking again, a little less passionately this time.

'I suppose, here, of all places, is the wrong place to air my grievances with God.'

'Oh, I think He has heard much worse in this space than what you have just said,' the monk answered with another small laugh. 'Be assured, He knows your pain, my dear one, and before you even uttered the words. You may not believe it, or feel that He cares, but He is your Father in heaven. He knows

110

the hairs of your head, your dreams and your disappointments. He feels your heartbreak, and weeps when you weep. I can assure you that He loves you, but you may have to find out that truth for yourself, and it might take time. He will wait.'

She doubted the truth of what he was saying, but it felt wrong to voice her doubts. He was being kind. It was his job to preach God's love to her.

'I can see you still struggle to believe my words. Perhaps you cannot feel Him here within these sanctified walls. You have not seen Him answer your prayers as you would wish Him to. It does not change the fact that He is close, and that He does care for you.'

He paused and Efa began to feel uncomfortable that she didn't know how to answer him. Yet his words carried such conviction, and deep down perhaps she wanted them to be true for her. God still seemed so distant.

'If you cannot experience Him here, let me ask you this. What about at Tregaron? Have you experienced God there?'

She looked up sharply at that. 'I cannot say I have sought God out at all.'

'Ha, that doesn't mean He hasn't been searching for you! Look to those who surround you in that home. See if you cannot see the kindness of God in them, feel His love demonstrated to you through their words and actions. We will speak again.' He smiled broadly. 'That is my promise to you. But now,' he rose to his feet, groaning slightly as he straightened his back, 'I must be somewhere else.'

At that very moment the scurry of footsteps heralded the arrival of a very flustered-looking plump monk, tonsured hair askew and cheeks rosy with exertion. He was breathing heavily, but came to an abrupt stop when he saw them. He bowed his head – but not to Efa. He made his obeisance to her monk companion.

'Father Ulrich, we have been looking for you. The bells are about to sound for Sext. You need to prepare yourself for leading of Mass for the Lady Annest.'

'Oh, do not fuss so, Prior Andrew. I have time enough. Please greet the Lady Efa properly.' He turned then and winked at Efa, before bowing to her himself and walking away, the prior scuttling behind him.

Father? The realisation hit her then that she had been pouring her heart out to no ordinary monk, but to the abbot of Ystrad Fflur. He had not introduced himself and she had not asked. Now she felt embarrassed but, remembering both his kind words and his laugh, consoled herself that it had been him making time for her. She felt honoured by that, and pledged to at least consider the words he had spoken to her. She also found herself hoping that they would indeed have cause to meet again. His presence and his words had soothed her soul.

Arise, my love, my beautiful companion,

and run with me to the higher place.

For now is the time to arise and come away

with me.

Song of Solomon 2:13, TPT

9
Haf

Summer 1222

That visit to Ystrad Fflur had changed things at Tregaron. For Gerallt, it had opened up a whole new world. Riding beside her on their return journey from the abbey, he had chattered enthusiastically about all he had seen of the monks' work in the scriptorium. The neat, precise script worked in fine black strokes, the beautiful illuminated capitals, the colourful illustrations. Efa had never heard him speak so much, or seen his face so animated. Cynan must have seen it too, because within a month of that visit, a monk by the name of Brother Paul began visiting Tregaron. A serious young man with dark hair and intense dark eyes, he came for two hours a day, three days a week. He brought with him books, manuscripts, parchment and inks. He also brought with him a well-read mind and a desire to share that knowledge with Gerallt. The boy lapped it up and thrived under his new tutor's attention.

Manon had been encouraged by Efa to also attend Brother Paul's lessons, and to begin with she had. She had even tried to flutter her eyelashes at the young monk, who in response had turned beet-red and quickly excused himself. It was no real surprise when Manon soon lost interest in the lessons, and thankfully in the poor young monk. Efa found the brother was also awkward around her, but in contrast he seemed to make a fast connection with Non. They often talked together in whispers, and shared smiles. They even took walks around the garden together, deep in conversation, Brother Paul choosing to delay his departure regularly to spend time with Non. Efa had begun to worry that an unhealthy attachment was forming between the two, but was loath to mention it; the young tutor, with his quick mind, was so good for Gerallt. He had even begun to leave pages of manuscript with the boy, for him to copy in his own hand. And the boy was meticulous in his copying, creating fine work.

This arrangement of tutor and boy had gone on for weeks, until suddenly the tutor was gone. Efa went to Cynan for an explanation, but he assured her that it was none of his doing. He had been initially unsure of the need to procure a tutor for his youngest son, but having seen how the boy had flourished, was as disappointed as she was that the lessons had ended. They would have to wait until their next visit to the abbey to discover if the monk would return or be replaced.

Efa's encounter with Abbot Ulrich at Ystrad Fflur had also stayed with her. She had spoken with Non of the things he had said, of the way he had described God as Father. For Efa, who had not known her earthly father, and only had experience of Llewellyn as any sort of a father figure, it was hard to see how a Father in heaven could be unconditionally trustworthy. Non smiled when she voiced her doubts.

'God is our perfect Father, Efa. We cannot compare him to any earthly father, even the very good ones. I too see failures in my own father, however much I care for him. But God is perfect in every way. He is infinitely kind, infinitely loving. He is just and compassionate, and truly cares for His children. Even when they need discipline, it is done with justice, kindness and mercy. Do you know the story that Jesus told of the prodigal son? It is one of my favourite stories of the Gospels.'

Efa had only the faintest of recollections, so Non had continued to share the story with her.

'A rich man had two sons. The elder son seemingly served his father well, but the younger son was more faithless. He asked his father for his share of his inheritance, and then left his father's household. He chose to spend that inheritance on worldly pleasures until finally the wastrel found himself penniless and friendless, dependent on the food thrown to pigs to satisfy his hunger. In a sudden lucid moment, that unhappy boy remembered the wealth and comfort that even his father's servants lived in. He decided to return home and throw himself on his father's mercy, to ask to be taken back as a slave. But his father ran to meet him on his return, and threw his arms around him, kissing him and welcoming him back as a full son. He clothed him with fine clothes and shoes and put a ring on his finger, and then threw a feast to celebrate his return.

'You only have to see how that father responded to his wayward son to get a glimpse of how God cares for each one of us. He waited, he watched out for him and he welcomed him back with open arms. He didn't care what his child had done; he just wanted to show his love and forgiveness, and reinstate his son to his place in his family.'

This made Efa think deeply. She still wasn't sure that God truly loved and cared for her that way. And she had run from Him, she knew that to be true. But if He did really want to be a Father to her, could she find her way back to Him? Would there be open arms waiting for her? He probably would not love her like He loved Non, or even Father Ulrich – which had reminded her of the other thing the abbot had said to her: that she should look for the kindness of God in those around her. And she could not deny it was there. Non, Eluned, Ifan – they each one had shown her so much kindness. They had welcomed both her and Siwan into their home. They had encouraged and supported her with the children. Each day she saw such loving care demonstrated, and Tregaron was a happy, safe and peaceful place as a result. She had to admit that Father Ulrich had been right. Perhaps God was trying to reassure her of His love and presence through those He had placed around her.

Efa had even begun to pray again, falteringly, and using learned prayers, the familiar words of the 'Our Father'. She paused every time she said it now. She so much wanted Him to not be the distant, disapproving, angry God she had always imagined Him to be, but rather a Father who would accept her as she was and hold her close to Him. She realised that she really wanted to know God as Non and Ulrich did. She longed to speak more with the abbot, but had not yet had the opportunity. They had visited Ystrad Fflur for the Easter celebrations, and again at Pentecost. But both times the abbot had been busy. She would never have dared to approach him anyway.

Efa had found a growing sense of contentment, being part of the family at Tregaron. She thought less about Swansea, and continued to shut thoughts of her erstwhile lover out of her mind. The pain was still there, and the tears would fall if she allowed them, but as the weeks went on, she discovered joy in many things that she had not expected to. Spring had turned to summer. The new season gave opportunity for Efa to visit Annest's garden early each day, before the sun rose to its zenith and the air grew too warm. She loved to sit with her face turned to the sun, enjoying its warmth and the sounds and scents of the now flourishing garden.

This particular sun-soaked morning she had company. Haf and Siwan were playing happily with Jac, who had grown, but not much. He was still a small dog, but now fleshed out and strong. He seemed to be coping remarkably well with three good legs; the fourth now rested on the floor when he stood still, but was held up when he ran. He had done well in developing strength and stamina, but not so well in learning obedience. He had been spoiled and fussed over by the girls. He did not know how to respond to a command, and was rarely chastised. At least he was becoming increasingly resistant to being picked up and carried around like a toy, now that he had found his feet.

Manon appeared, a sullen look on her face and what looked distinctly like streaks of flour down the front of her dress. She flopped down onto the stone seat, deigning to share space with Efa while keeping a safe distance. 'Siwan!' she raised her voice to get the girl's attention. 'Eluned sent me to find you, as she says she needs someone who can handle pastry gently, and I am too rough. She should be pleased that I am helping her at all.' This last was punctuated with a glare in Efa's direction.

Siwan smiled sweetly, and Efa could have sworn that behind the smile was a distinct look of triumph. Was there a quiet rivalry developing between the girls? If so, Siwan had won this particular battle. She disappeared off towards the house, leaving Haf still playing with the dog. Manon made no attempt to join her sister, but sat scuffing her shoes in the loose stones beneath her feet, making a study of the clouds of dust being released by the movement.

Haf came bouncing over to Efa, the dog at her heels.

'Can Jac come with us for our walk today? He is strong enough now, look.' She demonstrated his ability to jump by teasing him with the stick she had just been throwing for him, laughing as the little dog spun in the air trying to grab it from her hand.

'I can see that he is strong. But can he be trusted to come when called? Will he walk by your side and not run off, chasing a rabbit? I am not so sure he is ready, little one. He needs to be trained, and he is still young. I do not think he can join us outside the gates yet.'

Haf stopped laughing, creased her brows and pursed her lips. It was unusual to see the girl cross. She came to stand in front of Efa, folded her arms across her chest and stamped her little foot dramatically.

'I want him to come. He is my friend. He is sad when we leave him behind.'

It was a moment of defiance, but done so sweetly that Efa struggled to hide a smile. She would not be moved on this one, though. Untrained, the dog could prove a liability to the local wildlife, and worse, could run off and get lost. That would certainly break Haf's heart more than having to leave Jac at home.

'No, Haf. I am resolute on this. We will train him to come to command, and then see if he is ready. Or if not, train him to walk attached to a long lead rope, perhaps. But that won't be today, or tomorrow. It will take time.'

With that she stood and bent to cup her hand gently around Haf's chin, lifting her face, disconcerted to see tears in the girl's eyes. She hated to see the girl sad, and her resolution wavered for a moment. But she knew the wisdom of the decision she had made, and chose to stay with it.

'Soon, I promise, Haf, soon.' She wiped a tear from the girl's cheek and smiled, hoping for a smile in response but getting none. Efa sighed. She wanted the children to like and respect her, and in the most part this little one had shown her nothing but affection and trust. Unfortunately, there would be times when she had to enforce unwelcome rules, regardless of whether they liked her or not. This was one of those. 'You can play here with Jac in the gardens for as long as you want to. You know that will have to be enough for now.'

Efa stepped away from the girl who, to her surprise, ran to her sister and climbed up onto the seat beside her. In a rare display of sisterly affection, Manon put her arm around her sister and seemed to whisper words of comfort to her, as Haf was soon wiping grubby hands across her eyes and trying to smile.

The last thing Efa saw before she turned to return to the house was Manon shooting her a glower that revealed plenty. So in this battle for Haf's affection, Efa had lost, and seemingly made even more of an enemy in Manon. She hated that. This was why she hadn't wanted to be a parent to these children; why she hadn't felt ready to take on the responsibility. And to add to that, she had actually begun to really care about them. It hurt her to see Haf sad, and to see Manon angry with her. But deep down she knew she had been right to say no to Haf. Right in many of the decisions she had made to try to improve the children's well-being. Gerallt at least had been grateful for her interventions. She consoled herself with that thought as she headed back inside.

'Help, please, someone help!'

An hour or so had passed and the screech was unmistakably Manon. Efa rushed to greet her at the door.

'What is it?' The terror on the girl's face made Efa's own heart race in panic.

'Haf!' Between gulps of breath and racking sobs, Manon tried to speak.

'Where is Haf? Manon?' Efa found herself gripping the girl's shoulders and shaking her.

Manon took a deep trembling breath and pointed behind her. 'The river!'

Efa released her and ran, her skirts held high above her knees. She ran through the open gates, past a shocked guard who had to step briskly out of her way, and down the path towards the river, not knowing what she might find, and unaware of the footsteps of the one who followed her.

'Haf!' she screamed as she reached the water's edge, looking frantically for any sign of the girl.

'There.' Manon had appeared behind her and was pointing downriver to where a large tree hung its branches over the fast-flowing stream. Efa could see a flash of colour, bright red against the dull brown of a tree branch that was bent towards the water. She ran to the tree and, as she approached, could see both blonde curls and branch bobbing menacingly as the girl was repeatedly dipped into the water. There was no time, she had to act.

'Get help, Manon!' she screamed back at the girl, as she hoisted her skirts and stepped into the river. Shallow at first, it dipped suddenly and she found herself waist-deep in the swirling water, struggling to keep her feet on the slippery stones beneath. The water was cold too, despite the warmth of the summer sun, and she felt her breath being taken from her as it reached her chest. She was having to fight against the swirling current and was grateful when she could grab hold of the branch herself. Haf was finally within her reach. The girl was trapped by an arm, mercifully, as without the tree her lightweight body would have been swept under and downstream within minutes.

A thousand thoughts and fears raced through Efa's mind at what might have been. For now, she had to focus and act swiftly. Haf was unresponsive to her voice, and clearly exhausted. Efa thanked God for her own unwomanly height and strength in that moment, as she grabbed the girl around the chest and lifted her so that her arm came free. Only then did she realise how much of a dead weight Haf was, lifeless and drenched by river water. Efa swallowed back her fear, seeing the small white face with its blue lips. She had to move, had to get them both out of the water. She could not easily turn without letting go of the tree branch, and the current was threatening to drag them both down. She used every ounce of strength she could muster just to hold the girl's head above the water and to try to work her way back to the bank. Just when she feared she could hold on no longer, there were shouts, and a strong arm grabbed her own.

Ifan was in the water, a rope tied around his waist and two men taking the slack on the riverbank.

'Give me the girl!' he yelled above the sound of the water.

She shifted the weight of Haf into his arms and turned to cling to the branch, watching gratefully as Ifan waded out of the water with his precious bundle. She inched slowly along the branch until one of the guards could reach to grab her hand, and she fell in an undignified heap of sodden skirts onto the muddy riverbank.

Ifan had laid Haf on the ground and was putting his mouth to hers, giving him her breath. Efa watched, holding her own, until with relief she saw the girl splutter and cough, river water spewing from her mouth. But still she did not move or speak.

'Go!' Efa cried. Ifan glanced up at her briefly and then gathered the girl into his arms and broke into a run.

Efa sank back against the tree trunk. She needed to follow. She needed to do all that she could to fight for Haf's life. She also needed a moment to catch her breath. She willed her body to stop shivering, and as if she had voiced the need, suddenly a warm cloak was around her shoulders and a concerned face was bent close to her own.

'Can I help you up, my lady?' It was the same guard who had stepped out of her way as she had sped through Tregaron's gates minutes before. Behind him stood Manon, quivering with shock. Efa took the guard's outstretched hand and rose unsteadily to her feet. She was glad of his strength to lean on as she reached out to Manon and grasped her hand.

'We can talk about what happened here later. We need to get back to see how your sister is.'

'Jac! He went in the water, and couldn't get back. Haf went in after him. She moved so quickly I could not stop her.'

The dog was in the water? What were they all doing by the river alone, anyway? And then she realised. As an act of defiance, Manon had brought her sister and the dog into this situation. She had probably used her charms to persuade the guard to open the gates for them. The very same guard who now stood supporting her weight. He would probably lose his position over this, at the very least. And he knew it. She could not feel sorry for him now.

'There.' Manon was pointing to the other side of the river. A shrill bark and a frantically waving tail confirmed that the dog had survived his ordeal perfectly well. That would be small consolation if his human companion did not survive hers.

Haf had been carried back to the house where Eluned had stripped her of her sodden clothing and laid her down in front of a hastily stoked-up fire, covered by warm blankets. Once Efa had divested herself of her own wet skirts, she insisted that the child be brought up and laid in her bed. A pale-faced Ifan gathered the precious bundle into his arms and carried her there. There was still no sign of movement, not even a flicker of her eyelashes in response to their ministrations, just a gentle rise and fall of the little girl's chest.

As the afternoon wore on and the light began to fail, Efa and Non never left the girl's side, willing Haf to come back to them, longing for her eyes to open and her little face to light up and smile. They longed to see colour replace the deathly white, but when colour did come, it was in the form of vivid pink spots, high on her cheeks. The child's breathing was no longer shallow and gentle, but deep and rattling. Where her hair had been wet from the river, now it was dampened with sweat. Efa and Non looked anxiously at each other across the bed. Both knew the signs. Haf had survived drowning, but the fever induced by her fight with the river might yet take her. Tepid water was brought and they took turns to tenderly mop Haf's forehead, neck, upper chest and arms in an attempt to keep the fever from overtaking her. Ifan appeared in the room more than once, the same mirrored look of concern on his face.

The long hours seemed to drag on. Messengers had been sent to summon Cynan home, but he had not yet returned. As Efa and Non continued their vigil, there was no improvement in Haf's condition. Her breathing was still laboured, and every now and then it was accompanied by a racking cough that convulsed the little body. Then she was shivering and tossing, deliriously calling out unrecognisable words; there was nothing more they could do, other than what they were doing – except to pray. And as the evening wore on, Non spent more and more time with her head bowed, resting on her hands, which were clasped together close by Haf's head. Efa could hear her whispering words under her breath, but Efa could not find the words to pray herself.

Even before night had fallen completely, the household seemed unnaturally quiet. Efa just assumed that the other children had been put to bed. She knew that she needed to check on Manon and give her a chance to talk about what had happened, but for the moment she couldn't bear to leave Haf's side. At some point during the night hours Manon appeared, dressed just in her shift with a cloak thrown loosely around her shoulders, her dark hair in an untidy braid. Her face was pale and drawn, her eyes red from sleeplessness, or from crying, or likely both. To Efa's surprise, the girl walked around her sister's bed and came to stand beside Efa. She hung her head, standing mutely until Efa reached out a hand and drew her closer. And then her arm was around her and the girl was in her embrace, sobbing on her shoulder.

'I'm sorry, I'm sorry,' she was whispering over and over again, her words muffled as she hid her face. Efa rubbed her hand across Manon's back. What could she say? The girl needed to say sorry, but then Efa felt she too needed to be sorry. The children were her responsibility and she had let this happen somehow. How would she ever explain this to their father? How would she explain such lack of care?

Once Manon had cried herself out, Efa drew a stool over so that they could sit together at Haf's bedside. She knew the sight of Haf would shock Manon, but she could do nothing to prevent that. She heard the sharp intake of breath and watched Manon reach out and cling on to her sister's legs, covered as they were by light bedclothes. Efa realised she would have to say nothing to condemn Manon's disobedience. The girl could now plainly see the consequences of her defiant behaviour. And if Haf was to lose her life, then Manon would have to live with the guilt for the rest of her own. Eventually the older girl rested her head down on her arms. Efa wondered if she too was praying.

Efa bowed her own head and clasped her hands together, closing her eyes to the desperate scene in front of her. Why could she not find words? Perhaps she did not really believe that her prayers would make a difference in this situation. She'd only just begun to call God 'Father', only just begun to believe that He might actually care. And now He had allowed this to happen. Weariness overtook her and she found her own head resting on her arms just inches from Haf's chest, which mercifully was still rising and falling, but with such effort. Between the moments of delirium, the child lay unnaturally still and quiet, her sunny self subsumed by the darkness of the fight she was in for her young life.

Night after night I'm tossing and turning on my bed

of travail.

Why did I let him go from me?

How my heart now aches for him,

but he is nowhere to be found!

Song of Solomon 3:1, TPT

10
Prayer

Soft light had begun to creep around the edges of the shutters when Efa suddenly awoke with a start. She realised that she'd actually drifted off into a deep sleep, where she had dreamt of a father embracing his child. She looked up, desperate to see a change in Haf's condition. But still she lay fighting for breath, her face clammy. And the hand that Efa reached out to hold was now frighteningly cold. Non was missing from her seat, and maybe it had been the sound of the door opening and closing that had startled Efa out of her sleep. Next to her, Manon laid sprawled on her sister's bed, one hand still closed around Haf's leg, as if holding on to keep her with them in the land of the living. Efa felt hot tears rise, stinging her eyes. She knew she had to do something.

'God!' she cried, a little more than a whisper. 'Father in heaven, have mercy!' She wet the girl's cold hands with her tears. 'Father, have mercy!' she repeated the words. 'If not for my sake, then for love of Haf. Do not let her die. She must live! God in heaven, she must live. Merciful Father, I'm pleading with You. Please.'

Through closed eyelids she was aware of a bright light entering the room just momentarily; Non most likely returning with a fresh tallow candle, although Efa had not heard the door creak. In fact, a strange quietness now filled the room. Manon still snored quietly beside her, but she could no longer hear the sound of Haf's harsh breathing. She felt the wave of grief threaten, and could not bring herself to open her eyes to the inevitable. But then, the fingers of the small hand she still held in her own twitched. She looked up, relieved to see that the little girl's chest still rose and fell.

It took her a moment to register that Haf's breathing was different. No longer laboured, now it was calm and steady and quiet. Haf's face was different too, pink but not with the high flushed spots of colour that had been so worrying. She looked healthy, as if she were just sleeping. Wondering, Efa reached over to touch the child's forehead, which she found was no longer damp with sweat. Then Haf's eyelashes flickered and she yawned and stretched, opening her eyes to smile at Efa. She looked around the room, seeming confused to see her sister sprawled, asleep, across her legs.

'Where is the man with the kind face?' The words were clear and tuneful.

Efa was finding it all so hard to process. Not least Haf's words.

'What man?' she whispered in awe.

'The man that stood there.' She pointed to where Non had vacated her spot. 'He smiled at me and took my hand, and told me that Jac was safe, but that I needed to wake up now. Where is Jac?'

Efa was saved from having to think of how to answer her by the creaking of the door. Non appeared, and close behind her was Cynan, dishevelled and breathless from his panicked ride to get home. They stepped into the room, Cynan's face pinched with grief, just in time to see Haf raise herself up onto her elbows with a broad smile on her face. Non looked as shocked as Efa felt, almost dropping the tray that she carried. Cynan, for his part, moved so quickly over to the bed that he almost fell on top of his daughter as he grabbed hold of her and held on to her.

Manon stirred and sat up, brushing stray hairs from across her face. 'What happened?' she said, with a dazed look.

'The fever has broken,' Efa whispered. 'She's come back to us.'

Suddenly Non was there behind them both. 'I think we've just seen a miracle!' she whispered, placing her hand on Efa's shoulder and squeezing it slightly. Efa turned to face her friend and nodded. Tears were streaming down her cheeks, tears of relief and joy. Somehow God had heard her prayers, although she would find it easier to believe that maybe it was Non's prayers that God had heard and not hers. It did not matter whose prayers He had heard, the feeling of gratitude was almost overwhelming as she watched Haf and her father and her sister embrace one another.

Efa rose unsteadily to her feet, leaving the family to have their time together. She walked stiffly to the door, just glancing back once more to imprint the miraculous scene on her memory. Non followed her out and onto the landing.

'Did you pray?' Non asked, her eyes full.

'Yes. I tried to. But you were praying too.' Efa's voice shook with emotion.

'I was.' She grasped Efa's hand and squeezed it. 'He heard us both, Efa,' she smiled and shook her head in wonder. 'He gave us our Haf back!'

They held one another for a moment, and then walked slowly down the stairs together. As they reached the hall, Efa remembered Haf's words.

'She was asking for Jac the moment she woke. Have they found the dog?'

Non laughed softly. 'Yes, they found him and they brought him back. They felt it safest to lock him in Ifan's room, and that has been a good thing. The minute Cynan heard about the dog's role in Haf's misfortune, he was all for strangling the poor creature. I doubt he would have really done so, but it was best the dog was kept away.'

'Does he know about Manon's role? And the poor guard?' If Cynan was angry with the dog, Efa could only wonder as to how he would react to their involvement.

'He has had the full story, as such as any of us know it.'

'He will be angry. I will have to explain my part in it.'

There was food left on the table from where others of the household had broken fast. Efa sat wearily on a chair and helped herself to a chunk of bread. Non sat beside her.

'He will not blame you, Efa. Manon acted against your direct instructions.'

'But I should have known where the girls were. I should have noticed that they had left.' The two sat together thoughtfully as they both helped themselves to more food. Finally, Non spoke softly. 'I suspect that Cynan will be so overjoyed that Haf lives and is well that the events of yesterday, and who bears the blame for them, will be forgotten.'

Manon appeared then, joining them with a wary look, and shifting her gaze when Efa smiled at her.

'Haf is hungry. She is asking for food and something to drink,' she said quietly.

'Of course,' Non laughed. 'Just like the story in the Gospels, when Jesus raised Jairus' daughter.' She jumped up and hurried away to the kitchen.

Manon turned to leave, but Efa was quick to reach out and grab her arm. 'Manon, what you did yesterday was wrong. But I know you are sorry.'

The girl bowed her head. 'I was so scared. I thought she was going to die, and I was so angry with myself that I wanted to die too.'

'I know. I was scared too.'

Efa encouraged Manon to sit in the seat Non had just vacated, and the two of them sat in silence for a few moments reliving the trauma of the last few hours. Manon lifted her face to Efa then, her forehead pinched. She swallowed hard. 'You saved my sister's life. She lives because you put your life at risk to get her out of the river.'

Efa nodded. 'I truly believe that it is God who saved your sister's life, Manon. But I would do what I did for her again. I would do it for any of you.' She felt for Manon's hand and drew her closer to her. 'Do you believe that?'

Manon studied her face for a moment, her eyes filling with tears. 'Yes. You have tried so hard to be kind to us. You have always tried to do the best for us. Even when you have asked us to do things that we haven't wanted to.' She paused.

Efa smiled. 'Like making pastry for Eluned?'

Manon smiled shyly and then looked away. 'I haven't been very kind to you in return. I resented you marrying my father, and I did not want you to be my mother. I did not want you here at all. I thought I could make you leave again if I was unfriendly. And yesterday…' She paused again, and took a deep breath. 'Yesterday, I wanted to prove you wrong. I wanted Haf to think that you were just being cruel. I was jealous of the way she has attached herself to you. Jealous of how fondly Gerallt talks of you. But I didn't intend for Haf to get hurt. And you could have been angry with me. Instead, you stayed by my sister's side, you embraced and comforted me, and you prayed. And God heard your prayers.'

Efa brought her other hand up to cup Manon's cheek, her heart full of compassion and understanding.

'All of that is in the past now, Manon. And things can be different now. I will not always do or say things that you like, but I am trying to make life better for you. I would very much like it if we could be friends. At least for most of the time.'

Manon nodded. 'I will try to be nicer.' Their gazes met and something passed between them. A mutual understanding at last.

Non had reappeared with a tray laden with a feast for Haf. Efa laughed. 'There's enough for all of us there!'

'Come on, then,' Non laughed in reply. 'Let's go back up and celebrate together.'

That night, Efa had fallen exhausted into her own bed, Haf insisting on sleeping back in her room, enfolded into Manon's embrace. Efa had slept so soundly that she woke when the sun was already high in the sky. She rose from her bed and opened her door a crack. There were sounds of laughter from the hall below, including, to Efa's joy, the high-pitched giggle of a small girl and the excited yapping of a small dog.

'There you are!' Non appeared from the children's room. 'The rest of the house has been up for hours. We've been waiting for you, but thought to let you sleep. It seems everyone is waiting to greet the heroine who braved the wild river waters.'

Efa blushed and stepped back into her room, Non pushing her way in and closing the door behind them. Her usual smiling face now turned more serious. She stood before Efa and took both of her hands in her own.

'We did not realise. None of us did. Not until Manon told us, and Ifan confirmed it, that you put your own life at risk to save Haf.' Her eyes had filled with tears. 'We might have lost you as well! And that would have broken my heart. I am so, so grateful. To you, for what you did, both at the river and at Haf's bedside yesterday. And to God for saving you both.'

Efa squeezed her hands, her own eyes pricking. She nodded and then, feeling unsettled by being at the receiving end of such praise, quickly released Non's hands and turned her attention to getting dressed. Non stepped up to assist her, and they worked in companiable silence for the time that it took to get her fully clothed.

'My father is waiting to speak with you. I think he wants to offer you his gratitude also.'

'I would rather he didn't.'

Efa followed Non down the stairs. There was much activity going on in the hall. Children, dog, Ifan and Cynan laughing, Eluned heaping food on the table.

'My lady!' Cynan turned at her entrance and bowed deeply, taking her hand in his, a broad smile on his face. 'I understand we have much to thank you for,' he said quietly as she accepted his greeting.

'Please,' she said, her face flushing in embarrassment. 'I would rather we not speak of it. Non has praised me enough, and I feel more than I deserve. I could not bear any more praise from your lips.'

Cynan examined her face for a moment, and then nodded in understanding. 'Well, at least come and eat with us. We are having another, more planned, celebratory meal than our impromptu feast at Haf's bedside yesterday. And everyone must be happy and enjoy it.'

There was a scrambling, then, as the gathered family and friends found their places at the table.

'Tomorrow we will go to Ystrad Fflur.'

From the corner of her eye, Efa saw Gerallt's head shoot up at his father's words.

'All of us,' Cynan added. 'We will go to offer our thanks to God for the life of our daughter and sister.' He raised his cup at that and was met with a cheer from the others in response.

Efa added her own quiet cheer. She knew Ystrad Fflur was exactly where she needed to go. As excited as Gerallt was to visit again, so was she. This time, she prayed she would see Abbot Ulrich once more, and have time to speak with him.

The day was bright and dry, the wagon had been loaded with children, food and a fussing Eluned. She would not be left behind, but was obviously nervous, being away from Tregaron. She had been helped up into the back of the wagon and sat holding on to the side with white-knuckled hands, gasping every time the wheels hit a rut in the road. Haf and Siwan joined her but were more relaxed, sitting together giggling, leaning up against the side of the wagon bed, laughing when the wagon turned and they were flung from side to side. Gerallt was happy to join them in the wagon, as was Non, but Manon insisted on riding. She had a good seat, riding side-saddle, and Efa was jealous of her poise. She was less comfortable in the saddle, wishing she could have ridden astride, if fine clothes and decorum had not made it impossible. She rode alongside Manon, behind Cynan, the wagon rattling along after them with Ifan in the driving seat.

As the abbey came into view, Cynan pulled up and gestured for Efa to come alongside him.

'I have sent word ahead to ask Father Abbot if he can lead a *Te Deum* as part of the office at Terce this morning. I am hopeful he will accommodate us. I intend to give a gift to the abbey in thanksgiving for Haf's deliverance, and he knows its value.'

'I am sure Father will happily lead a song of thanksgiving for Haf's life, even if we were not prepared to donate to the abbey. I believe he is a good and godly man.'

He watched her for a moment, his eyes curious.

'I will take your word for that. My gift to the abbey is only a small measure of how much my daughter's life is worth to me.'

'I am sure they will receive it with gladness,' she replied, smiling over at her husband.

The *Te Deum* was beautifully sung by the monks, and prayers of thanksgiving enthusiastically prayed. Haf smiled at all the attention she was getting, but as soon as the service was done, she was ready to be let loose. Cynan had promised them a visit to one of the grange farms, where new lambs had been born a few weeks before. The brothers also kept goats and chickens, and there was mention of a cat with new kittens. Haf was jumping up and down with excitement when she heard this, and Ifan laughed as he helped her and Siwan, Non and a less-than-enthusiastic Eluned back up into the wagon for the short ride. Cynan would ride with them, but Efa touched his arm before he remounted and quietly asked for his permission to stay at the abbey for some time of private prayer. She explained that she was still tired from her unexpected 'swim' two days before, and the rest and quiet would do her good. At the reminder of what he owed her, Cynan was quick to agree to her request. Gerallt was also permitted to stay behind. He had been released to visit the scriptorium and find Brother Paul, who had promised him a tour of the library.

Efa knew exactly where she wanted to be, as she headed back into the church to find the same chapel where she had met the abbot before. She found herself alone as she entered the quiet space and for a moment felt disappointed. But she could not expect Father Ulrich to know she wanted to speak with him. He did not even know she was there.

She sat where she had before, on the cold stone seat in the alcove to the side of the small, simple altar. She leaned her head back against the cool stone wall and closed her eyes, letting out a deep sigh. The peace of the place was beautiful, calming. She used the time to revisit the events at the river. It struck her how close she had come to being swept away herself. She could have slipped and fallen, hit her head; she could have lost hold of Haf. Any one of a plethora of scenarios would have made the outcome very different. And yet Haf had still almost died despite her efforts. The only difference in it all was God. He had healed Haf, she was sure of it. The girl was so full of energy, and that would not have been possible if the fever had broken of its own account, a little over a day ago. But was it also possible that God had protected her, been with her in that cold water, helped her to stand against the current and hold on to the child?

'Thank You, God' she whispered, 'for Your help and protection. For saving my life as well as Haf's. And for answering my prayers.'

'Amen.' It was a familiar voice, and Efa smiled as she brought her head up and opened her eyes. This time Efa stood and started to dip, bowing her head to greet the abbot.

'Now, now. There is no need. We are friends, are we not?' Father Ulrich took her arm gently and gestured for her to resume her seat. He sat, as he had before, beside her. He too let out a sigh and then smiled warmly.

'So we meet here again,' he laughed softly. 'I do believe my favourite hiding place has also become yours.'

She smiled in return. 'I was hoping I might see you to speak to you today,' she said shyly.

'Well, I am here, and I am happy to speak with you. I believe you have an incredible story to tell me. A story of miraculous happenings and of answered prayers?'

He encouraged her to tell him the whole tale, and listened intently. He closed his eyes and whispered 'Glory to God' when Efa explained how she had watched Haf miraculously awaken. Efa could see that his eyes were glistening with tears, but his face was radiant with joy.

'She said that she saw a man with a kind face, who told her to wake up. No such man entered her room, so I believe it was a dream.'

'Oh, it was more than a dream. I think Jesus visited Haf's bedside, just as He did the bedside of Jairus' daughter. In the very same way, he told that little girl, who was already dead, to wake up and she did. Sitting up and asking for food!'

'She did the same!' Efa exclaimed. 'Well, after she had asked after the dog, anyway!'

They laughed together.

'You have witnessed a miracle, my lady Efa. How does that make you now feel about God? Have you forgiven Him?'

She was startled enough to turn at his words. 'Forgive me, Father, did you ask whether I had forgiven God? Surely I do not have the power to do so?'

'You are right, of course. God does not need forgiveness, because He only ever acts justly and perfectly. He is Almighty, after all. But sometimes I believe we hold things against Him. When He seemingly ignores our prayers, or allows hard things to happen to us. So in forgiving Him, what we are doing is choosing to wipe away any grievances against Him we might have.'

Efa was thinking it through and it was making some sense to her. 'I can see that I pulled away from God because of my hurt, believing that He did not care for me. I made a case against Him, which embittered my heart towards Him. He did not deserve that.'

'No. He did not. But in His grace and mercy He has begun to reveal more of Himself to you, the God who does care, who is kind, who does answer prayer.'

'I had already seen Him in Non and Eluned and Ifan at Tregaron.'

'Yes, I thought that you would.'

'And now I have seen Him do the most marvellous miracle, and in response to my prayers.'

'Indeed.'

They sat in silence for a few moments as the sun streaming through the glass above them painted patterns on the stone chapel walls.

At last Efa spoke, softly and reverently. 'God Almighty is indeed worthy of my praise and my love and not of my rebellious heart. I will ask His forgiveness and grace to release my case against Him.'

Father Ulrich reached over and patted Efa's hand.

'He knows your heart, my dear one. He knows.'

Efa bowed her head then and whispered her thanks again. She wondered if this was her moment of running back into the Father's arms, as the son in the story Non had reminded her of. She thought she could almost imagine His arms around her, and it felt wonderful. Could it be that she really was truly loved by God?

Moments passed before she raised her head. She hadn't heard the abbot leave, and sure enough he was still sat beside her. His own eyes were closed and his hands clasped before him, a serene smile on his face.

'Thank you, Father Ulrich,' she said.

He opened his eyes and broadened his smile. 'I am praying that you will more and more come into an understanding of how much your Father in heaven cares about you,

She smiled and nodded. 'I am grateful for your prayers, and I do want that understanding. I think my heart is opening to Him, and that is thanks, in no small part, to you, Father.'

A few more moments passed before Efa summoned the courage to question the abbot about the other matter that concerned her: Gerallt's wayward tutor.

'There is one more thing I wanted to ask you, Father.'

'Go on.'

'Brother Paul...'

'Ah, yes,' he interrupted her, leaning forward to rest his elbows on his knees. 'I feel we owe you and your husband some explanation. I am sorry that Brother Paul relinquished his duties, and let you and Gerallt down. I have to tell you that he believed he had no choice but to end his visits to your home.'

'Was something said or done to offend him?' Efa was disturbed by the thought.

'No, no, not that. It was more a matter of conscience, a recognition of a personal weakness.'

'Oh? He was always polite and behaved as was expected of a brother of this house.'

Ulrich sighed heavily, looking her directly in the face. The smile had gone.

'It was not in what he did that he found his struggle, rather than in what he was thinking and feeling. He felt himself drawn into an affection that challenged the vows he has made.'

Non! Of course! She had seen it, and wondered at the time. So he had become attached to her, and that was why he had left. She wondered if the feelings had been reciprocated on Non's part. She had not confided such to Efa, but then would not necessarily do so.

She looked up to find Ulrich still studying her intently.

'I am sorry. I saw his attachment to Non, and I should have stepped in to prevent it deepening.'

'Efa, it was not Non.'

'Not Non? But it was she with whom he spent time.'

'Yes, but only because they share the same vocation, Efa. She questioned him on life in the order, I understand, what she could expect. They talked of their shared devotion to God and their hopes for the future. Neither saw their relationship as anything more than acquaintances with shared interests.'

'If not Non, then surely it was not Manon? He seemed most taken aback when she tried to be coquettish with him. I think he was even a little scared of her!'

'No, my lady, not Manon. You do not see it, do you? You do not see how beautiful, gentle and kind a woman you are? It was you that drew him, lady Efa. The way you were with the children, your smile and your laughter. Your quiet grace in accepting a role you did not ask for, and a marriage that does not satisfy you. He found himself deeply admiring you, and knew how wrong that was.'

Efa was stunned by his words. She had not seen it at all. She could not recall ever speaking to the monk, except about the children's needs. But then, as she thought more about it, she remembered his easy blushes when she did speak to him, and catching him watching her from time to time. She had thought nothing of it.

'I am sorry if I did or said anything to encourage his feelings.'

'No. It was all in his own mind, Efa, and once he recognised that his heart was also becoming involved, he chose to withdraw himself. He will be able to reapply himself to his work, his vows and his devotion to God, now that he is back with us. Do not worry for him.' Ulrich had risen to take his leave from her. 'You do not see your beauty my dear, but God does.'

I do not see myself as beautiful, she thought to herself. *I have never had the face or build that most men would consider beautiful in a woman. Which was why Philip's love for me was so precious.* She felt the tears prick.

Ulrich was still there and still speaking. 'This is what God says about you: "Behold, you are fair, my love! Behold, you are fair!" Perhaps you should dwell on His words, and begin to see what He sees when He looks at you.'

He smiled then and made a small bow before leaving her.

Efa was glad that she could be alone now. She needed to speak to her heavenly Father. The One who loved her and wanted to embrace her. And the One who called her beautiful. The One who saw more in her than she saw in herself. She needed to ask Him to help her to believe it all.

Listen, my dearest darling,

you are so beautiful – you are beauty itself to

me!

Song of Solomon 4:1, TPT

11
Beloved

Efa stayed long after the abbot had left her, soaking in the quiet peace of what felt like her own little personal corner of the abbey. She didn't pray exactly; it just felt good to quieten her mind and meditate on all that Father Ulrich had said to her. The excitement of Haf's healing had also overtaken the trauma she herself had encountered. She was glad of time alone to rest her body, mind and emotions. Except she did not feel alone there. God's presence was in the very air itself, and not just because of the sacred objects all around her. She knew He was there; she could not explain it other than she felt safe, held, surrounded and soothed. Ulrich carried God, she had no doubt, but as he had left her, the feeling that a holy presence was still with her was so strong. She found herself reaching out a hand as if to grab hold of something elusive, but which also hung so thick in the air around her.

She must have fallen into a dreamless doze, which was surprising as the stone seat she sat on wasn't built for comfort. She was awoken by the sound of bells and then the sound of footsteps entering the echoing quiet of the church. It was time for Sext. She should have got up and left as the community of brothers entered, but she stayed, transfixed by the simple beauty of the sung liturgy. The monks' voices seemed to fill the church right up to the fine stone arches that supported the rafters. The sun was still streaming through the panes in the window above her. She breathed in deeply at the beauty of it all. God had not spoken to her in words, but she had encountered Him there and her heart was full; full of a joy and peace that she had not felt for a very long time.

She waited until the monks had completed their office and held back a few moments to follow them out. She was surprised to see that Gerallt had joined the monks for the service and was now walking beside Brother Aled, whispering excitedly. He held a rolled-up manuscript in his hands. He must have caught sight of Efa as he stopped and, nodding a farewell to the monk, turned to approach her.

'This is for you.' He held out the manuscript, a shy smile on his face and the hint of a blush colouring his cheeks.

Efa was slightly taken aback, but took the scroll from his proffered hand. He was still watching her, expectant, so she smiled and thanked him.

'Shall I look at it now? Is it a message? Something important I need to read now? Or should I save it for when we return to Tregaron?'

The blush deepened. 'Father Abbot came to see me in the scriptorium, saw that I was working on a script with Brother Aled and suggested I copy a special piece of scripture for you. He told me it was a piece rarely read out loud, but that he thought it would have special meaning for you.'

She unrolled the parchment to reveal a few lines of very neatly copied text. Gerallt had also attempted to illuminate the capital letter that began the scripture. The large 'Y' was decorated with the picture of a woman with long golden hair, her hand clasped by a man with a gold crown on his head. It was not finished, and would need more colour added to it, but it was stunningly beautiful nonetheless.

Efa was deeply moved. 'You did this for me? It is really very fine work, Gerallt. God has gifted you.'

He still looked flustered but smiled broadly, the light reaching his eyes. 'Do you think so? Brother Aled thinks I have potential. I only made a few tiny mistakes, and he was very complimentary.'

He proceeded to point out to her where a tool had been used to scrape back errors and fresh ink applied. The spots where he had done so were not obvious to the untrained eye.

'And Father Abbot asked you to do this for me?'

'Yes. He said you would understand.'

She looked down at the wording again, and one word leapt off the page: 'Bride'. Her eyes filled with unexpected tears at the kindness of the abbot. He had wanted her to have these words from God's own lips to her. She would read them again, meditate on them, ask God to make them real to her. But she did not trust herself to read them in Gerallt's company without being overcome. She re-rolled the parchment and asked Gerallt to carry it safely home for her in his scrip. For now they were being hailed by excitable voices, a wagon and horses standing ready for their return to Tregaron.

Later, Efa sat alone on her favourite bench in Annest's garden, precious parchment in hand. The sun was beginning its descent, the sky turning a glorious warm orange, but the summer air was still warm. She opened the scroll and read the words, slowly, tracing each line with her finger.

> *You have captured my heart,*
> *my treasure, my bride.*
> *You hold it hostage with one glance of your eyes,*
> *with a single jewel of your necklace.*
> *Your love delights me,*
> *my treasure, my bride.*
> *Your love is better than wine,*
> *your perfume more fragrant than spices.*

The words were a love letter. One she would have been overwhelmed to have received from Philip, if he had been a poet of any kind. But it wasn't Philip calling her a treasure, calling her his bride. That dream was dead and gone. She was now another man's bride, a man who would never speak such words of love to her either. Her heart had been broken and scarred by betrayal. She had been abandoned by her lover, and bartered with by her uncle. She had dreamt of being a bride in love, and had instead become a bride of convenience. But as she read the words again, she realised that she was not being wooed by a man, and that spoke deeply to her soul. The voice behind these words was God Himself. He was telling her how lovely she was, how much she delighted Him, how much their love for each other meant to Him. 'He calls me bride.' She whispered the words to herself.

She knew, of course, that women entering the Church would consecrate themselves as brides of Christ. She knew Non would have no trouble doing so; her devotion to her Lord was plain. But was the same possible for her? She who was wed to a human man, she who had promised herself to care for his children, she who had begun to make a life for herself here. She realised then that she had actually begun to really love her life at Tregaron, and feel deep affection for the children. For Non, Ifan and Eluned. Was God asking her to give this up and enter a nunnery? Was that what it meant to be His bride? She physically shuddered at the thought.

It was in this confused state that Non found her and came to sit by her. She showed her friend the precious piece of Gerallt's handiwork, commissioned especially for her by Father Ulrich. Non took it to read, concentrating hard. When she finally raised her head she looked at Efa with a glowing smile.

'Yes. Efa, I agree with Father Abbot. I think you needed to hear these words.'

'But is it a call for me to enter the Church?'

Non laughed deeply. 'No, my dear friend. I do not believe so. I think it is just the call of a God who loves you and wants you to know just how much.'

'But how can I be His bride and still be Cynan's?'

'This is a deep and spiritual truth that I may not be able to explain well myself, but I will try, Efa. When I enter the Church, God willing, I will take a vow to be married to no one but Christ. He will have all the affection that I would have otherwise given to a man. But as I have come to understand it, one of the ways that Jesus is described is as a bridegroom. A bridegroom whose bride is all those who believe in Him. So in that way, we are all His brides, even the *men* who love Him.' She chuckled. 'Although they do not need to wear a veil to greet Him!

'I think Father Abbot wanted you to have these words so that you would know that being in a marriage where you are not loved as a wife deserves to be does not mean that you are not lovely enough, or lovable enough to be a true bride. In God's eyes, you are beautiful. He considered you worth the death of His Son on the cross. If you choose to give your heart to Christ in response to His love for you, then you become one of those He calls His own. His daughter, and His bride! Does that make sense to you?'

Efa had listened, her heart stirring at Non's words. To be loved that much! Not only had God loved her enough to sacrifice His Son for her, but He also wanted her to be His bride? No, she did not fully understand it all. She had only just begun to see God as a Father she could trust. Now He wanted her to see Him as her bridegroom also?

'I must think on these things, Non. It all sounds so wonderful. But I do not feel worthy of His words as they are written here. Of His love.'

'Oh, my friend! None of us feels worthy. None of us *is* worthy. That is the beauty of it all. His mercy extends to us, and His grace, so that it is never dependent on us. His love is what makes us worthy, and it is a mystery how He can take our feeble attempts to love Him in return, and call us delightful! Although I for one love being thought of as delightful.' She jumped up and spun around, her face lit up with joy, laughing prettily, making Efa break into a wide smile herself.

She knew that Non had that loving relationship with God that those verses described. Efa had been envious of her for that. Now it seemed the same love was being offered to her. And she knew the truth – that it was up to her to accept it.

'Thank you for showing me what it looks like to be secure in God's love, and demonstrating how to love Him in return. I want what you have. I want to be worthy to be called both His daughter and… His bride.' She swallowed back the sudden emotion. This was big. Bigger even than what she and Philip had shared. She knew what followed would change her life forever. She reached out for her friend's hand.

'Pray with me, Non,' she whispered.

For you reach into my heart.

With one flash of your eyes I am undone by your

love,

my beloved, my equal, my bride.

You leave me breathless –

I am overcome

by merely a glance from your worshiping eyes,

for you have stolen my heart.

I am held hostage by your love

and by the graces of righteousness shining upon

you.

Song of Solomon 4:9, TPT

12
Christmas

December 1222

Efa shivered with the cold as she rose from her bed. Hot stones and heavy covers had warmed the bed the night before, but now she hurried to dress and get downstairs to where she knew the fire would be stoked and the hall warm. For weeks now she had abandoned using the *prie-dieu* that stood in the corner of her room. It had become a comforting habit, to spend time in personal prayer each morning, and kneeling to do so had seemed right. She needed that time speaking to her Father in heaven, needed it to keep her mind and heart settled. Asking for His wisdom, grace and strength each day; thanking Him for His love and provision; praying for those she loved. Even Philip. She could pray for him now without pain causing tears to fall. She prayed for his safety and his health, but most of all she prayed that he would come to experience the peace that she now carried.

She knew that coming to know Christ as her Saviour, accepting how much He loved her, had been the start of a deep healing of her heart. Abandoning the *prie-dieu* did not mean abandoning the prayer, although staying under the warmth of her bedcovers sometimes meant that the prayer slipped into dozing. She hoped God understood.

She thought she had risen early, but the household was already buzzing. Furniture was being moved, greenery hung from rafters and delicious smells were emanating from the kitchen. She found herself caught up in the excitement. Jac was running around the hall at speed, a stolen branch of evergreen in his mouth. He almost took the feet from under her and Efa, laughing, bent to stop Haf in her playful pursuit of the dog.

'I think it would be better if you took Jac outside to run off some energy. Just wrap up warm and don't go out of the gates!' The warning was not really needed. The young girl was now naturally wary of going outside the safe environs of Tregaron. Despite the fact that they had tried to teach Jac some discipline, and that he would come back when called now, he also rarely ventured outside of the gate. His favourite place, other than his bed beside the fire, was the stables. He had become an excellent rat catcher, despite his incapacitated limb.

The girl giggled and tried to catch the dog. After several attempts, and a near miss with Eluned who was carrying a tray laden with sweet and spicy-smelling pies, Jac was cornered by a laughing Non. Eluned wasn't laughing, and Efa was sure she had heard an unnaturally coarse expletive come from her lips as she almost dropped her load. Jac and Eluned had an uneasy relationship. He was fed with scraps from her kitchen and accomplished at keeping the vermin out of her stores, but he was also known to steal food and, like now, get underfoot at the most inconvenient times.

Gerallt was perched on a ladder, fixing up a bower of evergreen under instruction from Ifan, who stood at the base of the ladder, steadying it for him. The boy had grown, in stature and in confidence, since Efa had orchestrated his tutoring and supported his interest in writing and drawing. Brother Aled now visited Tregaron; not as regularly as Brother Paul had, being an older man, but his visits were welcomed by all. He included Haf in his lessons, skilfully adapting them so that she could keep up. And Manon and Non also often joined him as he sat at the table with Gerallt. He was a joy-filled man, and quick to laugh. He didn't mind being made fun of, and made his lessons fun. Gerallt was blossoming under his instruction, but also beginning to mirror some of his character. He was becoming a much more amiable and talkative boy, at home in his own skin.

Manon had also grown in character. She still had a tendency to moodiness, and was not always quick to engage with the things she was asked to do. But she was much more respectful of Efa, and there was a more natural warmth between them; an understanding born of shared experience. Seeing how Efa had risked her own life, and nursed and prayed for Haf devotedly, had certainly changed Manon's attitude towards her. Watching her sister nearly die had shocked her into being a more thoughtful and responsible young woman. She still had her moments of inappropriate behaviour towards men, and Efa had tried to speak to her of it. Manon had not reacted well; in fact, her words had been spiteful and unthinking: 'At least I have the chance to attract a young man. You are just jealous that you are stuck married to an old man. I won't let that happen to me.'

She had stormed off then, leaving Efa stunned into silence. There was truth to her words, after all, and there had been a time when they would have hurt Efa deeply. Not now. Still, being so forward was unlikely to attract Manon the right sort of husband. Efa was still looking for ways to explain that to her, but the opportunity had not yet arisen.

One surprising discovery that had come to light over the last few months was that Manon could play music and sing beautifully. With the weather deteriorating, there had been many occasions when the children could not take their daily exercise outside. This led to all-round frustration and resulting poor behaviour. Even Efa had struggled on those days to keep her temper, until Non suggested that they learn to dance. Efa had agreed. She had learned to dance both the formal dances favoured at Swansea and the less-formal dances of her uncle's court. She was more than willing to teach the children. It soon became obvious, however, that without music it was difficult to keep them in order. Counting, tapping of her foot, even clapping her hands were not effective ways to keep them in step, and the children soon got bored. Efa had to agree that it was less than fun.

The next time the weather kept them indoors, Non had appeared with a strange-looking wooden instrument in her hands. Rectangular in shape, with curved corners, it was strung with six strings, each with its own peg. The strings were stretched tight over a small flat bridge and smooth fingerboard. A cord threaded through a round hole meant that the instrument could be held against the chest to be played, with the cord looped around the neck to free the hands to play.

'Where did you find that?' Manon had jumped to her feet, and she sounded cross.

'Where you hid it.' Non was unmoved by Manon's anger, giving her a hard stare in response. 'It needs to be played, not hidden away under clothes at the bottom of a chest. Here!' She handed it to Manon.

The girl reluctantly took it and sat down, cradling the *crwth* in her lap. She began to lightly draw her fingers over the smooth wood and over the strings. She seemed to lose herself in her thoughts. Gerallt walked over and stood in front of her, but she didn't glance up. He cleared his throat and spoke, a noticeable tremor in his voice.

'Please play it, Manon.'

His sister looked up and locked eyes with her brother for a moment. Her eyes were moist and she was worrying her bottom lip.

Gerallt reached out and touched her arm. 'I know,' he said, nodding. 'But she would want you to play it, if she were here.'

Her eyes did not leave his as he sank to the floor to sit at her feet. Haf came over and sat beside her brother. It was unlikely that she understood the gravity of the moment, but something drew her. Efa sat a few yards away on one of the backless benches that were used by the children at the table. Non sat down beside her. Audience in place, it just needed the performer to find it within herself to play.

Manon put the cord over her head and positioned the *crwth* against her chest. She began to tentatively pluck the top two strings with her thumbs, grimacing at the tuneless notes they produced. She fiddled with the tuning pegs to tune the strings.

When she was satisfied she looked up, and realised that she was surrounded with expectant faces.

'I need a bow. I can't play without a bow.'

Before she had even finished speaking, Gerallt had shot to his feet and run up the stairs into their shared room. He soon reappeared with a bow in his hands. It was looking a little worse for wear; the gut most probably needed replacing. But he skidded to a halt in front of Manon and handed it to her. She took it from him, smoothed the gut between her finger and thumb and then applied the bow to the strings. Her fingers curled over the finger board, and she dipped her head, closing her eyes. It was not immediately faultless, but as she continued to play, the instrument began to sing under her fingers. She stopped more than once, shaking her head over mistakes, but they encouraged her on. And her confidence grew the more she played. She began to play a more complicated lively piece.

'Come on,' said Non, jumping up, extending her hand to Haf and pulling her to her feet. 'Let's dance!'

Soon Non and Haf were galloping up and down the hall in time to Manon's music, and then Efa persuaded Gerallt to accompany her in joining in their crazy dance. Soon they were all laughing, even Manon.

Suddenly Manon changed tempo, and the song of the *crwth* became more plaintive and haunting. And then she began to sing, and the dancing stopped. Efa had rarely heard a voice more pure and lilting. She stood transfixed, and felt the warm body of Haf as the girl leaned into her legs. Gerallt sat on the bench with Non and buried his head into her shoulder. Manon's voice took them into the very heart of her grief, as she sang of love and loss. And then it was ended and the silence left by the absence of the music was almost as moving as the song had been. Manon's cheeks were wet with tears but she was smiling, her eyes bright.

'Mama's favourite,' she whispered, her speaking voice strained in contrast to the sweet flow of the music it had just made. Non stood and moved over to her, taking a still sobbing Gerallt with her, and the three embraced awkwardly.

'She taught you well, my love. You have a real gift.' Non spoke as she lowered her face to touch the top of Manon's head with a kiss. Her own voice trembled with emotion. Efa knew she was witnessing a precious moment.

After that first time, the *crwth* was regularly employed – to accompany their dance lessons, but also when Manon could just be prevailed upon to play and sing for their amusement. She rarely refused. It was as if she had rediscovered a lost joy, and she came alive when making music.

Now it was December and the year was drawing to an end. The preparations that had greeted Efa as she entered the hall that morning were for the feast that they were going to enjoy later that day, in celebration of the first day of Christmas. To add to the excitement in the house, they were expecting visitors. Cynan's older sons were both expected to arrive at some time during the day, from different directions. Efa had met neither, and was nervous as to how they would respond to her presence in their family. But she put her nerves aside and busied herself to help prepare for their arrival. Cynan had been away from home for more than a month, so he too would be arriving in time for the feast. It was a rare thing for the whole family to be together in one place, and the air was full of anticipation.

Cynan's second son, Dafydd, arrived first, his horse clattering over the stones in the courtyard a little after noon. He was accompanied only by a single man-at-arms. They had ridden hard for several days, from Llewellyn's court in the north. As they entered the hall Efa could see that Dafydd was not tall, but was already beginning to develop the muscular build of a trained fighter. His hair was not as dark as Manon's, but he too had his father's unusual eye colour. He was reserved in his greeting of Efa, but polite enough. Haf seemed pleased to see him, and he in turn lifted her up and swung her around. He kissed Manon affectionately and shook Gerallt's hand. Eluned and Ifan were also greeted warmly.

Gruffydd, Cynan's eldest, arrived soon after, and with a much larger retinue, his father included. The normally peaceful courtyard of Tregaron became a mêlée, as horses snorted and neighed and men shouted orders and laughed raucously. Where Dafydd had entered quietly, Gruffydd entered with a flurry, clapping his hands together noisily. Tall and well built, with a shock of brown curls, he stepped into the hall as if he owned the place, looking around, taking in the décor and the table already half-loaded with foodstuffs. His perusal of the room also took in the family standing to greet him. He nodded at Ifan and bowed dramatically to Eluned, laughing as he kissed her hand. He cuffed Gerallt around the head, with more force than seemed necessary, and tickled Haf until she squirmed away from him. Manon was standing next to Efa. Gruffydd stopped in front of his sister and seemed to do a double take.

'My, Manon, how you have grown!' He bowed to her with a flourish and took her hand in his. As he kissed it, he lifted his eyes to give her an intense look. She blushed visibly. Efa shifted uncomfortably. His attentions to his sister did not feel natural.

Gruffydd released his sister's hand and moved to stand before Efa. She stood with her head held high as he looked her up and down, a barely suppressed sneer on his face. He did not bow, nor reach for her hand, and Efa felt her palms begin to tingle under his perusal.

'My wife, Gruffydd. The lady Efa.' Cynan was there.

Gruffydd hid the sneer behind a false smile, and dipped his head towards Efa. She was glad he did not reach for her hand. The look on his face was all she needed to know about how little he thought of her.

Among the group of young men that entered the hall with Gruffydd's party was a face that seemed vaguely familiar to Efa, but she couldn't place it. He was not tall; in fact, when he was presented to her, she could see that she had more height than he, and instinctively bent her knees slightly as she had taught herself to do. It was a practised way of trying to make herself appear less. And this man's presence made her want to shrink. There was something imposing about him, despite his lack of height. He was broad and his tunic stretched over a well-defined physique. His hair was the colour of rust and his eyes black as coal. He was not as young as Gruffydd, either, his skin more weathered and an old scar creasing his forehead.

'My lady wife, the Lady Efa, Maelgwyn.' Cynan presented her to him.

Maelgwyn reached for her hand, bowing to touch it with cold lips, holding on to it for longer than felt necessary. He was undoubtably handsome, but something unsettling lingered behind those eyes as he held Efa's. She found herself tugging her hand away, as he smirked at her response. She knew now why she had known his face. He was Maelgwyn *ap* Maelgwyn, son of the Prince of Deuheubarth, Maelgwyn *ap* Rhys. He had been to Abergwyngregyn, some years earlier, while she was still part of Llewellyn's household there. And he had come there to be betrothed to Angharad, Llewellyn's young daughter by the Lady Joan.

Efa watched him now as he was led over to the table. Gruffydd was thumping him on the back and they were laughing together. But it wasn't a pleasant sound, and she felt the hairs on the back of her neck rise, convinced that she was the object of their derision. She shook off the feeling, turning to smile at her husband as he offered his hand to lead her to the table. Only Gruffydd had taken her chair, and Maelgwyn had taken Cynan's. Efa turned quizzical eyes to Cynan. He shook his head slightly and bent to whisper.

'He is our honoured guest, Efa, so we will give way to him. Not by my choice, but to keep the peace.'

He held her gaze for a moment, his eyes carrying what looked suspiciously like regret. She allowed him a small smile in return and took her place with him on the seats to the left of Maelgwyn. Gruffydd was calling for ale, and sent Eluned scurrying. Dafydd and Gruffydd's other guests positioned themselves around the heaving table with its appetising spread. Non placed the children on the bench the other side of the table and Manon slid in beside them. Manon was wearing the purple dress that she had made with Non. The colouring and the cut of the dress were flattering to her burgeoning figure, and she had designed the neckline to dip with a deep slit at her throat.

The neckline was also beautifully highlighted with Efa's gold thread, but that helped draw the eye to the flesh visible between Manon's small breasts. And Efa wasn't the only person to have noticed. As Manon sat straight-backed and thrust her chest forward, smiling and tossing her long dark hair behind her shoulders, Efa saw that she had also caught Maelgwyn's attention. He was staring, unapologetically, and one side of his mouth had raised in half-smile, half-sneer. He raised his cup and tipped it towards Manon, causing the girl to blush and dip her head coquettishly. She was asking for attention and he seemed to be happy to oblige.

Throughout the meal, Efa tried to watch them, while still entering into the celebration and putting food to her mouth. The more she observed of the interaction between Manon and Maelgwyn, the sicker she felt, and the less food that passed her lips. She longed to be able to do something, but could say nothing. She could not draw attention to Maelgwyn's behaviour, would not dare to offend, for her husband's sake. And she could not chide Manon, not that the girl would listen to her. Maelgwyn's dark eyes had a definite predatory look.

After the men had eaten their fill and were well lubricated by the ale and the mead that had flowed freely, Gruffydd called for entertainment.

'I don't know where he thinks he is,' Cynan grumbled to Efa, his words slurred by drink. 'This is not Maelgwyn's father's court. He commands entertainment? What does he want? Me to jump up and act the fool for his friends' amusement?' He hiccupped loudly, drawing laughter from his son.

Efa knew she had to act to save face on Cynan's behalf. What was supposed to have been a joyous celebration feast was quickly turning into something else. Men had begun to bang cups and fists on the table demanding a song or a dance. Efa rose and walked around the table to where Manon sat. She bent to whisper into the girl's ear, and Manon nodded. Her cheeks were already flushed but the colour deepened. She rose from her seat and, picking up her skirts, dipped and smiled a full smile in her brother's direction. Only she wasn't looking at Gruffydd, and was rewarded by a narrowing of Maelgwyn's eyes and a parting of his lips. As she turned away she missed what Efa saw, the tip of Maelgwyn's tongue emerging to trace his top lip like a snake eyeing his prey.

Manon walked to where she had placed the *crwth* the day before and pulled over a stool, so that all sitting at the table could see her. She knew she was the centre of attention and played to the crowd, taking time to spread her skirts and toss back her hair before lowering the instrument into its playing position. She plucked the strings to check their tuning, and then, when satisfied that the level of conversation had quietened sufficiently, she began to draw the bow across the strings.

It was a song that Efa hadn't heard her sing before. A love song, it soared and dipped as if to illustrate the joys and the pains of love. The words were not overly suggestive at face value, but had connotations that Efa did not think Manon could have fully understood. That the men who listened to her did was obvious at the barely suppressed snorts of laughter and ribald comments. But with one lift of his hand, Maelgwyn quietened them. He was watching and listening, seemingly transfixed by the girl and her instrument. When she had finished, he stood to his feet and raised his cup again to her. Efa felt a sense of dread creep over her, and instinctively stood up and placed herself between Manon and her admirer. But if she was attuned to what was happening between the two of them, it seemed Cynan was oblivious. He too stood from the table, wobbling slightly, and raised his own cup to his daughter.

'Fine singing voice. Just like your mother's, God rest her soul. But for the love of God, Manon, play something more cheerful!'

His request was met with cheers from around the table, and Cynan flopped back down into his seat. Manon scowled momentarily, but dipped her bow to play again. This time she played a dance tune, and found herself accompanied by clapping and the slapping of hands on the table. A couple of the more inebriated guests stood and began to dance – their hands held clasped together and their feet tripping over one another in a parody of a well-known court dance. That was met with howls of laughter from their companions and calls for more music. Manon continued to play until many of the guests were beyond hearing as they laid slumped across the table or snoring on the floor.

Efa's bed had been calling for hours. Non had excused herself with Gerallt and Haf some time ago. Cynan was asleep with his head on his arms on the table. But Efa was not going to leave until she had ensured that Manon was safe in her bed. Gruffydd and Maelgwyn were still awake, still drinking. They talked in hushed whispers and laughed at private jokes. If they noticed Manon was still playing, they did not indicate it. Finally, Efa made her way over to the girl, who was struggling to sit upright, the *crwth* still hanging from her neck.

'You have done well, Manon. I think you need to retire now, as do I.'

Manon glanced over at the table, but her admirer was not looking at her. She sighed and looked up at Efa, nodding her assent. She rose and removed the *crwth* from her neck, placed it safely on the stool and moved the stool to one side of the hall. She stretched her back and rubbed her neck. Her movement must have caught Maelgwyn's attention, as he rose from his seat and sauntered over to her. If he was under the influence of drink, it was not obvious.

Efa stiffened and watched with distaste as he took Manon's hand and bowed his head to kiss it. As he stood up, he whispered something to her. A blush crept up the girl's neck, and she smiled back at him. He glanced sideways at Efa before strutting back to his seat at the table.

'What did he say to you?' Efa whispered as she took the girl's arm to lead her away and up the stairs.

'Nothing of note,' Manon lied, a defiant look on her face, pulling away from Efa as they reached the landing and stepping through the door into her room. Efa stood and watched the door close behind Manon, breathing a sigh of relief that at least she was safe from Maelgwyn's attentions behind that closed door.

So I must rise in search of him,

looking throughout the city,

seeking until I find him.

Even if I have to roam through every street,

nothing will keep me from my search.

Where is he – my soul's true love?

He is nowhere to be found.

Song of Solomon 3:2, TPT

13
Manon

'Efa, Efa, wake up. Manon has gone from her bed!'

Efa was startled awake by the shaking of her shoulder and Non's panicked whisper. Efa shook off sleep and sat up, pulling her legs from beneath the warm canopy that had lulled her into a deep slumber.

'Is it morning?'

'No. It is still the dark hours, no one else is stirring. Although so much ale was consumed last night, I doubt that most of our company will stir for hours yet. I looked down at that sprawling mess just now, looking to see if Manon was there. She is not in the hall. And neither could I see our honoured guest.' She spat the last words in what was for her an unusual display of contempt.

Efa's heart was now racing as she grabbed her miniver and threw it around her shoulders. She felt around for her discarded shoes and slipped her feet into them.

'You go and try to wake Ifan. Your father will not be much help, he was well into his cups. I will see if I can find her. Pray God they are not alone together somewhere, Non.'

She rushed from the room and down the stairs, Non close behind her. She stepped over more than one sleeping body, and after confirming that Maelgwyn was no longer in his seat at the table beside a slumbering Gruffydd, she headed for the door, grabbing a lighted torch from its holder.

As she stepped into the darkness the cold hit her, and she shivered violently, pulling the cloak tightly around her. She stood with the door open behind her, listening intently. Behind her she could hear snores and sleep-induced mumbling. From the still darkness outside she heard the screech of an owl. And then something else. A muffled screech of a different kind, coming from her right. She hurried in the direction the sound had come from, and raising the torch could make out the outline of two bodies in an embrace.

'Manon, is that you?' Efa called out, and the figure nearest to her turned, the torchlight picking out the face of Maelgwyn, his face contorted into a derisive sneer.

'Come to join in the fun, have you? I am willing, once I've enjoyed this little one first.'

Efa recoiled at his words, but she could see who it was that he had pinned up against the stone wall. He had the weight of his hips pressing against her, one hand around Manon's tiny neck, the other... Efa could only imagine where his other hand was. The girl was shaking in terror, her eyes bulging.

Efa moved towards him, brandishing the torch, swinging it closer and closer to his face. Maelgwyn was laughing now, a malicious sound, but he had at least loosened his hold on Manon's neck.

'Step away from her!' Efa spoke with all the authority she could muster, but still her voice shook.

'You must wait your turn, I have told you that. You are not the most attractive woman, but I have had worse-looking whores!'

Something rose up inside Efa and she ran at him, raising the torch to bring it down on his head. He spun away from Manon, his raised arm easily deflecting the torch and knocking it from Efa's hand. And then he was advancing on her. As she stepped back, she caught her foot in the hem of her cloak and stumbled to the ground. He loomed over her and, placing one foot either side of her body, knelt and reached down to grasp the neckline of her shift. His face was so close that she could smell the stale drink on his breath, his eyes wide with lust, or anger, or both. She tried to raise herself onto her elbows but he forced her down again and with his free hand began to feel around for the hem of her shift. She was pinned down beneath his weight and he was strong. But so was she. She was not going to let him steal what she had never given to a man. She stayed still for a moment and heard his triumphant laugh. Sending up a silent prayer she gathered all the strength she could muster. And then with one huge effort she flung her whole weight over to one side and drew one knee up so that it made contact with him. With a yelp he released his hold on her. At the very same moment there was a roar and a shout and Maelgwyn was being manhandled away from her.

Ifan! She sank back to the ground in relief, but only for a moment. Manon. She needed to go to the girl. She pulled herself to her feet and half-walked, half-staggered over to where the girl still sat huddled against the wall, her head tucked under her arms, her knees drawn up to her chest.

'Manon?' Efa crouched down in front of the girl and reached out her hand to touch her shoulder lightly. The girl recoiled from her touch, and huge sobs began to wrack her body.

Efa, shaking herself, sat down beside her and pulled her cloak around the girl's shoulders. Manon held herself tightly for a moment more before easing around and into Efa's embrace. And then Efa let her own tears fall and drip into the girl's hair. That had been too close, for both of them. She held her tightly, and they rocked together.

She lifted Manon's face from her sodden shoulder. 'Did he hurt you?' she whispered. The girl held her eyes for a moment and then there was the slightest of head shakes before her face was buried again. Efa was not fully reassured. She prayed that Manon was untouched, but more questioning would have to wait.

She looked up to find Ifan standing a few feet away from them, a look of anguish on his face.

'He is gone,' he said. 'I would have killed him! But there would have been consequences, given who his father is. He was reluctant to leave without his companions, and in the middle of the night. But I explained that Cynan would not have any qualms about running him through, regardless of who his father was, and that he would have the weight of Llewellyn in support of his actions. That was enough to persuade him to leave quietly. I understand he is betrothed to Llewellyn's daughter?'

Efa nodded. But she did not let go of the girl still sobbing in her arms.

Ifan stepped a bit closer and crouched down so that his face was level with Efa's. 'Did he hurt you, my lady?'

'No.' She answered honestly, although she knew there would be bruises on her body come morning.

'And Manon?' Efa heard the catch in his voice. Efa shook her head. She hoped not. She bowed to whisper something to the girl, who nodded.

'Can you help me get her to my room, Ifan?'

The tall man bent one knee to the ground and gathered the girl into his arms, standing to hold her carefully as if she were the most precious of treasures. Manon curled herself into his embrace and allowed herself to be carried towards the still open hall door. At that moment her brother Dafydd appeared, bleary-eyed and staggering slightly. He seemed to gather himself immediately he took in the scene in front of him. He looked from Ifan and the girl still weeping in his arms to Efa, standing bedraggled behind him.

He narrowed his eyes, and looked directly into Ifan's face.

'Who did this?' he snarled.

Ifan shook his head once in response. But Dafydd was not for being brushed off. He looked over at Efa who, realising her state, pulled the cloak tighter around her, but not before Dafydd had dropped his gaze and seen her torn shift.

'Who did this?' he demanded again. And then something shifted in his eyes and he looked back at Ifan. 'It was Maelgwyn, wasn't it?' His fists were clenched as they hung by his sides, his neck puce with anger.

'Dafydd,' Ifan's voice was calm but authoritative. 'We need to see to the ladies.'

The young man looked at Ifan again before stepping aside to let him pass with Manon in his arms. But he moved in front of Efa before she could follow Ifan into the house.

'I will find out what happened here. And he will pay,' he said, glancing over her shoulder into the darkness behind her.

'I will pray that you will let it go, Dafydd, for your sister's sake and for your own. She has suffered enough already by that man's hand. Do not do anything to shame her further, I implore you.'

He turned then to look at her, surprise at her words registering on his face. He clasped and unclasped his fists, gazed over her shoulder once more and then seemed visibly to shrink. He nodded, before stepping aside to let her pass by.

Ifan gently lowered his burden onto Efa's bed and then quickly excused himself. Non and Efa worked wordlessly to strip the girl of her outer clothes. The purple dress, its beautifully stitched neckline marred by a gaping tear, was thrown out of the door, out of sight. Manon was shivering, and as she laid down, she grabbed for Efa's hand. Efa climbed onto the bed and curled her warmth around the girl.

She did not sleep, watching Manon until the trembling stilled and the breathing steadied. All too soon the sun was rising, and Efa extricated herself to allow the girl to sleep on. She grabbed a dress and pulled it over her head, doing her best to secure the side laces herself. She covered her sleep-dishevelled braids with a wimple and veil. She was anxious to speak to Dafydd again. If he had told his brother or Cynan of the events of the night before, she dare not think what might follow. She did not care for Maelgwyn's sake, but for Manon's. She was so young and, yes, naïve. She did not need the shame of being compromised to taint her chances of a good and loving marriage in the future – in the far future, hopefully.

As she descended the stairs, Efa was greeted by bleary-eyed guests as they clumsily prepared to take their leave. A quick questioning of a stone-faced Ifan and Efa discovered that Dafydd had already left, before the sun had risen and while his brother and father still slept. She was sad for the family's sake that he had left, but also relieved.

It seemed that Gruffydd had also decided to leave and was harrying his entourage to get packed up.

'Does he know anything?' Efa whispered to Ifan as they stood watching what in other circumstances might have been comedic. Too many of Gruffydd's guests were still under the influence of the previous night's revelry, and much staggering and groaning accompanied their attempts to pack their belongings and take their leave. Gruffydd was lounging in his father's chair, one leg casually slung over the arm, a sneer on his face as he barked orders.

'No. I told him Maelgwyn left to find some female company. He decided himself that he wouldn't stay longer. He prefers the sort of entertainment he can get at Maelgwyn's father's court. Your father is disappointed that his sons are not staying longer, but I for one am not.'

'Me neither,' Efa sighed, before leaving his side to weave her way through the stinking bodies towards the sanctuary of Eluned's kitchen. It was best for Manon's sake that the house return to its normal peaceful state as soon as possible. Now she needed to find her something to eat and drink.

Non was one step ahead of her, meeting her with a tray laden with a dish of broth, some bread and warm ale. She nodded to Efa and passed her, heading for the stairs. Eluned was stood watching and as Efa turned to follow Non, she came over and took Efa's arm, her usual soft eyes creased with concern.

'How is Manon?'

Efa looked down into that kind face and found her own eyes filling. 'I don't know,' she gulped quietly.

'I will pray,' Eluned squeezed Efa's arm and turned away, wiping her sleeve across her eyes. Efa closed her own eyes briefly. Yes, she would pray too. For Manon, but for herself too, for wisdom to know what to say to the traumatised girl.

Manon was dressed in her simplest, most formless dress, a dull grey wool that drained even more colour from her already pale face. She was sat on the window seat and had pulled back one of the shutters. Watery sunlight did little to warm the room, but Manon sat huddled, gazing out of the window, seemingly impervious to the cold. Non had tried to get the girl to eat, to no avail. And now Efa hoped to get the girl to talk.

She sat down close to the girl, who pulled her legs up even closer to her chest. Efa spread the warm miniver mantle over both of them in an attempt to gain some warmth in the chilly room. She searched for the right words to say as the silence lingered between them.

The sound of horse hooves on stones drew Manon's attention.

'That was my father's horse. They have all gone, then?' Her tone was flat.

'Yes. They have all gone. It is just us left here. You and I and the children, Ifan, Eluned and Non. I'm sure Ifan has stoked the fire and it will be warm in the hall, if you want to come downstairs?'

'In a while.' Manon settled back with her head resting against the window jamb, her arms wrapped around her knees. Her careworn look aged her. Efa wept inside for Manon's loss of innocence.

'Did he hurt you? Physically? Did he touch you, Manon?' She spoke gently, resting her hand softly on Manon's arm.

The girl did not pull away. She slowly turned her head and met Efa's gaze.

'No. He tried. You saved me.' She turned back to staring out of the window.

Efa waited and, sure enough, the girl took a deep sighing breath and spoke again.

'He noticed me and I was flattered. I thought he just wanted to walk and talk. I expected words of love, not… I did not think he would… But he said that I had teased him with my smiles and glances, and that I had asked to be kissed. I let him kiss me, but then he grabbed me and tried to loosen my dress. I panicked then and cried out and he fought with me, grabbing my neck, tearing my dress, trying to lift my skirts.'

She buried her face in her sleeves. She was shaking again. Efa moved closer and took the girl into her arms, holding her as the tears came.

'Shush. It is all over now. He did not take what he intended to. And we ran him off. He cannot hurt you again.'

'But why did he treat me that way? That did not feel like love,' she mumbled into Efa's shoulder.

Efa pulled back and took the girl's face in her hands, wiping away her tears with her thumbs.

'No. That was not love. That was lust and power and cruelty. Manon, you are a lovely girl, but you do not need to use your eyes and smiles and physical attributes to attract love. If it is love you are truly looking for, then you will find it by just being yourself. Do you understand?'

The girl looked into Efa's eyes and raised her chin slightly, a faint blush tainting her cheeks.

'I wanted a man to love me, it is true,' she sniffed. 'I wanted to be loved because my mother left us, and then my father abandoned us, and my heart felt empty. I am lonely and I am bored, and to be a man's wife seemed like a way out for me. But I'm not ready. Not really. I didn't realise until it was too late, last night. What I thought I wanted – was not that… And marriage would mean *that.*' She shuddered.

'Oh, my sweet girl. I understand the desire to be loved. But you have so much yet to learn about what love truly is. You are young, and perhaps not ready, but one day I hope you will find a man who will truly love and respect you.'

Manon drew away from Efa's arms and settled back against the cold stone.

'I think that I would rather stay here for the rest of my life than marry at all. From this day forward I will not look at or smile at another man. I will not make the same mistake again. I am done with men. I do not believe they can truly love as I want to be loved.' She glanced at Efa again, and shook her head. 'And I don't want to end up like you. You are married to a man old enough to be your father, and he does not love you. Not even enough to share his home with you.'

If it meant to cut, Efa let it go.

'You are right – although I do believe your father respects me, Manon. And I have known love, the love of a good man. That is the sort of love I hope you one day find.'

Manon did not respond, her gaze transfixed again by some indeterminate object outside the window. Efa closed her eyes and sent up a swift prayer before continuing. She wanted Manon to hear about Philip, but reliving even the good memories would cost her. For too long she had not dared. But now she felt God's peace envelop her as she gave voice to them.

'Philip and I were close in age and he was my friend first. We used to talk and laugh and play silly tricks on each other. But as time went on, we realised that we sought out each other's company above all others. My heart felt warm when he was with me, and we shared our deepest thoughts and feelings with one another. I missed him when he was not there, and his face broke into the hugest smile whenever he saw me. I did not have to tease him with looks and smiles, and he did not have to impress me with his manliness. We just cared deeply about one another. Our love was based on much more than our physical appearance or needs, and we needed to play no love games with each other to keep that love alive.'

'But he still broke your heart!' Manon had heard every word, and the bitterness in her response shocked Efa.

'Both of our hearts were broken. And it was not of our doing.'

She realised, perhaps for the first time, the truth of her own words. She could not blame Philip any more for leaving her. His pain must have been as great as hers to have their dreams ripped away from them. But she could not think of that now. She needed to focus on the broken-hearted child sitting beside her. And she wanted to share something else that she had learned to be the truth, which might help Manon more than any other comfort that she could hope to give her. She only hoped the girl had ears to listen.

'I have found a truer love than even Philip's, Manon.'

She watched for a response, seeing confusion in the girls red-rimmed eyes. Manon's gaze was now locked on hers, her face tilting slightly as if trying to read whether Efa was being truthful. And then there was a flash of something that looked like anger.

'You have taken a lover?' She ground it out.

'No, no, my sweet.' Efa laughed nervously and grabbed Manon's hands to squeeze them. 'No. I have not betrayed your father. The love I speak of is truer than that of any man. It does not depend on how I feel about myself, how I behave, or misbehave, how alluring I am, or how ugly. The one who loves me tells me that He loves me despite myself. He loves me unconditionally and calls me beautiful. And I know that He loves me, not just because He has told me so, but because He has sacrificed Himself for me so that I can experience His love.

'Manon, I do not expect you to understand it all now. It has taken me some time to understand it for myself. Father Ulrich and Non have been helping me to accept that God loves me. That His Son, Jesus, loves me. And that even if I never know the love of another man, another human being, in my lifetime, that I can be reassured that He will never stop loving Me. I can speak with Him, I can sit with Him, I can walk with Him. And I can even hear Him and feel His loving presence. Now that I know Him this way, I don't ever have to feel unloved, fatherless, unknown or unwanted. I never have to feel that I am not enough, or have to prove myself worthy of love. God knew me when I was at my worst, and loved me enough to pursue me anyway. Does this make any sense to you, Manon?'

The girl had laid back her head against the jamb again, her eyes closed, but still she held Efa's hand. She seemed calmer. At last she opened her eyes, and they were glistening with tears.

'I want it to make sense to me, Efa. I watched your face as you talked, and I saw how your eyes shone. I have seen how much more contented you have been lately, much happier than when you first arrived here. And Tregaron is a happier place for your presence here. So if God has done that all for you, maybe He can do it for me?'

Efa leaned forward and cupped her hand around Manon's cheek, brushing away a rogue tear.

'Manon, I know He can,' she said.

Then I encountered the overseers as they encircled the

city.

So I asked them, 'Have you found him —

my heart's true love?'

Just as I moved past them, I encountered him.

I found the one I adore!

I caught him and fastened myself to him,

refusing to be feeble in my heart again.

Song of Solomon 3:3-4, TPT

Part Two

14

Gruffydd

Winter 1231

Efa shifted, the cushion she was seated on doing little to ease the dull ache from sitting too long in a hard chair. She would excuse herself soon; weariness and the warmth of the fire were making her eyes heavy. But she enjoyed these evening gatherings around Tregaron's hearth, now that the family were fewer in number and that Cynan was more with them. He looked tired too, but still his face creased with laughter in the firelight when Ifan shared an amusing tale he'd heard from a passing friend.

Eluned had joined them, with the ever-faithful Siwan sitting on a cushion at her feet, her own head lolling with tiredness. Beside Efa sat Manon. She had grown into a beautiful and elegant young woman, and sat poised and quiet, a small, serene smile on her face. Long gone were the days of flirtatious smiles and coquettish glances. After her encounter with Maelgwyn, Efa had seen the girl withdraw into herself for a time, but as she began to explore Efa's faith more she seemed to find a new place of contentment. That she was still at Tregaron was testament to the promise she had made that fateful night. She had sworn to Efa that she intended to stay away from men, and she had kept to her word.

Over the years there had been several attempts by Cynan to encourage his daughter to marry, but Manon had been unmoved by any of the potential suitors. If, as Efa suspected, it was a matter of mistrust, then she would continue to secretly pray that the girl would one day find a man she could trust herself to, out of love and respect. Cynan, for his part, had despaired of the girl and had turned his matchmaking attentions to Non instead. She fought back just as vehemently, perhaps encouraged by the effectiveness of Manon's intransigence. Eventually Non had found the inner strength to stand courageously before Cynan and ask to be allowed to take Holy Orders. If she had been expecting her father's resistance, she was surprised by the lack of it. He had sighed deeply, and then stood and embraced his eldest daughter, kissing the top of her head fondly.

'I was only waiting for this day,' he had said. 'I have long suspected that was where your heart truly lay, but I was hoping perhaps you would change your mind, perhaps marry and stay close, so that at least we could still see you. But now I see that you are meant to leave us. And you can go with my blessing. But know this, Non, it is a sacrifice for us, for me, to let you go. One that I hope God will honour.'

Within weeks Non had gone, and had indeed left a gaping hole in their family. But the joy on her face as she bade them farewell was all that was needed for them to see that she had found her heart's desire at last. They heard from her from time to time, and once a year visited her at Llanllugan. The rigours of monastic life had thinned her face and form, but the spark in her eyes had grown ever stronger as she served her God and her sister nuns. Efa missed her more than she could have imagined, but still she rejoiced with her.

Within weeks of Non's departure Cynan was faced with another inevitability. He could no longer find reason not to also allow his youngest son to pursue his calling. Gerallt had finally taken his novitiate vows at Ystrad Fflur, thriving in that atmosphere and proving himself a worthy addition to the community. He would become a deeply valued member of the team of scriptorium monks, of that there was little doubt. Efa and Cynan saw him on their periodic visits to the abbey, and he had turned into a self-assured and confident young man, still a little on the serious side at times, but well suited to the vocation he had found for himself.

Cynan did get one wedding at least. Haf had grown and blossomed and was becoming noticed, but was seemingly oblivious. Her hair had remained fair and hung long down her back, and she had retained her sweet disposition and her love of all things animal-related. If she knew how to be coquettish, she didn't show it, and several young men came and went, not able to attract her attention; not unless they had a sick animal for her to tend to or a flock of geese for her to muster. And so it was that Haf had stumbled across the perfect suitor, literally, as she chased a vagabond hen across the yard, her skirts tucked into her belt and her hair streaming down her back. She ran straight into the poor fellow and both went sprawling into a large muddy puddle.

Whether it was the shared laughter or the fact that Morgan Parry had run and grabbed Haf's hen to present to her, something sparked between them. He was tall and broad with a round face, and towered over the petite Haf. His clothes were finely made but hung as if they were not made for him. Mud-splattered, they complemented each other in happy dishevelment, Haf just as oblivious to the damage she had done to her fine dress. Unsurprisingly, the young man continued to appear at Tregaron more often over the next few months. Always he came with a gift – of honey, or fine flour, or a pair of kittens.

The day the kittens arrived, Cynan had been in residence. He was standing by the window that overlooked the courtyard and saw Morgan arrive, jump down from his horse and untie the basket from his saddle. He watched surprised as his daughter arrived on the scene as if from nowhere, and as Morgan made a show of presenting the kittens to her. He saw the smiles and heard the laughter. Efa came to join him and he turned raised eyebrows to her.

'Morgan Parry? Is he courting my daughter?'

Efa laughed. 'I'm not sure he knows that he is. But he has been a frequent visitor of late.'

'Has he indeed?' Cynan turned back to the window, his face inscrutable.

'Would you be opposed to the match?'

Cynan sighed. 'He is no Welsh princeling, or Norman lord, and I would have hoped for that for at least one of my daughters. But he is a good man from a hard-working family. His father farms Ystrad Fflur's most profitable grange, and it seems his son has inherited his understanding of the land and of animals. He would be able to provide a good home for Haf, and she would love farm life.' He turned back to smile ruefully at Efa. 'I think she has always been happiest when with the animals. She would find the life of a fine lady too restrictive for her carefree nature, I don't doubt. What think you?'

'I think we might have a wedding to plan at last,' Efa smiled and squeezed her husband's arm.

So it was now a much-reduced family group that huddled around the fire in the great hall on those long winter evenings. As pleased as Efa and Manon had been to see Haf happily wed, her bright laughter and sunny disposition were missed by them all, Jac included. The little dog had become too much part of Tregaron to leave with her, and Morgan's sheepdogs would not have welcomed him to the grange farm. He had attached himself more closely to Siwan at Haf's departure.

Efa glanced over again at Manon. She was glad to at least have the young woman's company still. She thought about how she might feel if Manon were also to leave Tregaron. Efa had found an unexpected contentment in being a friend and sometime ally to Cynan's children. She had grown to love them, and to seek and pray for their happiness. She had rejoiced when each one had found a good reason to move on with their life. Efa had also found a role in being wife to Cynan when he needed a lady of the house to host guests, and had become increasingly fond of him too. Her husband was more at home these days, less able to travel any distance, more content than ever to sit with them by the fire. His Iola had passed away quietly in her sleep a few months after Non had left Tregaron, and the grief had marked him. His hair had thinned, his skin yellowed, and his once proud stature become bent with age.

He was sat with them, his legs stretched out towards the warmth of the fire, his eyes glowing in the half-light as he regaled them with a story of dragons and maidens from Welsh legend. Efa smiled to herself as she listened to a tale she had heard many times and in many versions, each more exaggerated than the one before. Manon had some stitchwork on her lap but seemed more interested in watching the changing expressions on her father's face than the needle in her hand. Siwan had stayed to listen too, and sat leaning into Eluned's legs with a dozing dog on her lap. Ifan snored softly from his own chair.

The sound of hooves on cobbles and frantic shouting interrupted the cosy scene. There was a thunderous beating on the door, which had long since been latched tightly against the cold wind outside. Jac jumped up, his barking adding to the cacophony.

Ifan was the first to move, almost tipping himself onto the floor in his hurry to get out of his chair. Efa stood too and was only a few steps behind him as he reached the door. Whoever it was out there had been granted free entry through the gatehouse, but still Ifan raised his hand to signal for Efa to stay back. They weren't expecting visitors.

The frantic knocking continued as Ifan lifted the latch and opened the heavy door.

'My lord Cynan, Ifan, hurry, we need help. It is Gruffydd. He's grievously hurt.'

It was a guard from Tregaron's gatehouse at the door and behind him stood a tall black destrier, steaming and panting in the cool night air. On the horse's back was a crumpled form, held barely upright in the arms of a stranger. They watched as the stranger carefully eased himself out of the saddle, one hand still holding on to the other rider, trying to prevent him falling from the horse. Ifan leapt forward to help, and together with the guard they eased the man down. As Gruffydd's feet touched the ground there was a scream of pain and he collapsed against them.

Then Cynan was there with a torch held high. He let out a gasp. His son's once handsome face was contorted with pain and pale with fear.

More shouts, and more men appeared. Efa watched as the broken form of Cynan's proud son was carefully carried into the hall and laid on the table. Gruffydd made no further sound. One glance at his face and Efa could tell he had fallen into a stupor, and that was a mercy when the extent of his injuries became clear. There was blood, lots of it, but mostly dried. A shoulder wound accounted for some of it, but most was from his lower left leg. Tightly bound with a crude splint, his foot hung at a sickeningly strange angle.

The stranger who had brought Gruffydd to them stepped forward into the light. He was tall and dark-haired, lean, with sharp features and probing dark eyes. His clothes signified rank, and when he spoke it was in highly accented Norman French.

'His leg is broken, and the bone has split the skin. I did what I could at the side of the road, but he will need a bonesetter. And soon. We have ridden for more hours than I would have liked, and I am afraid he may have lost too much blood.' The stranger ran his hand over his cropped hair and looked for all intents and purposes as if he were ready to collapse from weariness himself.

'Our thanks for bringing him home.' Cynan stepped forward and grasped the stranger's arm. 'I would ask you your name, and why you aided him…' Cynan looked the stranger up and down, taking in his dress and bearing, the fine sword hanging from his belt, '…but for now, I must see to my son.' He released him and began barking orders. 'Ifan, send to Ystrad Fflur for the infirmarer. He must come at once.'

There was a scurry of activity at his words.

'Gruffydd must have my room,' Efa stepped forward. 'If he can be carried?'

Ifan nodded to Eluned, who disappeared and returned with a large blanket. Carefully they rolled Gruffydd onto his side and placed the cloth under him. He moaned but did not awaken. Sweat drops dotted his white forehead as men gathered around him and he was lifted from the table and carried slowly up the wide wooden stairs.

Efa took charge as her husband followed his injured son.

'We will need hot water, plenty of it. And clean linens, cloths. Honey, and maybe some strong drink.' Siwan scurried away in the direction of the kitchen, Eluned in hot pursuit.

The stranger had sunk onto a bench, his long legs almost bent double. He crossed his arms on the table and let his head drop to rest on them, letting out a deep sigh as if he had been holding his breath for a very long time. Efa's heart went out to him.

Manon had been standing back, watching from the half-shadows as the drama had played out before her. Efa moved over and touched her arm and Manon jumped, turning wide eyes to meet her.

'Manon, I must go to your brother, and Siwan and Eluned are also needed. See, our guest here has needs. Food and a good dose of mead, I would wager. Can you serve him?'

Manon turned her gaze over to the stranger now half-lying across the table. She glanced back at Efa.

'Do you think he is safe?' she whispered.

'I have no idea, my dear one. Except that he has just expended himself to try to save your brother's life. So I would say he is probably at heart a good man. And by the look of him, he is in no fit state to be of any danger to you, or any other person. Can you serve him?'

Manon nodded her head slowly, once up and down, and lifted her skirts to walk past him and towards the kitchen. The stranger wearily lifted his head and smiled as she passed, and to her credit, Manon paused to offer him the slightest of nods in return.

It was some hours later before all was quiet again at Tregaron. Brother Infirmarer had arrived as quickly as he was able, accompanied by a bleary-eyed Gerallt. Gruffydd had mercifully remained insensible as they had ministered to his injuries, his stupor aided by a draft of poppy juice trickled between bloodless lips. The leg bone had been pulled and reset, and a stronger splint bandaged in place. His wounds had been cleansed and dressed with honey-soaked linens, his soiled clothing removed and his battered body washed clean.

Lying still, in the middle of Efa's soft bed, Gruffydd looked more vulnerable than Efa had ever seen him. No brashness or bluster. No snide comments or mocking laughter. Just a young man with soft brown curls and a pale, still face, barely holding on to his life, his breaths worryingly shallow. In that moment she could imagine the boy he might have been before he fell under the malignant influence of Maelgwyn and his friends. Her heart broke for him, and her prayers intensified. Despite all of their best efforts, he would be fighting for his life. If either of his wounds festered, if he never recovered from the blood loss, or if the shock of his injuries took him... Efa looked over at her husband where he sat now, his knees pressed to the side of his son's bed, his head resting on his hands that held tightly to his son's hand where it lay pale on the coverlet. She cried out to God for him also.

Moving quietly, she left the room. Siwan had surprisingly insisted on staying there, taking up position on the opposite side of Gruffydd's bed to Cynan. Efa was grateful. Ifan and Eluned had gone to send the infirmarer off with some nourishment in him. Now Efa supposed they were snatching some rest for themselves before the morning light heralded the day's start, because they were not in the hall. The space where the stranger had sat was now occupied by Manon. And beside her, close to the fire, a huddled mass lay on the floor at her feet. The stranger slept, and it seemed she had taken it upon herself to guard him. She lifted weary eyes to Efa as she heard her approach. A faint smile touched her lips.

'He is sleeping. He ate a little and drank even less before the exhaustion took him. He barely spoke. I don't even know his name. But he thanked me and smiled. He has a kind face when he smiles. I did not want to leave him in case he rolled into the fire.'

Efa wondered at her words. She suspected that Manon's overprotectiveness of the stranger had more to do with her need to feel useful while the rest of the household busied themselves caring for Gruffydd than any real concern that he would set himself alight in his sleep. She nodded in response to Manon's hushed words, waiting for an enquiry as to her brother's health, but Manon had turned her attention back to her vigil, staring at the stranger's sleeping form, her own head nodding with tiredness.

Efa stepped forward, reaching down to touch Manon's shoulder. 'You need to rest yourself, Manon,' she whispered. Manon jumped at her touch and her foot inadvertently made contact with the body at her feet. The man grunted and turned onto his back, his eyes flickering open. He groaned as he raised himself up onto one elbow and Manon shifted her feet back quickly beneath her seat. She turned her face to Efa and glared, a look reminiscent of the many that had been directed Efa's way in Manon's younger days.

'Forgive me for waking you, my lord.' Manon stood to her feet, clasping her hands in front of her as she stepped a little away from him.

'No forgiveness needed.' He raised his free hand and rubbed the back of his neck, stretching as he did so. 'And please call me Gwil. It is what my friends call me.'

The smile, although tired, did indeed soften his sharp features. He groaned again as he rolled onto his knees and levered himself up onto the bench seat, close to where Manon had just been sitting. Manon made a small movement to distance herself still further from him. Her hands were grasped tight, but she managed a nod and a smile in response.

'I thank you for your hospitality and for use of your floor to rest my tired bones.' He was brushing stray rushes from his fine sleeves. If he were used to more comfortable sleeping arrangements he did not complain.

'I will get you some more mead, or ale if you prefer. And something to eat.' Manon spoke but did not move.

He laughed softly. 'I would be most grateful for a cup of milk and a crust of bread. That will suffice until the rest of the household is ready to break fast. I do not want to put you to trouble.' He shifted and stretched his back. 'I must speak with your father and then take my leave soon after.'

Manon had begun to walk towards the kitchen but she slowed and spun around at his words. 'But you need more rest, surely?' Her hand flew to her mouth as she realised her words had sounded suspiciously like a plea, and she flushed scarlet and hurried away.

Gwil was still smiling, watching Manon's retreat. 'She has looked after me well,' he said, turning his attention back to Efa. 'Is she a daughter of the house?'

Efa smiled. 'She is Cynan's daughter and I am his wife.'

'So she still lives in her father's house. And is yet unwed? Unless she has decided against wearing a wimple…' He might have been speaking to himself and Efa watched as his smile dropped and his brow furrowed. He had turned his attention to examining a scratch on his hand.

Efa lowered her own tired body onto the chair that faced him. She took in the man in front of her. He might have been handsome once but he carried a world-worn look. His face was marked by a scar across his right cheek, and there were lines around his eyes that indicated maturity of years. His whole visage changed when he smiled, however. Which he did again, lifting his head to meet her gaze.

'Forgive me,' he sighed. 'It is not my business to know.'

'She has no husband.'

Efa was not sure why she said it. He was right, it was no business of his as a stranger to their house. Except there was something about this man that made her warm to him. If he was interested in knowing more about Manon, the thought pleased her.

Gwil held her gaze for a moment before looking away as if uncomfortable with himself. They were both saved from further embarrassment by the appearance of Cynan, who dropped heavily into his seat beside Efa and felt for her hand, squeezing it gently, before releasing it. He closed his eyes and leaned his head back for a moment, before taking a deep breath, opening his eyes and addressing his guest, who had risen to his feet at Cynan's arrival.

'Forgive me for not welcoming you to my home, but you have been well served, I hope.' Cynan gestured with his hand for Gwil to resume his seat.

'More than well served,' Gwil answered, as Manon reappeared and placed cups and a jug shakily on the table between them. She scuttled off again.

Cynan grunted and started to pour himself a cup from the jug, scowling when he saw that it was milk and not ale. He put jug and cup down and turned back to his guest.

'My son sleeps, but we do not know yet if he will survive his injuries. I think we have you to thank for at least giving him a chance at life. May I know your name?'

Gwil looked up from his own cup and wiped his hand across his mouth. He seemed to swallow hard and paused for a moment before answering quietly.

'I am Guillaume Fitzherbert, nephew of Piers Fitzherbert, my lord.'

That Cynan knew the name was obvious. A flicker of something crossed his face. Mistrust? Concern? He held his visitor's gaze for so long that it began to feel uncomfortable. Finally, Cynan nodded and replied, 'I know of your uncle and you must know how we Welsh think of him. But you are not he. And you brought my son home when you could have just as easily ended his life. And for that you are welcome in my home and at my table. But I must now know the details of this matter, and how it came to be that a Norman knight carried a half-dead Welshman deep into Wales, on the back of a fine horse, and risking his own life? Perhaps you might begin with how my son got that hole in his shoulder. I have seen enough battle wounds to recognise that a well-aimed arrow pierced his flesh. And I have heard of no battle being fought that he might have been a part of.

'But first, you must eat.' He indicated the bread that Manon had just placed in front of him. 'And I will force myself to drink this milk to slake my thirst.' He grimaced as he lifted his cup to his lips, but still drank deeply.

I've made up my mind.

Until the darkness disappears and the dawn has fully

come,

in spite of shadows and fears,

I will go to the mountaintop with you —

the mountain of suffering love

and the hill of burning incense.

Yes, I will be your bride.

Song of Solomon 4:6, TPT

15
Gwil

'My uncle is currently holding the castle at Blaen Llynfi for the English king.' Gwil glanced up and caught Cynan's eye. That his uncle had been granted Welsh lands by the English king was unlikely to sit well with his Welsh host.

'Hmm. He holds it for now,' Cynan snorted. He waved his hand for Gwil to continue.

'On the day just passed, well before dark, the castle came under attack from what we assumed was a Welsh raiding party. We are well used to them.' Gwil paused and glanced up at Cynan again, a wry look on his face. 'Usually the attackers come at night to steal our livestock, or to set light to barns and farm buildings. They do not usually dare to venture close to the actual castle defences in the full light of day. But it soon became clear that this group was different. There were maybe eight or nine of them, all well mounted and well armed. They rode past fields of grazing sheep and barns full of grain, right up to the castle walls, and began to wave their weapons and shout obscenities. I won't repeat those here.' He glanced over at the ladies. Manon had settled herself beside Efa and she was watching Gwil's face intently.

'The leader of the group was the foulest mouthed, and seemed oblivious to the fact that he was placing himself and his men in mortal danger by riding so close and brandishing weaponry. The castle is well defended at all times and they must have known that more than a score of archers stood ready with arrows trained. To be sure he looked like a fighting man. He was well built with a shock of red hair, and he brandished his sword with skill. I did not recognise him, but one who stood beside me knew his name.'

'Maelgwyn.' They were all thinking it, but Manon had voiced it, her face white in the early morning light. Gwil nodded in her direction and Efa wondered if he had caught the fear in Manon's eyes.

'Yes, Maelgwyn Fychan, son of Lord Maelgwyn,' he spoke softly. 'And just as unpleasant a man as his father. Foolish in this case also. There was no hesitation given in ordering the archers on the parapets to take aim and fire. It made no difference who he was, Welsh lordling or no. I still don't understand what he hoped to achieve in approaching the castle with such a small party. Perhaps it was a misplaced show of bravado, or maybe he was drunk on ale or on his own sense of infallibility.

'He held his position astride a fine grey, even as the arrows started to fly, and more than one met its mark, taking down at least two of his companions. It may have been then that your son was hit. Certainly the raining arrows soon caused the other riders to turn and scatter, while Maelgwyn still thundered his vitriol. Eventually the gates were opened and a small group of well-armed knights rode out to pursue the offenders, myself among them. It was only then that Maelgwyn finally turned his horse, but he was still laughing as he sped away.

'As the Welsh had fled in more than one direction, we had to divide our party to track them. Maelgwyn and the majority of his party fled into the mountains. Perhaps they knew they would be harder to find there. I had noticed a lone rider heading more due west and chose to make him my quarry.

'I must have trailed him for some time and was at the point of deciding to turn back when I came across a riderless horse. And then a little way further on I came across a tree trunk across the track, and lying beside it the wounded man. He may have lost control while urging his horse to jump the obstruction. The arrow head was still protruding from his shoulder and he had evidently lost a good deal of blood. The leg break likely happened as he fell from his horse.

'As I dismounted and came to stand over him, I knew I had a choice to make. He was in no state to fight me so I could easily had drawn my sword to finish him. I did in fact unsheathe my weapon. But as I drew closer he opened his eyes and looked straight into mine, and whispered, "Have mercy."'

He paused then and closed his eyes for a moment, bringing one hand up to knead his forehead.

'I have heard men beg for mercy before, and God forgive me I have ignored their pleas. I have not always shown mercy, but I have come to know in recent years what it feels like to receive mercy myself. I have come to know a God of mercy. Perhaps it has made me a weaker man, I do not know. Perhaps it would have been more merciful to end his life then and there. But there was something in this young man's eyes. And a deep sense within me that I must save him. So I re-sheathed my sword and set about doing what I could for his wounds. The arrow I removed easily enough, but I knew the leg break needed greater expertise than mine. And I knew that if I took him back to Blaen Llynfi he would get swift justice there. We were in the middle of lands that I did not know, so I prayed for God's help and guidance. If He wanted this man to live, then I needed His help to save him.

'I asked his name and he was able to speak it, "Gruffydd *ap* Cynan, of Tregaron". The name or place meant little to me, but he told me to continue to ride due west; it would take many hours but that I could ask any Welshman or woman I came across for directions to Tregaron. So I loaded us both onto my horse and found that he was right. It did take many hours, but I did find more than one Welshman who responded to the mention of your name and gave me direction. I can only thank God for that. I just as easily could have met a Welshman more willing to cut my throat than to aid me. And here you find me. At your table, and glad of it.'

He paused then, taking a deep steadying breath and to swig from his cup.

'I have been grateful for your hospitality but I fear that I must take my leave before long, as I suspect a search party will have already been dispatched to find me – although they would be brave to venture so deep into Welsh lands in search of a single lost Norman knight, even one who bears the Fitzherbert name.' He let out a small laugh and shook his head. 'I have no idea how I am ever going to explain my actions to my uncle.'

He had held his audience entranced in the telling of his tale. And as the rising sun began to flood dappled light into the room, Efa could see that the audience had grown. Ifan had noiselessly appeared and was sitting on a stool by the fire, prodding the dying embers with a poker. Eluned was standing in the kitchen doorway, resting against the doorpost, drying wet hands on her apron. Manon was sitting with her head bowed, a single tear making its way down her pale cheek. Cynan sat back in his chair, his hands grasping the arms tightly.

Gwil leaned forward with his elbows resting on the table and his chin in his hands, his face pensive, as he waited for someone to respond to his tale. Eventually Cynan spoke with a weary sigh.

'I am angry, and I am perplexed that my son allowed himself to get into such a situation, and at the one who created it. But how I deal with that is for another time. For now, my overwhelming feeling is of gratitude to you, and to God. I am humbled, Guillaume Fitzherbert, by your kindness towards my son. You showed mercy to one who did not deserve it, and by doing so have done a great service for this family. My son was set on a path that would have destroyed him and I had no way of saving him from that. I unwittingly put him into the company of evil-minded men who think cruelty a game.' Efa saw the glance he gave in Manon's direction, and she wondered if he knew more than they had credited him of what had occurred between Manon and Maelgwyn. 'I thought I had lost my son. The son I knew him to be. And now by the grace of God, and your merciful actions, I might yet regain him. If God grants him life.' Cynan sat forward with a groan and eased himself gingerly out of his chair. 'Now I must go to Gruffydd and see if the morning light has brought hope and more colour to his cheeks. And you... friend,' he extended his hand to Gwil, who reached out to grasp his wrist in return, 'must avail yourself of all that you need before you leave us.'

He walked over to Ifan and bent to whisper something in his ear before turning back to Gwil.

'In addition, I would be pleased if you would take a horse from our stables and an armed man who knows the trails well to accompany you on your return journey. We will take good care of your destrier, rest him well for a day or two and feed and exercise him for you. And then you will have cause to visit us again to collect him?'

Gwil smiled and nodded. 'I would very much like to return. Both for my horse and to see how Gruffydd fares. And...' his eyes flickered over to Manon '...to partake of your wonderful hospitality again.' The slight inclination of his head towards Manon would have been missed by anyone not looking for it, but both Efa and Manon had noted it. Manon's face had flushed pink and her eyes held a brightness Efa had not seen for a long time. Efa looked between the two of them and wondered if maybe God was yet answering her prayers for her dear Manon. Only time and God's good grace would tell.

If they were expecting a changed or contrite man in Gruffydd, they would not immediately see it. His ordeal and indeed his merciful salvation did nothing to tame his temper. Yes, he had survived his injuries with a miraculously short-lived fever and recovered from his blood loss remarkably well. But he was still an angry young man. He cursed when they tried to cleanse his wounds and lashed out when offered food not to his liking. Nothing that was done for him was to his expected standard, and they were all fools to him. He hated being in that room, hated being stuck in that bed, and was scathing in his retorts when reminded that his brush with death was of his own reckless making.

That he was in pain was not in doubt, nor that he was deeply frustrated in the perceived uselessness of his left leg. It had healed but the bones had not knit together perfectly straight, and the muscles around the bone had shrivelled. Compared to his other finely formed leg, it was a miserable sight. His plight did evoke sympathy, and as the days and weeks of caring for him wore on, each of them willingly continued to bear the brunt of his outbursts in order to see that his needs were met. Efa, Manon, Eluned, Ifan and even Cynan took turns to tend to him, sit with him, try to soothe him. But it was a thankless service. It was becoming obvious that his very presence in the house had begun to wear on them all.

There was only one person that he never swore at, only one that he kept his temper with, only one that he seemed content to let sit at his bedside for hours, and that was Siwan. The shy, quiet girl who had arrived at Tregaron with Efa all those years before had matured into a sweet-natured young woman. She was no great beauty but was blessed with a mane of soft chestnut curls, and eyes that seemed to be perpetually smiling. Still slightly built, she was an unthreatening presence in any room, and did all that was asked of her with a good grace. Her work was done diligently and with a gentleness that dared anyone to do or say anything to alarm her. Gruffydd seemed to feed off her quiet calmness and was only ever kind and meekly responsive to her ministrations. So it was that the others were pleased to leave his care to her as much as possible, and in turn she seemed willing.

It was Siwan who finally achieved what they had all else failed to do. He had stayed too long in his bed on the excuse that his leg pained him, and yet had found it easy enough to move around the bed and turn over in his sleep undisturbed for days. It was not that Efa wanted her room back; she had actually really enjoyed sharing space with Manon. It was more that Gruffydd needed to exercise his damaged leg and rebuild some muscle strength. For his well-being he needed a change of scene.

One particular morning, Siwan and Efa had entered his room bearing his breakfast, and clean linens to change his bed. Ifan had followed close behind with a crutch fashioned out of a strong piece of oak. They had conspired between them all that this was going to be the day that Gruffydd would leave his bed and walk, at least as far as the window seat to break his fast.

He had glared at them as they entered. 'If you think I am going to use that crutch like an old cripple then you are sadly mistaken,' he had growled.

Ifan had moved closer, undeterred. 'You must leave this bed, Gruffydd. Because it stinks, if for no other reason.'

'The only way I am leaving this bed is if you lift me from it, and I don't think you are capable of that, old man, are you?' he spat back at Ifan.

Efa had rarely seen Ifan close to losing his temper, but just for a moment it looked like he would physically grab the younger man and drag him out of the bed and onto the floor. He had even taken a step forward and raised his arm with the crutch gripped white in his hand. Then suddenly Siwan was there. She moved swiftly, placed a steadying hand on Ifan's arm and slipped her small body between the big man and Gruffydd's bedside. Ifan lowered his arm and stepped back as Siwan bent her head so that her face was level with Gruffydd's. The words were barely above a whisper, but spoken with surprising authority.

'Ifan may be an older man than you, but you are the one who is showing the stubbornness and grumpiness more usually attributed to the old. You have laid here long enough, receiving kindnesses that you did not deserve from people who have showed you nothing but care. I think the least you can do in return is to try to behave like the strong, courageous man you purport to be. And get yourself up and out of that bed.'

'But my leg is useless.' He raised his voice, and then when she did not flinch, he lowered his tone again. 'I cannot stand on a crooked leg,' he ground out through gritted teeth.

'You do not know that if you do not try. And try you will.' She stood resolute, her face still only inches from his, one hand on her hip. 'We will not leave this room until you at least try.'

She straightened then and looked around, and a bemused Efa dipped her head so as not to laugh out loud. Ifan stepped forward, crutch in hand. Siwan bent closer to Gruffydd again and this time she spoke so softly that it was hard to catch what she said; it sounded as if Siwan was telling him not to let fear have the better of him. The look that passed between the two of them spoke volumes. So maybe it was fear that was speaking through Gruffydd's voice and he was genuinely scared of what was going to happen when he stepped off that bed. It seemed that something about Siwan, and the things she said to him, eased that fear.

And so it was that the softly spoken Siwan persuaded the most obstreperous of patients to do what he did next. Sitting up, he swung both legs over the side of the bed. He reached his left hand for the crutch that Ifan offered him, placed it into his armpit and used his right hand to push himself upright. He staggered slightly as his right leg bore his weight. Ifan moved to steady him, but Siwan was quicker, fitting herself neatly under Gruffydd's right arm. Using her as his support, he hobbled over to the window, tentatively trying out his injured leg. It was noticeably shorter than the right and it seemed likely that he would never walk without a limp. What more he would ever be able to do with his injured leg was a question for another time. For that day it was good enough to see him upright, and once up, he seemed content to sit on the window seat and let them see to his bed linens.

And so a new pattern emerged and Gruffydd consented to move out of his bed and around his room every day, until the day came that it was suggested he try the stairs. He scowled and grumbled but eventually manoeuvred himself out onto the landing and positioned himself at the top of the stairs. Then he froze in place until Siwan yet again came beside him and whispered something only he could hear. Ifan moved around them and stood on the stair beneath him. As Gruffydd unsteadily made his way down one step and then the next, Ifan stepped down a step in time with him. Gruffydd made it almost all way down the stairs before the crutch slipped on the wooden step and he lost his balance. A flurry of legs and arms and crutch ensued, but Ifan held on until Gruffydd stood unsteadily on the rush-covered hall floor. Efa hurried to grab a stool for him to be lowered to sit on. His face had gone white and his breathing quickened. He lowered his head to gather himself and then looked up, his face now flushed red. Glaring at the audience that stood around him, he bellowed, 'Are you done watching me make a spectacle of myself?'

His outburst shocked Manon enough to back away, and Eluned scuttled off back to the safety of her kitchen. Efa and Ifan looked at each other, unsure of what to do next, aware of Gruffydd still staring at them, his rage barely controlled. He was stuck now, sat on a stool in the middle of the room, exposed and vulnerable. Yet again Siwan stepped up. She moved to stand in front of him and, bringing her fingers to her lips, let out a high-pitched whistle. From the direction of the kitchen a white flash emerged, as Jac bounded at speed across the rushes and came to an abrupt stop at her feet. His tail was wagging furiously and he yapped and jumped until she bent to fuss him. Once he was satisfied she had no morsel as a treat for him, he went over to make an exploration of the rushes on the floor beneath the table, snuffling around and being rewarded for his efforts with a discarded rind of cheese.

Siwan had turned her attention back to Gruffydd. She was standing with both hands on her hips, waiting until he looked up at her.

'What?' he hissed.

'Did you not see Jac run across the room to me? Did you not see him jump with joy to see me, and then did you not see him make himself useful in cleaning up the scraps from our meal? And watch now – he will return to the kitchen and keep it clear of vermin for Eluned. He will be rewarded with a bone, no doubt, and he will enjoy that immensely. Do you not see how he is living a good dog life, despite the fact that many thought he wouldn't? He was condemned because he had one useless leg. Does he let that leg stop him? He does not!'

She stood and he met her gaze, his top lip twitching into a half-sneer and his head shaking slightly.

'So I am no better than a dog, and a three-legged one at that? Is that what you are saying?'

Siwan lifted her hands in exasperation and let out an exclamation of frustration.

'Gruffydd! You take what you will from what I have said! If I have offended it was not my intention. All I wanted you to see was that having a weakened leg does not mean that your life has to end. It is up to you to decide whether you will give up, or whether you will fight to make the best out of the life that is now yours.'

Her voice was increasing in volume and colour was creeping up her face.

'You know, we prayed that you would survive your injuries, and God granted that. We served you and cared for you, to ensure that you would heal and live. And for what, if you refuse to help yourself? You have a good family and a good home; you have much more than very many have. And yet still you are unpleasant and ungrateful and... urghh!'

With that she spun around and stalked away in the direction of the kitchen herself, not once glancing back at Gruffydd, who she had left stunned into silence.

Eventually he swallowed hard and spoke, his voice cracking slightly with the effort to speak more measuredly.

'Ifan, I wonder if you would help me to move from this stool? Perhaps I could borrow my father's chair at the table. And then I could sit to eat with you all. If Eluned and Siwan will ever deign to cook for me again.'

Ifan shook his head and let out a small bark of a laugh as he moved over and bent to help Gruffydd stand upright. 'Oh, I don't think they have fought so hard to keep you alive to let you starve now. But don't be surprised if the bread comes burnt and the pie over-salted.'

Once he was comfortably sat, Gruffydd turned his attention to Efa.

'I hope you will join us at the table, my lady?' It was mumbled and it was not an apology, but it was an olive branch and Efa was glad to take it.

Cynan arrived home late that evening and his weary face was transformed into a look of amazement at the scene that met him. At his table sat his wife, his daughter and his dear friends Ifan and Eluned. They were laughing and sharing stories, passing dishes to one another and eating and drinking. And there at the heart of it all sat his eldest son, Gruffydd, with a broad smile on his face and with Siwan by his side.

Now you are ready, my bride,

to come with me as we climb the highest peaks

together.

Come with me through the archway of trust.

Song of Solomon 4:8, TPT

16
Changes

Early spring 1232

Ystrad Fflur emerged out of the morning mist, the spring sunlight playing off glass windows and smooth stone walls, and it was a welcome sight. The abbey always felt like it welcomed and embraced Efa, and the peace she felt as she entered its sheltered enclaves was especially appreciated on this day. Not only was it good to escape the damp air, but she was also glad of the chance to breathe deeply of the stillness. The last few days had felt hurried and busy and had left them all a little fraught. But here they were now, being welcomed into the abbey by the smiling porter and led towards the church. The bells were being rung to welcome them, the chimes echoing around the broad, green-grassed valley.

Efa drew the edges of her beloved miniver closer together. The sun was finally dispelling the early mist, but riding through it this morning had left her feeling damp and chilled. She was glad at least that her hair had stayed tucked neatly beneath her veil and wimple, as the moist air would have tightened her curls into a wild mass. She looked over at Siwan and saw that she had not been so fortunate. Her chestnut waves, which had been brushed to a shine before they had left Tregaron, were now hanging dank down her back. But she did not seem in any way perturbed by the wild state of her hair, as she laughed and threw a loose tendril back over her shoulder and adjusted her simple veil. Nothing could steal the joy from Siwan's face, for this was her wedding day, and the man she loved was beside her, leaning on a stick but with a face as joy-filled as hers.

Following behind them were another beautifully attired couple ready to make their marriage vows. Gwil stood tall in dark, wine-red finery, his tunic and cloak trimmed with fur, gold clasps holding both belt and cloak in place. Manon was beside him, a shy smile lighting her face. Her dress was made of silk, turquoise shot with silver, and she looked every bit the lady she was about to become. She would leave Ystrad Fflur that day a Fitzherbert.

Cynan stood with Efa as the procession of couples passed them, and then he took his wife's arm to lead her into the abbey church. Efa did not miss his sharp intake of breath as her husband took his time to ascend the church steps, gripping her arm for support. Concern for him tempered her own joy. Her husband was ailing, and the deterioration had been marked in the last weeks. Plans for the weddings had been simplified and made in haste when all had realised how Cynan was sickening.

But this was a joyous day, and he was smiling through his pain. Efa was deeply moved, seeing Manon and Siwan so happy to be brides, seeing how well loved they both were. There may have been a time when she might have been jealous to witness what she herself had been denied, but any disappointment had long since fled. God had healed her heart, she knew it. She had found love at Tregaron. Love of a different kind, perhaps, from what she had known with Philip, but a love that had filled her heart and her days. This family loved her. She smiled as the wedding party was swelled by the arrival of Haf and Morgan, Eluned and Ifan. And more than that, she knew that God loved her, and she loved Him.

Gwil and Manon stood before the priest first. They made their promises and received the priest's blessing. Efa smiled to herself at the remembrance of how many times Gwil had made excuses to visit Tregaron after he had first come to retrieve his destrier. To begin with, he used his concern for Gruffydd's recovery as his reason. But the true motive for his visits became increasingly apparent. His wooing of Manon had been gentle and patient. She in turn had responded to his kindness by opening up her heart at last to the possibility of love and marriage.

More of Gwil's history had emerged. He had been married before, an arranged marriage that had grown into a love match. He had shared with Manon how he had been a man of war and how his wife had tamed him, her faith in God a balm to his own troubled soul. He had been devastated by her too-early death and had thought never to marry again – until he had met Manon. It was her gentleness and timidity that had touched something within him, and he had felt himself irrevocably drawn to her. She in turn had found in Gwil a man who knew how to love well, and had blossomed under his affection. And so it was that Efa saw the answer to her prayers for her young friend being enacted out before her.

Gruffydd and Siwan now stepped up to the altar. This wayward young man, used to having any woman he wanted, using and discarding hearts at will, now stood before the priest with a young servant woman by his side; incongruous, perhaps, and yet he seemed utterly devoted to her. That an attachment had been forming between them had been observed from those first days of her caring for him. And when Cynan had noted it himself, he had seemed happy to see his son happy – until marriage had been mentioned. Then Cynan had baulked, and a conflict between him and his son had ensued, their tempers a match one for the other. The truth was that Gruffydd was now in line to inherit Tregaron, as Dafydd had made his home in Gwynedd and had forfeited his half share. A wealthier or well-connected wife for Gruffydd was his father's aim, to help ensure Tregaron's future.

It was the decline in Cynan's own health that had finally softened him towards the match. Gruffydd was going to inherit sooner than expected, and Siwan at least knew and loved Tregaron. She had proved her worth in supporting Gruffydd in his recovery, and seemed to have a calming effect on his wilder tempers. Gruffydd trusted her, and was determined that she would be his wife, so Cynan gave his blessing to the match. At least Cynan's eldest daughter was marrying into the nobility, albeit Norman nobility.

As the priest pronounced his final prayers, the brothers of the abbey sang the *Te Deum*, the sweet sound seeming to fill the air beneath the vast stone arches above them. Cynan had somehow found the energy to remain upright throughout the service, but he seemed to shrink and stumble as they were led out to the guest hall that had been laid with refreshments for them to enjoy. Ifan appeared and took his old friend's arm, lending him his strength as he sank into a chair. Pain etched Cynan's face and Efa hurried to bring him a cup of spiced wine. He drank deeply and handed the cup back to her.

As the wedding party and other guests began to fill the small space there was laughter and shared embraces as they were served from the abbey kitchens. It was simple fare – bread, cheese, dried fruits, and river trout dressed with herbs, and dishes of savoury-smelling barley stew.

'Can I bring you anything else, my lord husband?' Efa pulled a stool to sit beside him and leaned close.

He patted her hand in response. 'No, no, my dear. I want nothing more than to sit here and enjoy my children's happiness.' He smiled feebly, his eyes bright for all his obvious weariness. 'They are happy, are they not?'

'It would seem they are, my lord. And long may that happiness continue for all of them.'

Cynan nodded. 'I was wrong to try to dissuade Gruffydd from marrying Siwan. It would have been acceptable for him to have her unwed, and still to marry for politic or wealth.' He sniffed then and a wry smile crossed his face. 'But then I tried to have the best of both, a lover and a wife, and I ended up causing both unnecessary pain. To my great regret. And then I caused you pain too.' He touched her hand again, and Efa was shocked at how cold his was. She placed her other hand on top of his, hoping to lend him her warmth, hoping her words would warm his soul.

'I forgave you a long time ago, Cynan.' She spoke so that he alone could hear. 'I bear no ill will towards you. But I believe that you have made the right decision to let your children marry for love. I believe Gwil and Manon will be happy together, although their marriage will take them far from us. I have some concern that Gruffydd and Siwan may well have to work harder to keep the happiness they now share.'

She glanced over to where Gruffydd was stood leaning on a chair back to relieve the pressure in his weaker leg. He was laughing as he bent to allow Siwan to feed him dried apricots from her fingertips.

Cynan followed her gaze. 'Indeed. I want to believe that Gruffydd is changing, that he is rediscovering the man of character he was before being led astray by Maelgwyn. And maybe his love for Siwan will help him in that.' His face had darkened at the mention of Maelgwyn and Efa could see that his eyes had moved to where Gwil and Manon stood together, their heads dipped together in conversation with Gerallt, who had been permitted by the abbot to join the wedding celebration.

'That man near ruined two of my children's lives,' Cynan ground out. 'He should by rights be held to account for that.'

'God will hold him to account.' Efa squeezed the hand that had still not regained its warmth.

Cynan sighed heavily. 'You speak the truth, my lady wife. Anything I do now would only open old wounds and cause my children more pain. And I am tired...' His voice trailed off and he closed his eyes.

Efa watched his face as he breathed slowly and deeply, occasionally screwing his forehead with whatever pain was plaguing him. She felt a wave of tenderness towards this man. Whatever had passed, he had gifted her with a safe and happy home and a family and friends to love, and she was grateful for that. She did not know how much longer she would have her husband, but for however long God gave him, she would give herself to caring for him. Loving him. Not as Manon loved

Gwil, or as Siwan loved Gruffydd. But as Christ had loved her. Willingly and sacrificially. Serving him as God called her to.

Efa had not thought to be so soon back at Ystrad Fflur, but so it was that barely a month after they had celebrated those joyous weddings, they came again to the abbey to lay Cynan's body to rest. It was a small and sombre party. Manon and Gwil were far from Tregaron, visiting his uncle in Yorkshire, and Dafydd had not travelled south to be there. Haf and Morgan were in attendance, and Gruffydd and Siwan, Ifan and Eluned. They stood together as the Mass was said and sung, and then they all gathered to watch Cynan's body being lowered into the ground, grief tangible in the air around them.

He had not died an easy death, and when the end had finally come it had been a blessed release. Whatever ailment had assaulted his body had left Cynan often writhing in agony and calling for death. He had found only short-lived relief from the herbal infusions Ystrad Fflur's infirmarer had sent for him. Efa had stayed as close to him through his last days as she could, ministering to his physical needs, but also praying for him and reading words of Scripture over him. In his moments of rest and lucidity, he seemed most soothed by the sound of Efa's voice.

One evening he had grasped her hand, stopping her midway as she read to him, his voice so weak that she had to lean into him where he lay reduced in her comfortable bed, his head cushioned by her soft pillows.

'I have made provision for you, Efa.'

She was flustered for a moment, and placed her other hand over his. 'You have done enough for me, do not concern yourself. Gruffydd will see I am provided for. You must rest now.'

'No.' His voice rose slightly in volume and he lifted his shoulder so that he could awkwardly roll to face her, his features creasing with the pain the movement caused him.

'No. Efa, I took you away from your life and tied you to Tregaron as my wife. When I die, I want you to be free, if you wish to be. I have instructed Gruffydd... with Ifan as my witness, that you will have a good sum of money for yourself, and a yearly annuity for as long as you need it. You need never marry again unless by your own choice. That is my gift to you.'

He sank back into the pillows with a sigh and closed his eyes. Efa did not know how to respond and sat watching him as his breath hitched and then eased. She had been stunned at his words. It was more – much more – than she had expected. She had not really thought beyond Cynan's death and what her future would be; hadn't thought of what life at Tregaron might be like for her without her position as his wife.

Watching Cynan now, she bowed her head and prayed again for him, thanking God for him and his generosity towards her, asking God to relieve him of his pain. And for his soul, that it would rest in God's love for him. She thought he slept, but as she raised her head he had opened his eyes and was watching her.

'You pray for me? I am grateful for your prayers.' He smiled weakly. 'My dear lady wife, you have brought much goodness and joy to my home. I thank God for you.' He paused. 'I have sought His forgiveness, Efa.' Cynan squeezed her hand feebly. 'My sins have been many, but I believe God has absolved me and I am at peace.' He stopped to take a sharp breath as another pain seized him. She felt her eyes moisten, seeing his struggle, but he was not done. 'You carry Him, you know,' he whispered. 'You, Non, Ifan, Eluned. You have made God real to me, more than any priest or monk has, despite their well-intentioned efforts. I hope your prayers have been answered and that we will meet again in God's kingdom. And now, my dear, you are free.'

Though she stayed close by him for the remainder of the scant hours that he lived, her husband did not speak again.

And so now Efa stood by his graveside, and the sense of loss was real. As the priest finished his words, the other mourners began to move away, but Efa stayed. It was not that anyone had said anything or done anything to make her feel so, but she suddenly felt very alone. Seeing Cynan's body finally laid to rest, she was confronted anew by her change of circumstance. She would return to Tregaron a widow, and Siwan would take her place as mistress of the house. There were no longer any children for Efa to mother, and there was no longer a husband to serve.

Efa left the grave fillers to their task, but did not follow the others. She wanted to be alone to pray and think before she returned with the family to Tregaron; not her family by blood, and yet they had become dear to her – more dear to her even than any other family she had known. And they would make room for her to stay at Tregaron, she was sure of it. She had rightly surrendered her fine apartment to the master of the house and his wife, on Cynan's passing, but had been gifted Manon's old room to occupy as her private space. She was content enough with that, but still the unease would not leave her.

She made her way back inside the cool quiet of the abbey church and found herself instinctively heading for the chapel where she had met with Father Ulrich so many times. She did not expect to meet him; they had been told that he was too frail now to leave his bed. He would have been at Cynan's Requiem Mass, she felt sure of it, had he been well enough to do so. Efa sat on one of the stone seats cut into the wall, as she had so often before. She felt chilled. Despite the daffodils being in full bloom and the first lambs appearing in the fields, a heavy, grey-clouded sky had stolen the day of its warmth. And with no sunlight streaming through the glass panes above her, even her dear chapel felt a dreary, lifeless place to be. It suited her mood. She grieved Cynan's loss, but his death had brought a deeper sense of loss. Her life as she had known it, the life that had been gifted her, that she had grown to love, was now also lost to her.

She laid her head back against the cool stone and closed her eyes, longing to hear a comforting voice, be it human or divine, but all was quiet. She knew she needed to pray, to ask God for direction. What purpose would her life take now? She was not the same young girl who had been forced into a marriage that terrified her. Neither was she old and ready for her own grave.

God had gifted her with health and vitality. How should she be spending the remainder of her days? Perhaps she should join Non and the nuns at Llanllugan? It was a noble thing for a widow to do, especially one with wealth of her own. She did not know how wealthy she was; that was a conversation she was yet to have with Gruffydd. But she did not doubt that Cynan's gift would be more than enough to endow an abbey for her keep.

She sighed heavily and drew her miniver close around her, its familiarity soothing her. The peace of the chapel fed her soul, and finally she could utter a few words of prayer. 'God, guide me. Show me my path.' She heard nothing in response, but deep in her heart she felt she had been heard. 'He knows,' she whispered to herself as she opened her eyes and stood up from her resting spot.

'Here you are, my lady.' The voice startled her and her hand went instinctively to her throat.

It was the prior. And in his normal state of agitation, as if the whole of the world excepting himself needed to be herded into line. His face was creased and his cheeks flushed.

'I was sent to find you, and you were not with the party from Tregaron. They are yet availing themselves of our hospitality, and seem in no hurry to leave.'

Efa could swear he frowned momentarily.

'I am sure they are most grateful for your kind hospitality,' she answered him. 'And the abbey has a reputation for caring well for its guests. You must be proud of your part in upholding that?'

'Yes, yes. Of course. As long as it does not distract the community too long from its work and prayers.' He was flustered now, and Efa dipped her head so that he could not see her barely supressed smile.

'Come, come,' he said, turning from her, with the tone of one used to giving orders. He began to move away, glancing back to see that she followed. But she had stood her ground, forcing him to stop in his tracks.

'Forgive me, Brother Prior, but where are you hurrying me away to?'

His face flushed crimson. He brought his hands together in front of him and began twisting them palm against palm.

'My apologies, Lady Efa. Did I not say? Father Abbot has asked to see you. And we must go now, while he is awake, and before the bells for the next office sound. He wants to see you before you have to take your leave to return to Tregaron. He asked especially for me to find you. He said you might be here in this chapel. I should have come here first.'

Efa smiled genuinely then, feeling just a little sorry for the poor prior's discomfort. Her heart swelled with the thought that she might talk with Ulrich again. Perhaps in this God was already answering her simple prayer for direction. Ulrich might have God's wisdom for her.

'Brother Prior, I will come. I thank you for your diligence in seeking me out. Lead on and be assured that this time I will follow you willingly.'

For you reach into my heart.

With one flash of your eyes I am undone by your love,

my beloved, my equal, my bride.

You leave me breathless –

I am overcome

by merely a glance from your worshiping eyes,

for you have stolen my heart.

I am held hostage by your love

and by the graces of righteousness shining upon you.

Song of Solomon 4:9, TPT

17
Come Away

Father Ulrich lay propped up in a curtained bed, a fur coverlet covering his slight frame. Brother Paul was there, attending the abbot, arranging a cloak around his thin shoulders. He stood and stepped away as Efa was ushered into the room, nodding in her direction but keeping his eyes averted. The abbot held a trembling hand out towards Efa, and she hurried to clasp it and bring it to her lips. His face was shockingly drawn and his hair had noticeably thinned, but his eyes still shone brightly as he beckoned her to sit on the stool beside his bed. He turned his head slowly towards her and gifted her with a warm smile.

'I have been praying for you today especially.' The voice was surprisingly strong from one who looked so frail. At his gentle words, Efa felt the first tears she had shed that day roll unhindered down her face. 'They think that I sleep more than I am awake,' he whispered to her conspiratorially. 'I feign sleep so that I can escape their overzealous ministrations. And it gives me much time to pray.' He glanced over to where the prior still hovered by the door. 'Brother Prior, you may leave us.' The authority still rang in his voice. 'You must look to the needs of our guests in my place. Brother Paul will stay.'

The prior looked less than pleased to be dismissed. Brother Paul had now seated himself in a far corner of the room. His eyes were closed and his hands clasped together within his habit sleeves.

'I trust Brother Paul not to eavesdrop, and if he does, he will keep our confidence. I do not have the same certainty with our dear prior. He is a good man at heart, but he fusses. Indeterminably so. And gets easily anxious if he does not feel he has control of a situation. His words have a tendency to run away with themselves.' He winked at her. 'Now we must talk. *You* must talk.' He patted her arm gently.

'I do not want to tire you, Father.'

The look he gave her was full of compassion.

'You need someone to talk to, and I am happy to be that person, if you would grace me with the honour. I see you carry a burden, questions, uncertainties. My legs may have ceased to work as they should, but my brain is still very much alive, and so is my spirit, my child. And God knows, as do I, that there are things weighing heavily on you. I asked Him to allow me to speak with you one more time. And here we are. So speak, as you have spoken with me before. I know you must grieve for Cynan at least a little, but it is more than that?'

Efa sighed and drew her hand across her face, wiping away the stray tears.

'You are right that I do grieve my husband. But I believe he is free from pain now and in the Father's embrace. His passing was a mercy in the end.' She glanced up at Ulrich. 'I grew fond of him, never loving him perhaps as a wife should, but more as a daughter might. I had long forgiven him for taking me for his wife against my will. To be truthful, it seems a lifetime ago that I was brought to Tregaron as his bride.'

'And now with his passing you are no longer his bride, no longer a wife. And all of Cynan's children have grown to maturity. So they no longer need you. Perhaps you do not know what your role or purpose should be now?'

She shook her head. He understood, with his God-given insight.

'But you are still a bride, Efa. Do you not remember that God Himself calls you His bride? You are not alone, can never be alone, my dear friend, wherever life might take you, or whatever may become of you.'

She bowed and the tears flowed freely again. It was the truth. God's love for her had not changed, her identity as His beloved was not altered by her changed circumstance. She needed that truth to settle in her heart and mind.

'Now I have something else that I want to share with you,' Ulrich continued. 'It may sound strange to your ears at this moment in time, but I do believe God has laid it on my heart for you to hear this. It is from that same portion of Scripture that we read together, many years ago now, in that small chapel space. Do you remember? The Song of Solomon. Brother Gerallt wrote some verses for you on parchment, to carry with you.'

'Yes,' she sniffed and smiled, meeting his eyes. 'I do remember, and they have stayed with me, and I have read them often to remind myself of how God sees me.'

'Well, this is what I believe He is speaking to you now. My eyes can no longer see to read, but these verses are etched on my own heart. Because, you see, He has used them to call to me. I too have longed for love, and I know what it is to be wooed by a God who wants my whole heart...

> *My beloved spoke, and said to me:*
> *"Rise up, my love, my fair one,*
> *And come away.*
> *For lo, the winter is past,*
> *The rain is over and gone.*
> *The flowers appear on the earth;*
> *The time of singing has come,*
> *And the voice of the turtledove*
> *Is heard in our land.*
> *The fig tree puts forth her green figs,*
> *And the vines with the tender grapes*
> *Give a good smell.*
> *Rise up, my love, my fair one,*
> *And come away!"'*

Efa let the beautiful words roll over her. She could not make sense of them, except that they somehow spoke hope to her troubled heart. What did it mean? 'Come away'? Come away to where?

As he had finished speaking, Ulrich had laid back again, his head sinking deeper into the pillows and his eyes closing. Brother Paul appeared noiselessly beside her and bowed to whisper.

'He has tired himself out.'

'Yes, of course.' Efa rose reluctantly to her feet, not taking her gaze from the dear form lying still in the bed beside her. She bowed her head and lifted his pale hand to kiss it one more time, and then turned to follow Paul from the room.

'Efa!' The voice came from the bed as she reached the open doorway. She turned and he had opened his eyes once more. He took a deep breath and gave her one last exhortation. 'Listen for His voice, Efa. And when He calls, be sure to follow. He has new paths for you.'

The grass was lush and green, and there were flowers in bloom everywhere. Efa turned her face to the warmth of the sun and, closing her eyes, reached her arms out to twirl like a child, her skirts swishing around her, her hair loose and wild. The trees were in full leaf and birds sang sweetly from their branches. Efa took a deep breath and let it out, relinquishing the months of cold and sorrow and confusion. It was as if she were beginning to see and feel more clearly. The sky was azure blue above her and it felt good to be there.

The sound of children's voices made her turn around in surprise as two young boys raced past her, chasing each other around the trees. She shook her head – she could not understand why there were children again at Tregaron. Who were they? Why were they running free in Tregaron's gardens unaccompanied? She walked towards them and they stopped their game. They turned small faces towards her, and she could see in them a familiarity that she could not place. She wracked her brains as to who they could be. Had Gruffydd invited them, and where were their guardians? She turned back to see if anyone had followed the children from the door of the hall, but the familiar stone walls of Tregaron had gone. She brought both hands to her mouth and stifled the gasp. She was not in Tregaron; it was Swansea's castle walls that loomed above her.

Efa sat up in her bed, her heart still pounding. It took her a moment to focus in the half-light, but she was back in her room, the children's old room, in Tregaron. The linens of her bed were crumpled and she fought to free her feet as she swung around to sit on the edge of the bed, waiting for her breathing to steady. Now fully awake, she stood and grabbed the coverlet to throw around her shoulders against the early morning chill. Efa made her way over to the window embrasure and opened the shutter. She sat watching as the rising sun slowly dispelled the shadows outside. It was promising to be a warm day. Outside the grass was lush and green, Annest's garden was coming into bloom, and the trees had begun to blossom. Spring was bursting into life, like the scene in her dream. But her dream hadn't been of Tregaron; it had been of Swansea. And the two boys, the faces that had perplexed her so... She knew now who they reminded her of. Although youthful they had borne a distinct resemblance to John and Philip de Braose. Why had she seen them in her dreams?

'Come away with Me.'

She felt rather than heard the whisper. The words came unbidden to her mind and she recognised the voice of God's Spirit in her heart. She closed her eyes and listened to see if God would speak more. All she heard were the same words again.

'Rise up, My beloved, and come away with Me.'

Was God was calling her to return to Swansea? She had considered the idea of going back at Cynan's passing and had quickly dismissed it. She felt that she had been too long gone, too long estranged from her cousin Marared. And seeing John again, with all the memories of his part in her heartache... Efa believed she had forgiven him in her heart, but could she live under the same roof as him? And what of Philip? From what she knew he had never returned to Swansea, but if he did, and she was there? Could they rekindle what they had lost, when so many years had passed? Philip could be a married man by now for all she knew.

Yet the dream had been vivid, and she had felt free and released and joy-filled. Had God spoken to her in a dream? She had heard of Him doing so for others, and so wished she had Non or Ulrich there to confirm it in some way for her.

The sounds from outside her room signalled that the household was coming to life, and she made herself move from her contemplation, finding yesterday's discarded clothes and dressing herself. She tied her braids up, reaching for Marared's gold barrette over her more usual plain one, and tucked her hair under her wimple, securing her veil in place. She was a widow now, not a young carefree girl twirling her skirts in a grassy garden as she had in her imagination. She left her room to face the day, vowing to find time to speak to God when she could think a bit more clearly.

As she had anticipated, things had changed at Tregaron. Siwan had taken on the responsibilities of mistress of the house with remarkable ease. Gone was the shy, retiring girl who had hidden behind Efa's skirts on her arrival. Every day the young woman grew in confidence in her new role, asking questions when she needed to, working alongside Eluned and Ifan, always with a smile on her face. She knew her place in the family, and the others at Tregaron served and encouraged her willingly.

Despite the fact that they were still in mourning for Cynan, there was much laughter in the house. Yet still Efa carried a wistfulness for times past when she had known her place at Tregaron. The unsettled feeling deepened when she realised she now had little to fill her time. While she had concentrated on caring for her husband in his last days, the world of Tregaron had gone on without her. Gruffydd and Siwan were now well and truly master and mistress of the house.

She joined them to break her fast, smiling as she watched and listened as they shared with each other their plans for the day. Theirs seemed to be a true partnership, founded on a genuine love for each other. Gruffydd still had a tendency to imperiousness at times, but Siwan teased and cajoled and mellowed his moods. In turn he treated her as any lady would hope to be treated, with an unexpected gentleness and respect. Efa had yet to see them argue with any fierceness, but she suspected it would come, knowing what she did of Gruffydd's character, and the inevitable pressures that stepping into his father's shoes would bring. She prayed Siwan would fare well in any clash that did occur, that their love for each other would be enough to weather the storms. She prayed fervently that they would seek to make God a part of their marriage, to have Him as their anchor.

Gruffydd dipped to kiss his blushing wife as he left the table, leaving Siwan sitting alone with Efa.

Siwan turned to smile at Efa. 'Do you have plans for today, my lady?'

It was a genuinely kind question and Efa was dismayed that it irritated her so. Was she actually jealous of this dear, sweet girl sitting by her side, who had so much to occupy herself with? The wimple and veil Siwan now wore as a married woman still seemed incongruous with her carefree character. And she seemed oblivious to how the question bit into Efa.

Efa trained her features into a smile, but before she could answer, Siwan spoke again.

'I only ask because I would really appreciate your assistance this morning. My husband has presented me with a problem that I cannot fathom on my own.'

Efa could have laughed with the relief that flowed through her, the pleasure of feeling needed for something, and felt deeply ashamed at her moment of jealousy. This time her smile in response to Siwan was fully genuine.

'What is this unfathomable problem? I am at your service to help if I can.'

At her words, Siwan flew from her seat and hitched up her wide skirts to scurry in a less-than-dignified fashion over to where a large wooden chest had been deposited against the wall under the window. It stood in the same place where Gerallt had sat at his little desk all those years ago and dreamt of the life he was now living. Siwan bent and with some effort raised the heavy lid of the box. Jac had been dozing in a patch of sunlight on the rush-strewn floor, but he jumped up, tail wagging at the sudden excitement.

'Come. Come and see,' she giggled, as Efa rose from her own seat and moved over to peer into the chest. She could see it contained bolts of cloth. Good, fine cloth.

'Gruffydd says that I must dress like the noble wife that I now am. And that this one dress is not enough.' She fingered the soft wool dress she wore. It was the same burnt orange one she had worn on her wedding day. 'For years I have worn the same dress day in and day out until it wore out, or until I grew out of it. And now he expects me to change my dress every day!' She scoffed. 'What he does not realise is that I am no needlewoman, so unless you can help me do something with this...' She lifted a length of beautiful red cloth in her hands and then let it drop dismissively, ' ... then he will have wasted his time and his money.'

Siwan flopped to sit heavily on the floor beside the chest. Her veil was knocked awry as she leaned her head back against the stone wall. Jac sat too, his head on one side and his tongue lolling. He was still expecting a game. Siwan sighed loudly.

Efa laughed then and stood over her, bending to offer her a hand. 'Come now, you cannot let a chest of cloth defeat you!' She pulled and Siwan stood, brushing rushes from her skirts. Efa stepped around her and bent over the chest, lifting cloth and examining the 'problem' – which would have been the happiest of problems for most young women, she suspected. 'There are some very lovely fabrics here. Why don't we start by lifting them out of the chest and carrying them over to the table? We can see what your husband has bought and decide what best to do with them. You can choose one that you can imagine yourself wearing, and we will make something of it together. A tunic dress of simple design, perhaps, and I will show you how to cut it and seam it. The actual sewing is no different from what you have done in repairing tears in sackcloth, or darns in your shifts. Just done with a finer needle and finer thread. I am sure you are more than capable, with a little encouragement – that I am happy to give.'

Jac flopped back to his original spot and let out a doggy sigh as Efa and Siwan proceeded to empty the chest. They lifted out one bolt at a time, until the table was spread with a glorious array of colours and textures. Even Efa was surprised at how much Gruffydd had spent. There were fine wools in russet red and warm brown, in sky blue and daffodil yellow. There were silks too, and the one that caught Efa's attention was of a soft green colour. It was so like the silk of the dress she had borrowed from Marared! The one she had worn and torn and almost destroyed on her journey here. She could not even recall what had happened to that original dress. She had certainly never worn it again. But as she fingered the soft silk now, she remembered, this time without any pain, the young frightened bride she had been. And she remembered Marared's kindness in lending her the dress, and the barrette that she had subconsciously put in her hair that morning. She felt a sudden longing to see her cousin again. And Marared was at Swansea.

'Are you quite well, my lady?' Siwan stood close, her forehead creased with concern.

Efa realised she had worried the silk as her thoughts had wandered, and it now lay creased and crumpled in her fingers. She smiled at her young friend – the one who had kept her company on her journey here, and had in turn blossomed and flourished at Tregaron. And who now found herself its mistress.

'Siwan, do you remember that once I sat with you and promised that if you ever wanted to return to Swansea, that I would make that possible? If you ever found yourself unhappy here and wanted to return to your family?'

'I do.' Siwan's smile was sheepish. 'I chose to stay, and it seems to have been a good decision, to see where I am now. Married, and mistress of Tregaron. I am so very happy here.' She laughed and then suddenly her face straightened and her eyebrows knit together. 'But why do you ask? Do you think I should go back?'

'No!' Efa placed a hand reassuringly on the girl's shoulder and laughed at the panic in the young woman's face. 'No, your place is here. And Jac agrees.'

Siwan laughed as she looked down and stroked the dog that had settled with his head on her feet. Efa smiled with her, but the words she spoke came from the heart.

'I find that I now have a request to make of you, Siwan, and of Gruffydd. You see, I think that *I* am the one meant to return to Swansea. And I may need your help to make that happen.'

The one I love calls to me:

Arise, my dearest. Hurry, my darling.

Come away with me!

I have come as you have asked

to draw you to my heart and lead you out.

For now is the time, my beautiful one.

The season has changed,

the bondage of your barren winter has ended,

and the season of hiding is over and gone.

The rains have soaked the earth

and left it bright with blossoming flowers.

The season for singing and pruning the vines has

arrived.

I hear the cooing of doves in our land,

filling the air with songs to awaken you

and guide you forth.

Can you not discern this new day of destiny

breaking forth around you?

The early signs of my purposes and plans

are bursting forth.

The budding vines of new life

are now blooming everywhere.

The fragrance of their flowers whispers,

'There is change in the air.'

Arise, my love, my beautiful companion,

and run with me to the higher place.

For now is the time to arise and come away

with me.

Song of Solomon 2:10-13, TPT

18

Swansea

Late spring 1232

Swansea Castle loomed large. Efa had never approached her old home with such trepidation before, and the high stone walls of the newly built castle keep did nothing to dispel her unease. The building work had been started while she was in residence and been completed in her absence, and it was a formidable sight that greeted their travelling party. The large square keep was surrounded by a vast rectangular timber palisade that enclosed the bailey. She supposed that too would be replaced with stone in time, to complete Swansea's defences, although she did not think that while the de Braoses maintained good relationships with both King Henry and Prince Llewellyn there would be much risk of serious attack.

She could appreciate how an enemy soldier advancing on Swansea Castle might feel, as her insides twisted with apprehension at their approach. And yet letters had been sent and received and her welcome had been assured. The gates would be swung open, no doubt, and she would ride unchallenged through them. With her was Gruffydd himself, come to present himself to John de Braose as his father's heir, and beside him, looking small on a large roan, was Siwan. From her pale features she seemed to be as anxious as Efa was about their reception at Swansea, especially as she had left there a nobody and was returning a wealthy wife.

Efa had been surprised that Gruffydd had offered himself and his wife, as well as half a dozen good men, to ride with them as her escort back to Swansea. It seemed that Siwan had already spoken with him and mooted the idea of how good it would be for them to accompany her – Gruffydd to offer a hand of friendship to the Lord of the Gower, and she to see if any of her family still lived. Gruffydd had surprised Efa again by presenting her with a small, bronze-banded wooden chest, and with it a large key on a finely woven leather strap. Key matched lock and the lid of the chest sprang open. It contained several pouches of coin, and Efa's eyes widened as she fingered it, finding both silver and gold among its contents.

'It is too much,' she whispered, her eyes questioning her benefactor.

'It is what my father wanted. And there is more, if you should ever need it.'

Efa watched Gruffydd's face for any sign that he was unwilling for her to have it, and saw nothing to suggest that he was.

'I thank you. It is more than enough.'

'Well, it is for you to use as you need, or to give away if you so desire. All I know is that my father promised you freedom if you wanted it. And now that you have chosen to leave our care, this must go with you. He was adamant that you should never find yourself solely dependent on the will of another man, unless he were one chosen by yourself. He wanted you to have the means to choose how to live. A means of assuaging some long-held guilt, perhaps.'

Efa had dipped her head at that and offered up a quick prayer of thanks – to God for His provision and for stirring Cynan's generosity.

The key now lay heavily against her upper thigh, secured tightly to a belt hidden beneath her tunic, as she sat astride her horse. The chest was well hidden among her possessions in the cart that followed them, wrapped about with the miniver cloak that, like her, was returning to its former home. She was returning to Swansea a wealthy woman in her own right, and with far more to call her own than she had left with.

A single rider wearing hauberk and sword came out to meet them as they approached the castle, not a man that Efa recognised. He received Gruffydd's words of greeting and good will and turned to lead them back to the gates, which were now being wound open with a creak to welcome them. They clattered into the compound and reined in. Men appeared, some with weapons carried conspicuously on their hips, most in the humble attire of servants. Grooms and boys stepped up to take their mounts; menservants began to unload their wagon. There was noise and activity, but above it all Efa's gaze was taken to a figure standing at the top of the stone steps that led to the door that gave entrance to the keep. She was dressed finely, in a gown of dark blue, with her veil secured by a silver circlet bearing polished stones that caught the light. Marared. She had aged little apart from having filled out slightly around her waist. She did not automatically descend the stairs, and from a distance her face was hard to read. Efa took a deep breath and, with it, courage to lift her own skirts and propel her weary bones towards her cousin. She stopped as she reached the base of the stone steps, waiting for the invitation to ascend. And then there was a squeal and a shout and two young boys appeared from behind Marared and hurtled down the steps and whooshed past Efa. They were far more interested in the horses and what was being unloaded from the wagon than in their mother's visitor, it seemed.

'William, Richard.' Marared's voice rose above the mêlée and the boys skidded to a halt. The older turned to face her, his face scowling in disappointment. The younger boy slid behind his brother's back.

With a regal grace, Marared slowly descended the steps until she came level with Efa. For a moment she examined Efa's face, her own still expressionless, before she turned back to the boys and lifted her fingers to beckon them over. And then Efa found herself looking down into two faces that unmistakeably bore de Braose features, if softened and framed with boyish grubbiness.

'William and Richard de Braose, let me introduce you to the Lady Efa. My cousin and your kinswoman.'

William, the elder, stepped forward and made a small bow. Richard, the shyer of the two, held back, his hands clasped behind him and a toe swinging in the dirt as he swayed his little body from side to side. Efa felt a wave of compassion and, forgetting her aching knees, she bent them so that her face was level with his. She extended a hand and smiled, and kept smiling until he stopped his motion and slowly but surely released his hands so that one snaked around and extended a little way out from his body. Efa quickly leaned forward and grasped his hand, shaking it formally.

'I am happy to know you, cousin Richard, and you too, young William.' She turned to his brother and was happy to see his lips curve upwards in a shy smile. 'I so hope we can be friends.' She waited, the smile never leaving her face, as first one and then the other boy nodded their agreement. She rose then to find their mother watching her, her lips twitching as if trying to hold back a smile, her eyes warmer than they had been before.

'You two can go now.' She spoke again to her children, shooing them in the direction of the horses and wagon still being unloaded. 'But do not get underfoot or you may get trampled, and then we would have to scrape you off the ground and roll you up like a mat.'

She broke into a broad smile as the boys giggled at her words, and Efa was pleased to see a glimpse of the Marared she knew of old. Her cousin was still smiling as she turned back to her.

'So you can still charm de Braose boys, it seems.'

It was not said with malice, and as she spoke Marared raised one eyebrow, a twinkle in her eye. Efa burst into laughter and then the two were in each other's arms, the years and the hurt falling away as they held on to each other, oblivious to all that was going on around them.

Beyond the castle palisades, on a long strip of grass leading down to the River Tawe, an orchard of sorts had been planted.

The cherry trees were just shedding their pink blossom, and the apple and pear trees were coming into full leaf, small buds of fruit already appearing. Efa loved the space. She always had, in the days of her youth. She had played with a youthful Philip among those trees. Now she chose it as her place of escape from the noise and busyness of the castle. Here she could be alone with her thoughts and with her God, the branches of the trees her chapel roof and the cool green grass her abbey floor to kneel on. She was not always able to enjoy peace for long as William and Richard would inevitably hunt her down, their flustered nursemaid struggling to keep up with them. As they ran and chased around the trees, picking up handfuls of blossom to throw at one another, it was eerily reminiscent of the dream that had turned Efa's mind to coming back to Swansea.

She did not know why God had directed her way back to Swansea. It was not that she was unhappy. Her days were fuller than they had been at Tregaron, with sharing happy hours with Marared and enjoying the company of two boisterous boys. Even John had formally welcomed her to Swansea. He had aged more than his wife, his once svelte figure now soft and rounded, the first flecks of grey visible in his dark hair. The look that his eyes had carried on greeting her had held a wariness that her warm smile had seemed to dispel. They did not have the same ease of friendship they once had enjoyed, but Efa strove to show him due respect, reminding herself often that God had forgiven her so that she could find the grace to forgive John. It would have done neither of them any good for her to carry offence in her heart towards him for something that had happened so long ago, and for circumstances that God had ultimately turned to so much good.

John had also done his duty in offering hospitality and the renewed hand of friendship to Gruffydd. Siwan had, for her part, reconciled with a brother who still lived and worked as a tenant farmer on de Braose land. He and his wife and young child had been loaded up onto the wagon to return with Gruffydd and Siwan to Tregaron within a few days of Efa's arrival at Swansea. There had been tears in the farewells and promises made of return visits. Whether Efa would ever return to visit Tregaron, or they to visit Swansea, was not a certainty on either part. But it was a promise made with warmth of feeling.

Swansea carried reminders of Philip, of course. And this was perhaps the most unsettling of the things that Efa struggled with. Often she questioned God why He had brought her back. She perhaps began to understand more of His plan as her relationship with Marared and her sons deepened and grew. This was a precious gift. Reconciliation and more – God had orchestrated it so that healing could happen. Her renewed friendship with Marared, and the honesty with which they could share their life experiences, was a gift she had not expected to have been given. Life had not been easy for Marared in the time they had been apart. She had lost babies, including a longed-for daughter whom she had named for her mother. And her husband was often far from home.

It gave Efa the greatest joy of all to be able to share with her cousin her newfound faith, and how God had called her and revealed His love for her. Marared listened intently and politely but did not easily accept Efa's words. Efa hoped and prayed that the change God had wrought in her character would shine stronger still than her feeble attempts at explaining His work in her life.

Despite the memories that being at Swansea evoked, Philip was a subject not talked of. One time, in the first few days after her arrival, Marared had taken Efa's arm and pulled her to one side, as John and his retinue had entered the great hall for their evening meal. It was to be a celebratory feast marking the end of a few days of successful hunting. Perhaps because the scene was reminiscent of the one where Philip had openly challenged his brother, or because the ale was already flowing freely – whatever had sparked it, Marared had cautioned her with a whisper.

'We do not mention Philip's name, not in John's hearing. And most especially when he is entertaining guests.'

Efa's brow creased. 'And at other times, when guests are not present, are we allowed to speak his brother's name?'

Marared had sighed and shaken her head almost imperceivably.

'I'm sorry, Efa. It is best if his name is not heard, especially from your lips. Such anger, and yes, remorse, still boils beneath the surface with my husband. I am not sure how he would react. And I so want you to stay now that you have come back.' Her eyes were pleading.

It did not sit peacefully with Efa, but she agreed to honour Marared's wishes. To her embarrassment, her own voice broke slightly as she asked her next question.

'Have you heard news of him since he left?'

Marared turned to face her and took her hand gently in her own.

'Forgive me, Efa. I should not have mentioned him to you either. I should have known it would still pain you.'

'No,' Efa reassured her with a smile and a slight lift of her shoulders. 'But I do wish him well, and would have been pleased of news of him. If that news were good.'

'We have heard, but never directly from Philip himself. Rather from those who have come across him, or heard of his exploits. He fled to France and is still there, we believe. He was fighting for a cause but the latest news was that he had become a mercenary.'

'Oh.' Efa was not sure why she was so disheartened to hear that he was a fighter now. And a fighter for hire, no less. It did not sit right for her to think of him as a cold and ruthless killer. She had hoped and prayed for more than that for him. But while he lived there was hope, surely? Hope that God might rescue him from himself? Give him a chance of a better life?

She spoke no more of him, as she had been asked. And she prayed with a new vigour for him, now that she knew something of where he was and what he had become. Sometimes her dreams were plagued with images of him with blood streaking his face and his lips curled with cruelty, riding headlong into some mêlée and fighting with unbridled ferocity. When she woke from such she invariably crawled out of her bed and knelt on the stone floor, pleading with God to save him.

Efa sat in her usual favourite spot, at the foot of a large apple tree. The sun had shone for several days and the grass beneath her was dry. The last few remnants of fallen blossom had shrivelled and been blown by the breeze into small piles. She was watching the boys as they gathered from those piles to make one large pile, into which, no doubt, they would be throwing each other in due course. Efa had sent their exhausted nursemaid back to the castle for a rest, happy to supervise William and Richard for an hour as they played. It was a lovely, fresh, late spring afternoon, and good to be outside.

She half-dozed, and so started when she heard her name called. It was not the boys, who were still engrossed in their game. She heard the voice again and glanced up to see Marared approaching. She was half-running and her face was flushed pink. The look in her eyes worried Efa enough that she got to her feet to greet her.

'What is it?'

'Philip.' Marared held her gaze and Efa knew with sudden clarity that it was not good news. She closed her eyes and, swaying slightly, stretched her hand out to find the tree trunk to steady herself. When she opened her eyes, Marared was watching her, her eyes wet with unshed tears. Marared reached out a hand, and Efa found herself stepping back. She could not bear to be touched or embraced in that moment.

She swallowed hard. 'Dead?' she asked.

Marared nodded and tried again to reach for Efa, who shook her head and raised her hands to fend her off.

'Do not be concerned for me.' She tried to smile. Tried to reassure her cousin. She had not convinced her, for she felt her knees give way, and as she sank back down to the very spot she had been so happily occupying just moments before, Marared dropped to her knees beside her.

'I am so sorry, Efa, to bring you this news. I am even sorrier to tell you that it is old news. John only just received word of it, but it seems Philip met his end many months ago. Perhaps even a year past. No one is sure.'

Efa let her head drop back to rest on the gnarled trunk and closed her eyes. Along with the shock and grief of his passing came other emotions. Anger. Disappointment. Disbelief. All those months that she had been pleading with God to save Philip, he had already been dead. All those prayers and pleadings for him had been in vain, and God had not spoken, had not given her any indication that she should stop praying for him.

She felt the tears come and did not try to wipe them away. She kept her eyes closed as she heard Marared rise and call for her sons. She supposed she had been left alone at last. And that was a blessed relief. The maelstrom within her caused bile to rise to the back of her throat and she retched. She needed to calm herself, calm her emotions, calm her thoughts, but still her heart pounded with pain. Pain of loss, and pain of betrayal. Not Philip's betrayal, or Llewellyn's, or John's, but God's betrayal. She had trusted Him to answer her prayers for Philip's salvation. And He had betrayed her trust in Him. Her prayers had fallen to the earth as withered as those windblown blossom flowers. Useless.

She curled herself into a ball under that tree, feeling cold despite the warmth of the sun that still shone out of a cloudless sky. She could hear the birds singing, the sound of the river as it splashed over rocks, the distant sound of lambs bleating. There was life all around her, new life, and yet she felt so alone.

Then she was aware of a presence beside her. She did not open her eyes to see who it was, assuming that Marared had returned. But it did not feel like Marared, and the voice that spoke was not her cousin's.

'*Efa.*'

She did not need to open her eyes, because the sound of her name had echoed in her heart, not her ears.

'*You are not alone, My beloved.*'

And then she felt it, as if someone had sat down beside her and entwined their arms around her. She knew there was no one there, but still she felt Him. She felt held and she felt loved –

overwhelmingly loved. And as her Saviour held her, she allowed the tears to fall freely. She sobbed and wept for Philip and for herself. Finally spent, she allowed her arms to drop from her knees, stretching her legs out and leaning the weight of her exhausted body back against the solid trunk behind her. Still she felt Him there, and she closed her eyes so that she could picture in her mind's eye what He might look like. She imagined that she could see the face of Christ, and knew Him for the love in His eyes. Love that did not waver, love without condition, love that held the answer to all her questions, love that healed her heart. A love that would be her place of safety and security for all eternity.

'Will you trust Me still, beloved?' His lips did not move but she knew it was He who had spoken. And from the deepest part of her heart she whispered, 'I will.'

Who is this one?
She arises out of her desert, clinging to her
beloved.
When I awakened you under the apple tree,
as you were feasting upon me,
I awakened your innermost being with the
travail of birth
as you longed for more of me.
Fasten me upon your heart as a seal of fire
forevermore.
This living, consuming flame
will seal you as my prisoner of love.
My passion is stronger
than the chains of death and the grave,
all consuming as the very flashes of fire
from the burning heart of God.
Place this fierce, unrelenting fire over your
entire being.
Rivers of pain and persecution
will never extinguish this flame.
Endless floods will be unable
to quench this raging fire that burns within you.
Song of Solomon 8:5-7, TPT

19

Llewellyn

As spring warmth began to give way to summer heat, Efa found she preferred to slip away to the orchard in the early mornings, sometimes even rising early enough to watch the sun rise. The grass was inevitably damp with dew, so she did not sit beneath the trees so much as wander through them and down to the riverside. The Tawe ran low and muddy in the dry season, but swans still swept by in the central current and kingfishers perched precariously on bent reeds, ready to dive for minnows in the shallows. Efa found a quiet joy in those solitary walks, not caring if her skirt hems were soiled, often removing her shoes to feel the damp grass beneath her feet. She would take the time to speak with God, and to listen for His voice. She would put all other thoughts and concerns aside for that time, so that she could strengthen her soul in the awareness of Him. It was usually her stomach that told her when it was time to return. She had never mastered the art of fasting, despite trying more times than she could count. She supposed those who entered monastic life must grow used to it. That life was still an option open to her, but she was yet to feel any conviction that God wanted that for her.

One morning, as breaking her fast called, and as she made her way back up through the flourishing trees, some already bearing ripening cherries, she met Marared coming to find her. For a moment Efa stopped in her tracks, stealing herself, wondering if she could bear it if her cousin bore more bad news.

But Marared was beaming, her skirts and veil flying behind her as she hurried towards Efa.

'Efa, I have good news!' She came to a halt in front of Efa and reached out for both of her hands. 'I hope it is good news for you too.' The smile left her face for a moment, and a sudden wariness appeared in her eyes. 'I'm sorry, I did not think that what might be good news for me might actually cause you pain.' She tried to pull her hands away but Efa resisted, laughing.

'That really depends on what your news is. You haven't yet told me!'

Marared let her smile return. 'It is my father, Efa. He hasn't visited Swansea for so long, and we have just had word that he is expected to arrive later today. And more than that – he brings my mother with him! I'm sorry if that makes things awkward for you. I am just excited for my mother to see my boys, and for Llewellyn to see how his grandsons have grown since last he was here.' She paused and squeezed Efa's hands. 'Will you be happy to see them?'

'Of course!'

Efa pulled Marared closer and embraced her, feeling how her cousin's body tingled still with excitement. Actually, she had mixed feelings about meeting Llewellyn again. So many years had passed and so much heartache with it. She was a very different woman now from the young girl who had idolised him, or the young woman who had been played as a pawn in his hands. As she had forgiven John, so she had come to a place of forgiving Llewellyn too. But she knew that he would no longer have any power to direct her life. God's voice would be the first and only that she would heed now. Still, there was a lingering fondness for the only human father figure she had known, and she held nothing against the Lady Joan, who had always shown her kindness. It was not a hardship to join in Marared's excitement in welcoming her parents to her home, and do all that she could to help them prepare.

'There is so much to do!' Marared turned and started to walk briskly back the way she had come, only she still had hold of one of Efa's hands and was pulling her along with her. Efa shook her head and laughed as she hopped into step with her cousin and they ran together back towards the castle.

Despite their hurried preparations, the arrival of Llewellyn and the Lady Joan and their considerable entourage created considerable upheaval. They arrived as the sun was setting, just as Swansea's cooks were beginning to mourn that all the fine dishes they had prepared would spoil. Even John looked flustered as the Welsh prince and his royal-born wife were ushered into the great hall and offered the best seats at the table on the dais. Servants began to stream in and out with steaming plates and dishes. Jugs appeared and cups were filled, as men jostled to find places at the two long tables that had been set to accommodate them. John offered his hand first to his wife, who he seated next to her mother, and then to Efa, who he seated beside Llewellyn. He then took his place beside Marared. Llewellyn had been leaning in conversing with his wife, but as Efa took her seat quietly beside him, he turned his attention her way.

'Efa? I did not think to find you here at John's table?.' He spoke quietly, without any accusatory tone. He did not smile but his eyes were soft, almost apologetic, as he held hers.

Efa looked upon a face that she had once loved as a daughter loves a father, and saw that it had aged. Grey streaked his hair, the lines around his eyes had deepened and he looked weary. Yet his presence still dominated the room. She looked at this powerful prince sitting beside her and remembered also how he had orchestrated her heartbreak. But in that moment she felt no animosity towards him; instead, she felt pity. It was as if God gave her a glimpse beneath the surface of the man, to see beneath the princely exterior, to see a person just as unsure and lost as any.

She smiled. 'It is good to see you again, my lord prince. I am glad for my sake that I am here, so that we could meet again.'

He watched her for a moment, and then allowed himself a wide smile in response. '"My lord prince"? There was a time you called me Tad, Blodyn!' He grinned then. 'Will you at least call me Llewellyn?'

'I will, but I prefer Efa to Blodyn these days!'

His face straightened again, although his eyes still shone. 'Of course. I hear you are a wealthy widow now. I was sorry to hear of Cynan's passing. He did well by you, I hope.'

Efa dipped her head at the reminder. 'He did. And I am grateful for it. He was a good man.'

'So you were happy?' Llewellyn had reached over to take her chin in his hand, a gesture than felt too familiar, and uncomfortable. She paused to reply. How much should she tell him? Would it help him to know of her unhappiness? Would it be politic to remind him?

'Eventually I found happiness with Cynan's family. His children became my joy, and God became my salvation.'

He nodded slowly. 'You are not the same girl that left here, that is evident.'

'No,' she replied softly, lifting her chin slightly so that his hand fell away. 'I am not, and I am free to choose for myself how to live the rest of my days, with God's guidance.' If a modicum of defiance found its way into her voice, it did not seem a bad thing.

He watched her for a moment more, his eyes probing. When she held his gaze without flinching, he was the first to look away. 'Ha!' he said, half to himself. 'The *blodyn* has grown into a *derwen*, it seems!'

On only the second day of their visit, Llewellyn was making moves to take their leave from Swansea, but for an unforeseen event that threatened to hinder their departure. The waiting woman who had travelled as companion to the Lady Joan had fallen ill with some ailment that had left her bedridden. Llewellyn's wife was not inclined to travel without her, but was even less inclined to be left behind at Swansea without her husband. Joan was a small, slight woman with the raven hair and dark eyes of her kingly father and she had inherited King John's stubbornness to match. Llewellyn had little sway over her, once she had set her mind. Efa and Marared giggled together, from where they hid in the stairwell, to hear the great man figuratively brought to his knees by his wife's quiet resistance. Eventually, Llewellyn gave way to his wife and agreed to stay a further night at Swansea. But it seemed the great strategist had himself been devising an alternative plan, and this he threw into action when it became clear that Joan's maid was still not well enough to travel.

He sought Efa and Marared out, finding them together in the kitchen garden, where they had gone to escape the sounds and smells that now permeated the living quarters of the castle. There were too many unwashed and overfed men, with too little to do, loitering in every free corner of Marared's usually sedate home. The fresh garden air was a welcome relief as they wandered through ripening vegetables and sweet-scented herbs.

'Ah, my daughters!' Llewellyn approached them with a suspiciously fixed smile. Efa excused the greeting; she had once been his daughter only by adoption, and had long since ceased seeing him as her father. But still he demanded respect as her prince so she dipped her knees and head in greeting, as did Marared.

'I have a proposition for you, Blodyn.' She bristled a little at the endearment but chose to say nothing, as he grabbed her by the arm with a firmness that cause her to flinch. He led her over to a seat and gestured for her to sit, and Marared bedside her, while he chose to pace backwards and forwards in front of them. 'And Marared, this involves you too, daughter. I must ask your indulgence to take your cousin away so that she can be a companion to your mother on our journey back to our homelands. You would like to revisit your place of birth, would you not, Efa? Of course I would ask you to come, Marared, but you have your sons and your husband to consider. And Efa, she is free, is she not? She can leave Swansea at will.'

He spoke without looking directly at either of them, only stopping his pacing as his words ran out. He stood, his hands on his waist, his eyebrows raised, expectant of an answer. He had surprised Marared, that was apparent, but somehow Efa was less perturbed by his request. She had not felt settled at Swansea, not since she had heard the news of Philip's death. And while she loved being with Marared, and loved her boys, Swansea did not feel like home.

Llewellyn was obviously anxious for a reply, as he began to shift from one foot to the other. Efa tried not to smile to see the man so discomforted. She thought to play him along a bit, make him beg, even, but chided herself at her disrespect. Instead, she replied with honesty.

'I thank you for your offer, Llewellyn, and I promise I will give your request due consideration. You will have your answer within the hour. But first I need to pray.'

He stopped his motion and looked full at her, and then, surprisingly, bowed from his broad waist in her direction. He dipped his head towards Marared and then made to leave them, before turning back with a laugh.

'Of course, we keep with Norman customs here, Efa. But if you come home with us, once you cross over into my lands you can remove that hideous wimple and let your glorious hair flow freely down your back. Wouldn't you love to ride with the mountain wind in your hair?'

'And the mountain rain down my neck?' she laughed in response. 'You will have your answer, my lord. I gave you my promise. But know that if my answer is yes, I will keep my freedom. No more husbands, except for my choosing. You will make me that promise at least.'

'You have my word.' He bowed again before striding off.

'Well, you are not afraid to challenge my father, it seems,' Marared said, her eyes widening with surprise.

Efa smiled. 'I think we have an understanding. He must know that if I agree to go with them, he will never again force me against my will. What think you? Should I go?'

Marared turned from her for a moment, before sighing. 'I think that it may be God's provision for you to go. And you know that I do not have your faith in God... yet. But I was looking for a way to tell you that we too will be leaving Swansea within a sennight. John wants to spend the rest of the summer in Bramber. He says he has business there, but I suspect it is more to do with the hunting that his English lands afford at this time of year. He is bored with being here. And he wants me and our sons to accompany him, and I have agreed to it. The boys run a little too wild here and will respond to a little more order and routine at Bramber, where a good tutor awaits them. I was thinking to ask you to come with us, but I think my father's offer might suit you more.'

Efa felt the relief flood through her. Marared was releasing her, so there was nothing to keep her at Swansea. The idea of seeing Abergwyngregyn, the mountains and the sea of her home, appealed more than she realised. Now she just needed to be sure it was God who was leading her and not just her will.

'Thank you, Marared.' She grasped her cousin's hand warmly. 'For welcoming me back here and embracing me into your family. If I leave you, it is not because you have driven me away, but because I need to take another path than yours. And I will always be grateful for the time God has given me here. I pray that I will return to be with you all again. Now I must speak to my heavenly Father before I speak again to your father.'

She rose from her seat and left Marared sitting alone, but as she walked away she already knew she had her answer. Her heart was filled with warmth, and a peace she had not felt for weeks filled her soul.

Efa's forecast of a rain soaking did not come to pass. In fact, the sun had shone relentlessly and the heat had increased as their journey had progressed north. As those familiar mountains of Llewellyn's Gwynedd began to loom into view, she would have blessed that cooling rain as she rode astride a steady roan. Even though she wore the lightest of veils with her hair streaming across her shoulders, the sweat trickled between her shoulder blades and her head throbbed, almost as much as her hips ached from being in the saddle. They were almost at Cymer, the small Cistercian abbey that nestled among the hills at the gateway to Snowdonia. Llewellyn had decided they would break their journey there. He expected they would be well received, fed and watered by the small community that benefited from his patronage and protection. And he had business to do. Abbey Cymer bred horses for him.

Llewellyn had pushed them hard, irrespective of the presence of the ladies in the party, in his desire to get them safely back into his northern stronghold. He had been right, of course; there had been parts of Wales they had journeyed through where the prince was still not confident of his welcome. He had chosen their stopping places carefully, and expected them to ride for long hours between. But now that his beloved mountains with their dense woodlands rose before him, Llewellyn had seemed to visibly relax. Efa was as glad as any for the chance of a rest.

They descended towards a solid wooden bridge which crossed the River Mawddach, its water sparkling in the sunlight. The cooling breeze coming off the water was welcome. Her horse seemed to be anticipating the break as much as she was, as he lifted his head and began to trot as the abbey grew nearer. She laughed at his sudden and unusual burst of energy. And then they were on the bridge, the horses' hooves creating a cacophony as they met the wood. But even with the noise they made, the sound of fishermen calling to each other caught her attention. She glanced sideways as her horse followed close behind Joan's. One of the fishermen, a monk, drew her attention. He stood within feet on the bridge, his habit tucked into his belt and his sandalled feet just out of the water. His head was tonsured, and his head and arms were brown from the sun. He was looking directly at her. He was not tall but his frame was lean and strong, and his face was that of Philip de Braose.

She closed her eyes and shook her head, swallowing hard. The shock that permeated her body, followed by a wave of emotion, caused her hands to tighten on the reins and her knees to clasp against the poor roan's flanks. Thankfully the temperate old horse just tossed his head with a disgruntled neigh and plodded on, coming to a stop as the other horses did and lowering his head to examine the dusty ground for a blade or two of grass. Efa slid from his back, before even a hand was offered to help her dismount. She blindly followed the prince and his lady through the abbey gates, past the smiling porter and a more agitated monk. Their arrival had seemingly caused a stir, and a not altogether welcome one.

A lay brother appeared carrying a tray with simple cups, and Efa stepped forward to take one and drink deeply of the cool, fresh spring water. Her throat was dry, and not just from the heat. She wanted to glance back to check that she had been wrong in what she saw. But she was sure she did not need to, as she knew the truth. Philip was not here in Wales, but dead on French soil.

As soon as she could, Efa broke away from the party, knowing she was unlikely to be needed. She had spotted the church. It was smaller, much smaller than the one at Ystrad Fflur, but still it stood proud among the other abbey buildings, and it called to her. She needed to get out of the heat, she needed to get away from the noise and bustle, and most of all she needed to pray, to calm herself. As soon as she stepped through the wooden door into the coolness beyond, she felt God's presence.

She tried to make sense of what had just occurred. Why had she seen Philip in that poor man's face? Maybe the sun had addled her brain, and she needed to just rest and eat? Yet Efa knew the uncomfortable twisting of her stomach had little to do with hunger. She needed to compose herself and find a place of peace again. She needed to breathe and she needed to speak to her heavenly Father. God had a reason for her being on this journey, she was sure of it. She needed to reconnect with Him, and recommit herself to His purposes, not dwell again on the man who had loved her and left her, and yet who still held a place in her heart; the man she had prayed for and thought that she had released to God. The wave of renewed grief had surprised her, and the lump in her throat surprised her still more. 'Philip,' she whispered, and an involuntary sob escaped her.

She made her way softly to the steps that led to the altar. The great window above it was not made of the finest glass, but its simplicity appealed. And the shafts of sunlight that poured through it spoke comfort to her soul. Lifting her tear-stained face to the window, she closed her eyes and stood, as if God's own glory were bathing her in light. Her hands came together as she prayed.

'Father God, let me release my grief at his loss to You.'

The light seemed to permeate her whole being.

'I feel You are here with me now, and that gladdens my heart. Give me Your peace, Father, and heal my heart again. I give myself to You.'

He alone is my beloved.

He shines in dazzling splendor yet is still so

approachable —

without equal as he stands above all others,

outstanding among ten thousand!

The way he leads me is divine.

His leadership — so pure and dignified

as he wears his crown of gold.

Upon this crown are letters of black written

on a background of glory.

Song of Solomon 5:10-11, TPT

20
Abbey Cymer

Summer 1232

Efa stood, feeling her breathing steadying, becoming less aware of her pounding heart and more aware of the stillness all around her. The coolness emanating from the stone walls refreshed her and the solid floor beneath her feet grounded her. She knew God had heard her as peace began to fill her again. She sighed softly and heard her sigh echo back to her. But then she heard another sound and knew this one had not come from her. She glanced over her shoulder. The sound had come from behind one of the columns that held up the arches soaring above her head. She turned and leaned her head to one side. At the base of the column she could make out a sandalled foot and an arm clothed in Cistercian white. A monk at private prayer? She felt she had somehow encroached on his space and hastened to make her apologies.

'Forgive me for disturbing your prayers, brother. I thought I was alone.'

A voice replied from behind the column. 'Be at peace, my child.' The voice cracked slightly. 'Don't let my presence disturb your own prayers, my lady.'

She took a step towards the column and saw him pull back his foot and stand up. Was he leaving because of her? She stopped and made the decision that it should be she who left.

'Please don't leave on my account, brother. I had a shock, that is all. I saw someone and thought he was someone else. Someone I lost years ago. God knows my heart, and He has met me here. I can compose myself now. I was drawn into this beautiful sanctuary, but it is your place of prayer above mine.'

When he did not reply she resolved to leave him to his quiet contemplation. It was time she rejoined her party anyway. She turned one last time to the sunlight streaming through the high window and brought her hands up to her face to wipe away any sign that she had been weeping. She could not do with being questioned.

'Efa.'

At the sound of her name, she spun around.

'You know my name, brother?'

The monk shifted and stepped around the column and half into the light.

'I do know your name. And I know your face, that form, those eyes, that voice. Efa, you were not mistaken when you saw me by the river.'

He stepped closer and she saw his face, now lit up by the same window light that had bathed her person just moments ago. Philip? Suddenly the whole world was spinning and she stumbled. He reached out a hand to grab her before she fell onto the stone steps behind her. She sank down until she sat hard on a step. His hand was still holding her arm. She looked up at him, taking in his monk's guise, his leather sandals, his rough, undyed robe and his shaved head. And yet it was his face. She was so confused.

'I mourned you as dead, killed in battle in France. How can you be here? How can you be... a Cistercian? It doesn't make sense.' She pulled her arm back so that he released her, and staggered to her feet.

'Efa! Look at me. Truly.'

He reached out his hand again and this time his fingers brushed hers. The touch was as familiar to her as the voice and the face, and she gasped despite herself. She closed her eyes for an instant, and when she opened them, found him gazing at her.

She took in his features, his familiar warm brown eyes that held such a look of intensity. He was not the youth of her memory; it was a mature man who stood before her, but it was unmistakeably Philip.

Bells clanged above their heads.

'Come quickly. With me.' Philip spoke quietly but with urgency, grasping her hand firmly. He led them to a side door that stood ajar, and out into the full sunlight. He kept walking, her hand still in his, she a few steps behind him. It felt like she was in some kind of waking dream. Ahead of them was a field of grazing sheep, and he led her through that and into the trees beyond. He did not stop until they came across a fallen tree in a small clearing.

'We cannot be long. I will most certainly have been already noted as missing from Sext, and you will be missed too.'

Philip was breathing heavily, and her breathing matched his. He gestured to the tree trunk and they sat together. She shifted, feeling uncomfortable at his closeness and yet revelling in it all the same. Her hand was still in his, resting on the rough bark between them. Was Philip really here, talking to her? Very much alive and seemingly well? She did not know how to think or feel. But he was speaking again and she needed to focus on what he was saying.

'There is so much we could say to each other, and we must talk quickly. But first, Efa, I must say sorry. Sorry for causing you pain, causing you grief, abandoning you.' He squeezed her hand.

She saw the regret etched in his face and wanted to smooth the lines away with a touch of her hand. Instead, she chose words to absolve him.

'You had no choice leaving me, Philip. I no longer blame you for that. We neither of us had any choice. We had our lives and our love stolen from us.'

His closeness was becoming increasingly disconcerting and she pulled her hand from his. She took a deep, steadying breath and moved still further from him. She could feel him watching her, but tried not to meet his gaze.

'Efa, you married him!' He sounded angry. Or hurt, perhaps. He must have heard it himself, for he moderated his tone as he continued. 'I know you had no choice, but I could not bear it. And I could never forgive John; he knew my hopes, how I felt about you, and yet the good opinion of Llewellyn was more important to him than his own brother's happiness. I could not stay to see you with another man, or live with the anger I felt towards John. I could have killed him.'

Efa involuntarily found herself reaching out to touch her fingers to his cheek, as if they were back in that dreadful moment and she was comforting him as she would have done then. But this wasn't then and she was no longer his lover. She dropped her hand and her head.

'I wept and railed at the injustice of it all too, Philip. I wept for our lost hopes, I wept for our pain.' She paused, the memories tinged with guilt. 'But then I was done with weeping and my heart grew hard. Life had to be lived, and I determined to make the best of it and not allow my heart to be hurt again. Yes, I married Cynan, and he was not a bad man. It was not a bad life, just not the life I had dreamed of. Over time I even grew fond of him, but more like a daughter than a wife, he was so much older than I.'

She glanced over then to see the effect of her words. She hoped she could offer him more in the way of reassurance, perhaps to help him come to terms with the pain of broken dreams, as she had. She owed him full honesty at least.

'Philip, he didn't want more children. He made no demands of me that might have led to more.' Efa paused and saw the subtle widening of his eyes in understanding. She felt emboldened to continue. 'He wanted a wife for his children's sake, and in caring for them my heart softened. And then God took hold of me, and my heart softened still more. I chose to forgive those who had wronged us. I chose to live free of bitterness. I chose a better way.'

Silence sat between them for a moment.

Philip spoke quietly. 'You spoke of your husband in the past tense.'

'I am a widow now, yes,' Efa replied. 'That is why I am with the Lady Joan. Llewellyn asked me to accompany them back north as Joan's companion fell sick and had to be left behind. I agreed on one condition – that he would not force me to remarry. I would not be a pawn in his hands again.'

'And he agreed?' Philip lifted one eyebrow.

'He did. And I am quite determined. I will not be bartered for any price. My husband left me well provided for. I can live independently. Or perhaps I will find myself a place in a convent.' She looked at him in his monk's habit. 'It seems to me that you made that choice yourself?'

'Not exactly. It was chosen for me.' Philip sighed heavily. 'You have told me your story. It is only fair that I tell you how I came to be here.' He shifted and clasped his hands loosely between his knees, dropping his voice to barely above a whisper. 'It is true that I wanted to escape my life, and lying wounded in a French ditch, I longed for my life to end. Or for the strength to take my own life. But God had other plans for me... in the shape of a Cistercian by the name of Brother Hywel. He found me and tended to me, and brought me back here. We agreed for me to be disguised as a full brother. I did not want to be recognised, to be dragged back to a life I had despaired of. I had to have a new identity. Philip de Braose had to die in France.' He glanced over at her.

Efa remembered the moment she had been told of his death and remembered the grief. She remembered too that she had thought her prayers for him had gone unanswered. And yet now she realised that all the time she had been praying for his salvation, he had still been alive. And God had been rescuing him through the hands of a Cistercian monk! It was almost too much to take in, grief overtaken with unexpected joy.

Her eyes were moist but she could not keep a tremulous smile from her lips.

'News reached me some months ago that you were dead, and all of the grief of the past so carefully packed away in my heart came flooding back, and I wept again for you,' she said quietly. 'When I saw you today, standing by the bridge, I thought I had dreamed you into being. It was such a shock. I thought perhaps I was hallucinating, from grief or from the heat of the sun. That I had imagined your face onto that of another man.' She half-laughed.

He smiled and it lit up his face. 'It was the same for me, seeing you, or thinking that I had seen you, and yet not believing it could be you.' He took her hands again in his. 'So much of my old life, Efa, has been put to death. By my choice, and through the healing grace of God. And yet you, the memory of you, I could never erase, nor wanted to. You were the brightest, most alive part of my life. You were a dream I returned to again and again in my darkest moments. Even though I could not be with you, you never left me.'

She let her hands lie in his. For all those years they had been apart he had taken comfort from the memory of their love; he had not forgotten her. She knew that she still loved him. God had heard every one of her prayers for him. But the man before her was dressed in a monk's habit and might even have taken vows. That meant they could have no future together. This might be the only moment she would have with him. She wanted to savour it for as long as they were given.

'And so Philip de Braose is dead? And this is your life now?'

He looked sheepishly at her then. 'I wanted him dead, yes. But now… now, I don't know. I am content, I have learned so much, and have lived a different, better life here. I have even considered taking my vows to commit to this life in truth. But seeing you again… knowing that you are free…'

Something stirred in her heart at his words. But this was not a dream, this was a very different reality from what they had known.

'We cannot go back to what we were.'

'No,' Philip sighed. 'It is more than I could have hoped for to see you, touch you, be near you again.' He reached up a hand to cup her face. 'The truth is that I am not whole yet, Efa. I have been broken and have been mended, but I am not fully whole. Not just my body and its physical scars, but my heart, soul and spirit. Do you understand?'

She thought for a moment that she could glimpse into his very soul. She did understand, all too well. And the God who was doing a healing work in her would do the same for him. She was sure of it.

'I do understand, Philip,' she nodded. 'I will pray for you.' She bowed her head, looking at his hands still holding hers. 'Will we see each other again?'

'I think that must be left in God's hands, Efa. It is too much for me to even understand what it is I desire most in this moment. Or what God desires for me, for us both.'

His words wounded. She wanted him to desire her above all else. But even as the thought entered her head, she knew he was right. And had she not sworn that she would only go where God led her from now on? She had to trust Him with it all.

'Then pray for me also, Philip, that our hearts' desires and God's will be as one.'

At the sound of a distant bell, they reluctantly disengaged their hands and stood. They began the slow walk back towards the abbey. As they left the shelter of the trees, he grabbed her hand and pulled her to a stop. His voice was strained.

'You will keep my secret?'

She wanted to shout it from the rooftops that Philip was alive. Her heart so desperately wanted him to be a free man, and not the monk who stood beside her. But it was not that simple.

'Your secret is safe with me.' She smiled at him, but the smile was forced now as she was the one who had to leave him this time, and it tore at her soul. But she could be resolute; she had to be. She strode out, leaving him behind, not daring to turn until she was almost inside the abbey walls. Only then she allowed herself to look for him again. He was standing where she had left him at the edge of the trees. She swallowed back the tears that threatened, and smiled. The hand that still tingled with his touch she raised to her lips so that he could see it. And then she stepped beyond the walls and beyond his gaze.

Llewellyn had pushed them yet harder as they had ridden away from Cymer, and Efa had been grateful for that. No time to converse, no need to explain why tears still wet her cheeks. She had joined them at the table in the abbot's rooms but not much of the generous spread had passed her lips. Nobody had noticed as she had pushed the food around her trencher. Now that she had walked away from Philip, she wanted to leave quickly the place where he was. She could not bear the thought of catching another glimpse of him. It was better that she did not, for fear of exposing herself and him.

They had reached Dolwyddelan as the sun was almost set, late, and weary to their bones; grateful for the shelter and warm beds that the castle afforded them, grateful for a few days at least out of the saddle. However, Dolwyddelan was little more than a fortress tower, and while Llewellyn loved it there, Joan was less keen to stay longer than she had to. Before a sennight had passed they were mounted on their rested horses and on their way north again, Efa thankful that it was only one more day of hard riding to get to Abergwyngregyn. The terrain was not the easiest, but the steeper the mountain paths they rode, the closer they got to the sea. The cooler mountain air was also most welcome, and the clouds that thickened as they rode. As the sea came into view at last, they began their descent to Abergwyngregyn just as the first drops of rain began to fall.

Her childhood home did not seem to have changed, to Efa's mind, in all the years that she had been absent. The same long, white-painted hall, with its kitchens and stables, surrounded by a formidable wooden palisade. The melodious sound of her native tongue as servants busied themselves to greet them. The sound of the sea crashing against the rocks beneath them and the cry of seabirds as they flew above. As she dismounted her faithful roan, Efa stepped into the embrace of Llewellyn's *Llys*, hoping that here she would find solace in the familiar. And that, in time, she might forget that the man who held her heart was alive and well on the other side of her beloved Welsh mountains.

O my beloved, you are lovely.
When I see you in your beauty,
I see a radiant city where we will dwell as one.
More pleasing than any pleasure,
more delightful than any delight,
you have ravished my heart,
stealing away my strength to resist you.
Even hosts of angels stand in awe of you.
Turn your eyes from me; I can't take it anymore!
I can't resist the passion of these eyes that I
adore.
Overpowered by a glance, my ravished heart –
undone.
Held captive by your love, I am truly overcome!
For your undying devotion to me
is the most yielded sacrifice.
The shining of your spirit
shows how you have taken my truth
to become balanced and complete.
Your beautiful blushing cheeks
reveal how real your passion is for me,
even hidden behind your veil of humility.

Song of Solomon 6:4-7, TPT

21
Bride

One thing Efa had not missed about her northern home was how, as the summer ebbed away, cold wild winds came blowing off the sea to herald the autumn. Here, the leaves fell more easily from the trees than they had in either Tregaron or Swansea. The chill infiltrated the layers of her clothing more noticeably, and the rain fell more often. It did not help to lift her mood that she could spend less and less time outside, walking along the seashore, or up into the woods, climbing up to stand in the spray of the majestic waterfall that crashed over the rocks above Abergwyngregyn. All these had helped to keep her mind from too much imagining and her emotions in check. It was in those times that she had prayed and sought God for Philip, and for herself.

Efa had kept her promise and Philip's secret continued to lie heavy on her heart. God was the only one she could talk to about it, and she became increasingly dependent on Him. She had no human friend to confide in, or indeed who would have understood her deep reliance on God. She wondered again if she would not be suited better to the monastic life, where she could live out her devotion to God unhindered. But still something checked in her spirit every time she gave thought to joining her friend Non at Llanllugan, or the gentle sisters at Gwytherin not so many miles away from where Efa was now. Her days dragged by. Joan had little need of her company now that she was back among her household, and Efa struggled to find tasks to occupy herself. It was as it was at Tregaron after Cynan had passed, and the same listlessness threatened.

To add to her despondency, they had received sad news not more than a fortnight after they had reached Abergwyngregyn. News that for a moment had her wanting to turn around and fly back to Swansea, taking Philip with her. A missive came informing Llewellyn that his daughter's husband, John de Braose, had died suddenly as the result of a hunting accident. Efa's heart had broken for Marared and her young boys. But it seemed that a return to Swansea would have accomplished little, as Marared had chosen to stay at Bramber to bury and grieve her husband there. All Efa could do was pray for them, and that was the greatest gift she could give. She could not escape the sad knowledge that she also knew what Philip did not know – that his brother was dead. How she wanted to be able to get news to him, but that would mean breaking her oath and telling Llewellyn that Philip de Braose lived.

One dull afternoon as the rain had pelted down and driven them all inside to huddle around the blazing fire, another messenger had arrived with news for Llewellyn from his daughter at Bramber. His face was hard to read as he examined the parchment in his hand; Efa prayed it was not more bad news. Eventually he looked up and, finding Efa watching him, he beckoned for her to come to sit by him.

He placed his large hand over hers where it sat on her knee. 'It is not bad news, Blodyn, but it is concerning news. It seems Marared has found herself a new husband. Not a man of my choosing but an English knight of property and influence who will see that she is cared for. I think she lacks your self-sufficiency. She would not fare well as a widow, wealthy or not, and she has her boys and their inheritance to think of.'

He shifted his position and sighed. 'That leaves me with another problem, though. I do not like the idea of Sir Walter Clifford having power over the de Braose territory in the Gower. He is an unknown and I do not know how the other Welsh lords would respond to him. We have kept a fragile peace in that area for a long time. In my view he would do better to concentrate on maintaining the de Braose lands in England for young William to inherit and leave the Gower to me.' He glanced across at Efa. She was not sure whether he meant to voice his concerns in her hearing. What had it to do with her, except of course for her link to Swansea and her love for Marared and her sons? 'Perhaps it would have been too much to ask for John to have set someone up to oversee his Gower lands in the event of his death. Someone that would keep his children's inheritance for them. Someone that both he and I trusted.' He was grinding his teeth.

A younger brother, perhaps. The thought came to her mind, but thankfully not to her lips. At least she did not think she had spoken the words aloud, but Llewellyn was looking at her with a puzzled look on his face.

'You have gone quite pale, Efa? Is all well?'

Efa closed her eyes, trying to clear the noise in her head, trying desperately to hear the familiar 'still small voice' of her heavenly Father. She knew whatever she did next might change the course of her life. Either she would lose Philip's trust for breaking his confidence, or she could keep silent when the most obvious solution to Llewellyn's problem lay in her knowledge.

Father, help me, she prayed.

Speak, child.

She glanced up, knowing it was nobody in the room who had spoken. She cleared her throat and brought both hands together in her lap, calling out to God for courage.

'Philip de Braose lives, my lord.'

Llewellyn's eyes darkened and his brows creased.

'What?'

'John's brother, Philip. He lives, my lord. I have seen him and spoken to him, not many months ago.'

'I remember him. That whelp who thought to have you as his bride. He deserted his family, did he not, and ran away? I thought he lay long dead in some French ditch?'

Efa felt the blood rising to her cheeks. She thought better of directly challenging Llewellyn's words, seeing the mood that had descended on him. Instead, she told Philip's story. Keeping her voice soft, she told him of a certain monk, a changed man, who had been saved by the hand of God and the friendship of a Cistercian brother, who had chosen a new way of life, and who was becoming a better version of himself than he had ever been before.

Llewellyn listened to her, and his face softened as she told him how she had recognised Philip at Cymer, how they had forgiven one another, but how he had chosen to remain unknown; how their hearts still longed for each other but how they had given their future into God's hands, unsure of whether they would ever meet again.

Eventually, when she had stopped speaking, she realised that it was not only Llewellyn who had listened to her tale, but the whole room had quietened in a kind of reverent awe. The tears spilled readily as at last she was able to unburden herself of her oath.

Llewellyn touched his hand to hers again and leaned in. She could have sworn the great prince had tears in his own eyes. His tone was much gentler than she had heard it in years.

'Efa, Blodyn. I did not know how much this man meant to you, all those years ago. I did not mean to cause you grief by separating you. I thought you too young to know what was best for you, and your marriage with Cynan offered a security and way of life many in your position would have envied. I admit, it served my purposes too.' He patted her hands and leaned back again. 'I would put it right now for you, my dear one, except that if Philip is a monk, as you say, then he would have to break his vows to have you as wife.'

Wife? Her breath caught at the sudden realisation of what Llewellyn was saying. Philip could take her as his wife – if he still desired it. Llewellyn wasn't offering only the Gower lands to Philip's care, he was minded to offer Philip Efa as well. She swallowed hard as the next words she uttered rode on a wave of emotion.

'But he has made no vows. He is no true monk. At least, he was not when I saw him. It is all a pretence, a means of him returning unrecognised to Wales. He had grown accustomed to the life and had found some joy in it, I believe, but I am not certain he would not give it all up if he had the chance to follow his heart. If God wills it.'

'And if I will it!' Llewellyn growled, but it was not with menace. 'So…' He slapped his hands on his thick thighs. 'We write to your monk who is no monk, and we invite him to be a de Braose again. He can have Swansea, to keep in good order for his nephew's sake. And he can have you! If he wants you. Although I would never force a husband upon you that you did not want.' He grinned. 'I keep my promises too!'

She dipped her head, and when she lifted it again, she could not keep from smiling. She knew her heart. 'I pray God wills it, for I will have Philip, if he will have me. But he must yet decide. Nothing will be settled until he knows the full story and has time to consider it for himself.'

She spoke as much to herself as to the prince. She could not be fully sure of Philip's response. She may yet have to deal once more with heartache and disappointment. Although this time she prayed it would be easier, knowing that she had a Father in heaven who would love her and comfort her. The love of Christ for her would not change, wherever her future path lay. She must take courage from that thought.

Llewellyn heaved himself to his feet. 'Now, get that letter written quickly, Blodyn! I will write to that horse magician, Brother Hywel, and you can enclose your letter in mine. That way Philip can keep his secret until he decides how to respond. I suspected something when I saw that fine dark destrier among Hywel's ponies. Not the usual sort of animal he acquires. He was cryptic in his answers when I questioned him about how he came to own such a fine beast. Now I thoroughly suspect that was de Braose's horse in Cymer's stables.' He turned to his address his wife. 'How does a visit to Chester's cloth merchants and silversmiths appeal to you, my love? If we are going to visit Cymer again, I will visit the horse fair and find myself some more horseflesh to add to the breeding stock there. Hywel also has a young horse that I think will be ready to return with us too. And Efa will accompany us, of course! That fool de Braose will have to tell her to her face if he is wont to reject her.'

He did not wait for his wife's response as he turned to leave the room in the direction of his private quarters. Efa saw the half-exasperated, half-resigned look that passed across the Lady Joan's face as she put down her needlework and rose to follow his broad back out of the room. It did not take many more minutes before she returned to announce that they were indeed leaving for Chester in the morning, and to wear warm clothing. Efa would not pack much, but she would wear Marared's miniver and fix her gold barrette in her hair. She would travel to Chester and then on to Cymer, praying all the while that God would finally give her the desires of her heart. But first, she had a letter to write.

Llewellyn was laughing as they clattered over the bridge and approached Abbey Cymer. He had thought it a joke to not announce their arrival, and already the agitated form of the prior could be seen running backwards and forwards, barking orders. Strangely enough, no one seemed in any hurry to respond to his shouts. Llewellyn drew up beside the poor man and sat back lazily in his saddle. He tried to keep his face straight as he explained to Prior William that they did not need a meal. No one would need to be put out by their visit, not even the abbot. They only had business with Brother Hywel and then they would be on their way. The poor monk was left still jumping from one foot to the other as Llewellyn nonchalantly turned his horse in the direction of Cymer's stables.

'Will you at least stop to have a cup of wine with the abbot?' the prior called out in a shrill voice.

'After we have done our business, perhaps. Now if you will excuse us, brother.' Llewellyn spurred his horse into a trot before the prior could say more.

Efa felt sick, her emotions veering between joyful anticipation and nervous apprehension. She still did not know what decision Philip would make. Had he already made his vows and chosen the monastic life? Would he turn his back on those for her? Was his love for her still as strong as ever? And then, if they did leave together, did marry at last, what would life be like for them? They were near strangers now, and had experienced life-changing events in their time apart. What would they have in common? Would the plans and dreams they had once shared still have weight? And she realised, with a sudden pang, this time around her marriage would be a true marriage. A love marriage, expressed in every way, with even the possibility of children of their own. Was she ready for that?

There were just five of them in the prince's party that fresh autumn morning. Llewellyn, his wife, two men-at-arms and Efa astride a beautiful grey. Younger and more spirited than the horse that had carried her from Swansea, Llewellyn had purchased the grey to be left with Brother Hywel at Cymer. But Efa and the horse seemed to have formed a connection with one another and Llewellyn had declared that she could keep him as a wedding gift.

The grey was not the only purchase made for Efa in Chester. At the inn in Dolgellau where they had spent the previous night, and where the rest of Llewellyn's retinue still rested, were packages containing bolts of rich wools and silks, and fine gossamer veils. There were also a pair of matching silver rings, fashioned to look like entwined vine leaves, each decorated with a rich amethyst. The Lady Joan had insisted on dragging Efa to the finest of Chester's merchants to furnish her with wedding clothes and enough cloth to sew a whole new wardrobe, and the two rings to be exchanged with their wedding vows. Efa had resisted at first but had found it hard not to get swept away by her lady's excitement. Now all that shopping might have been in vain if Philip rejected her.

Llewellyn's party approached the abbey horse yard, which consisted of a range of stabling and a large, rectangular, enclosed exercise yard. A fine, jet-black destrier with a proud bearing stood tied loosely to a fencepost, but he was tossing his head as they reined in. Llewellyn and his two men-at-arms dismounted and the prince strode forward to grasp the hand of a tall, well-built monk with a friendly, open face. A second monk had quietly appeared but did not approach the prince. Instead, he came to Efa's grey and took the reins from her hands, whispering to the horse as he did so. Philip lifted his face and their eyes met. She held her breath, but he was smiling, a smile that reached his eyes. He nodded then and winked, and she felt her cheeks warming. Was that his yes to all that her letter had contained?

Llewellyn had joined them. 'So this is him, then?'

The prince towered above Philip, and if he sought to intimidate him by standing close beside him, Philip did not shrivel. Instead, he released the horse reins and took a step back, turning to face him. There was a moment when Efa could not be certain that Philip would not advance on Llewellyn, except he was, of course, unarmed. They stared hard at one another for a few heart-stopping moments, and then finally Philip dipped his head in a respectful bow.

'Yes, I can see it now, he has something of the de Braose look about him. Not as ugly as his grandfather, mind; he should be thankful for that.' Llewellyn was enjoying Philip's discomfiture, and Efa's too, no doubt, as he made an examination of the other man. 'I remember him as a scrawny lad. This man is not that. A fighter, by the looks of him. Not big, but strong enough.'

'I can handle a weapon, my lord,' Philip retorted. 'I hope never to have to lift a sword in anger again, but I can defend myself, and those I am called to protect.'

'Hmm. I don't doubt that you could. So, Philip, you are not dead, just hiding, eh?' Llewellyn was unsmiling, but Efa could see the glint of amusement in his eye.

'Some might call it that, my lord. I call it finding the man I was designed by God to be. I am not the Philip de Braose I was. Not in looks, and not in character, thanks be to God. But some things have not changed.' Philip paused. 'I still care about my family, I still miss the Gower lands and I still love this lady.' He glanced up at Efa who, feeling her cheeks warm again, dipped her head. Finally, she could allow herself to believe that this was really happening, as all doubts as to his intentions ebbed away.

'So you will agree to my proposition, then? You will return to life outside of the Church, to the Gower, to serve your family, for my grandson's sake?' the prince continued.

'I will. If you keep your side of the bargain?' Philip had a glint in his own eye, but it did not look like amusement.

'Huff. You mean the lady here? Well, unless I get a better offer for her!'

Efa let out a strangled sound and glared at Llewellyn.

'Ha!' The prince bellowed. 'I was only jesting!' He was grinning broadly now. He turned his attention back to Philip. 'We are staying at a local inn tonight, but will be back here at first light. You'd best be ready. I assume you are bringing that great beast with you? Looks ready to retire to me.' He nodded over to where the destrier still stood. The horse had lifted a hoof to paw at the ground, and let out a snort that sounded suspiciously like the sound Efa had made not a moment before. Philip moved quickly to grab the horse's bridle, soothing him with a word.

'Yes, Noble will be coming with us. But like me, his fighting days are over. Will we,' he glanced up at Efa, 'be heading straight for the Gower?'

'No. I plan for you to wed at Abergwyngregyn, in full sight of everyone, so that no one will question your right to the position I have asked you to take. Or your right to marry Efa.'

It was a statement, not a question. Efa was glad of Llewellyn's intent to bless their union, and the protection that would afford them. But she needed no fancy wedding. She would stand before the priest with Philip now, in the abbey church here at Cymer, and say her vows before God. Except that the community here, Hywel excluded, did not know who Philip truly was. Brother Robert, as he was known here, would not be marrying her today.

She glanced over to see that Philip had drawn a blade, but not in anger. He was offering it to Llewellyn, who was nodding his approval. It was incongruous to see a monk carrying such a fine dagger, but it looked familiar to Efa. And as Llewellyn handed it back to Philip, she recognised it as the same blade his brother, John, had gifted him, many years ago. So much had happened since then. It warmed her heart to think that perhaps that dagger had been kept by Philip as a reminder of his brother. She wondered if Philip had grieved John, and if he had come to a place of peace with his past. She wondered too how he would leave the abbey, what lies, or truths, he would choose to tell. She wondered what it would be like to actually be married to the man she had loved for so long. She wondered a lot of things, but she knew she had to choose to trust God in it all.

Come away with Me, God had said. She had tried to listen to His leading and follow Him in obedience. She had found that God's love had given her life and purpose. It had strengthened her and given her courage. It had healed her brokenness and spoken peace to her soul over and over again. And His love had given her an unshakeable knowledge of who she was. She was His daughter, and His beloved bride. But that wasn't enough for God, it seemed. Now He was gifting her with the chance of a life she thought lost to her. She was at last to be her lover's true bride.

'Now, Hywel, where's this young horse of mine?' Llewellyn seemed satisfied with his assessment of Philip and now was keen to move on to other business. There were horses to be inspected. He wandered over and was soon in deep conversation with Brother Hywel. The Lady Joan joined her husband as a young yearling was brought out of the stables for the prince's inspection.

Philip was left with Efa. He had moved quietly back over to stand beside her horse's head. She wanted so much to dismount, to feel his hands in hers again, to lean into his embrace, but they were in full view of prying eyes. He leaned in to give the impression of adjusting her horse's bridle.

'Thank you,' he whispered.

'For what?' She smiled at his trembling hands. He was as overwrought as she.

'Everything. The letter, breaking your vow to keep my secret… wanting me.' Efa felt like her heart might burst, but one doubt still threatened her joy.

'You won't regret leaving here for me?'

'No. No more regrets. Only hope.' He turned his face back to her and continued to stroke the horse's neck. He went to reach out to take her hand where it rested on the horse's mane, but she withdrew it quickly, glancing over her shoulder, before turning her attention back to him.

'Tomorrow, my love, tomorrow,' she whispered, her voice as full as her heart.

I could have chosen any from among the vast

multitude

of royal ones who follow me.

But unique is my beloved dove – unrivaled in

beauty,

without equal, beyond compare,

the perfect one, the favorite one.

Others see your beauty and sing of your joy.

Brides and queens chant your praise:

'How blessed is she!'

Song of Solomon 6:8-9, TPT

My darling bride, my private paradise,

fastened to my heart.

A secret spring that no one else can have are you –

my bubbling fountain hidden from public view.

What a perfect partner to me now that I have you.

Song of Solomon 4:12, TPT

Author's Note

This is the third time I have written a full-length story full of monks and abbeys, Welsh mountains and rivers, and the third time I have found myself drawing on spiritual truths that God has personally revealed to me. In telling Efa's story I have drawn on my own. Although her spiritual journey is not the same as mine, I too have experienced heartache and loss, I have felt unloved and unlovely, I have been disappointed and close to despair. And yet, I too have discovered a divine love that refuses to let me go.

I have not always seen God as a loving Father, but that realisation came when I needed it most. He is a Father who adores His children and longs for them to know Him in a deep and personal way, through His Son, Jesus. He is the perfect Father, He never lets us down, and His love is truly unconditional. And His love does have the power to heal our brokenness and transform our lives, if we let Him.

I have also known what is feels like to be wooed by the Lover of my soul. He is my Bridegroom, and I am His bride. There are lots of interpretations of the biblical book the Song of Solomon. Was it just a love poem from King Solomon to his Shulamite bride? Slightly odd in its imagery and bordering on the erotic? Is it a picture of Christ wooing and cleansing His bride, the Church? I can see truth in that. But I have found such comfort in making the words of this ancient love song personal. As part of His bride, I can be that Shulamite, and receive the beloved's words as balm to my soul. That is why I have chosen to use verses from The Passion Translation of the Song of Solomon as end-of-chapter markers. I sat in this beautiful poetic book for all the time that I wrote *The Bride*, revisiting its message over and over again, trying to soak the truth of it deep into my soul. He loves me. I am His beloved bride. And He loves all of His own with the same intensity. My prayer is that you, too, will know this truth for yourself. In Him you can never be unloved or unlovely.

For more information about the author and the story behind *The Bride*, as well as Joy's other books, visit joymargetts.com

Historical Note

Readers of my previous books will know that I like to weave real characters and events into my stories to give them an element of historical authenticity. Efa, as a character, is a figment of my imagination, but John and Philip de Braose were real people. The de Braose family were powerful friends of the English crown and John did hold the Lordship of Gower at the time of Llewellyn *ap* Iorwerth (Llewellyn *Fawr*, or 'the Great'). He also married Marared (Margaret), a daughter of Llewellyn and Joan, his wife, who was in turn an illegitimate daughter of King John. John de Braose died young in a riding accident and Marared married again, to a Sir Walter Clifford.

Tregaron as described in *The Bride* did not exist, although there is a town named Tregaron in modern Ceredigion, which received a Royal Charter in 1292. It lies approximately six and a half miles from the Abbey of Strata Florida. At the time my story is set, Strata Florida (Ystrad Fflur) was a relatively new but well-established abbey. It was founded in 1201 as part of the Europe-wide Cistercian expansion. It became the burial place for many Welsh princes and noble patrons, including Maude de Braose. The ruins of the abbey are still spectacular, including portions of highly decorated coloured tile floors, and it is well worth a visit.

I based my descriptions of the manor house of Tregaron in part on the amazing Stokesay Castle. It was built by a wealthy merchant in the late thirteenth century, and is situated not so far from the Welsh border in Craven Arms, Shropshire. I didn't think it was too much of a stretch of the imagination to have a smaller version of this fortified manor house built by a wealthy Welsh landowner. Cynan and his children came from my imagination. Maelgwyn and his father, Maelgwyn *ap* Rhys, did not. They were notorious for their cruelty.

As always, my apologies if I have corrupted or misrepresented people, places or customs in my attempts to add authenticity to my writing.

Acknowledgements

Thank you to the publishing team at Instant Apostle. Your professionalism and attention to detail mean that once again you have taken a very rough manuscript and turned it into a thing of beauty.

My special thanks to the wonderful people who agreed to endorse The Bride: to Joanna Watson, Joy Vee, Jo Regan, Claire Musters, Liz Carter and Donna Fletcher-Crow. Your words of appreciation for both the story and the message of the book were a huge encouragement to me. And to my ever-growing community of supportive writer friends, thank you.

Thank you to a wonderful group of praying friends. Your prayers got me through some tricky moments and I am so grateful to God for you. To Joy Velykorodnyy and Joanna Watson – my Kingdom Stories compatriots – your love, support and friendship have helped me to grow, to stretch my faith and to dream big dreams. Thank you.

Tim, my husband, thank you for giving me the space to write and for your shared belief in my calling. Thank you for your unfailing support and encouragement. Thanks to all my family and friends who have championed me, and a special mention to my children, and to my adorable grandchildren, Judah and Olivia. You inspire me every day to do the very the best I can do.

My thanks to every person who has picked up one of my books and read them. Thank you for your kind reviews and encouraging messages. I write because God gives me the words, but I also write because of you – my lovely readers.

To be able to write is a gift, and it all comes from the One who loves me, and who gave Himself for me. He inspires the stories and His work in my life inspires the message. It is all for you, Jesus, Lover of my Soul. Thank you for enabling me to do this, and for Your immeasurable grace, mercy and love.

List of Bible references

Chapter 9
Pages 115-116: Luke 15:11-32

Chapter 10
Page 129: Luke 8:40-56
Page 138: Song of Solomon 4:1, NKJV

Chapter 11
Page 142: Song of Solomon 4:9-10, NLT
Pages 143-144: John 3:29, Revelation 21:2-3

Chapter 17
Page 211: Song of Solomon 2:10-13, NKJV

If you have enjoyed *The Bride*, check out *The Healing* and *The Pilgrim*, where you will encounter some familiar and much-loved characters.

'A feel-good exploration of forgotten times that leaves a final lump in the throat.'
Ian Hampson, Lay Reader, Church in Wales, and student of Welsh ecclesiastical history

'Impossible to read without encountering hope.'
Billy Doey – Senior Pastor (Retired), Welcome Evangelical Church, Witney

'A timeless journey of love, loss and redemption played out across a compelling medieval landscape.'
Anne E Bailey, Historian, Oxford University

'With a real sense of place and time, and characters that pop from the page, this novel is a masterpiece of historical fiction.'
Wendy H Jones, author and writing coach